The Head in the Ice

RICHARD JAMES

First published in 2019

This edition published in 2020 by Sharpe Books.

For Charlotte.

CONTENTS

Prologue	1
Chapter One	16
Chapter Two	23
Chapter Three	27
Chapter Four	34
Chapter Five	40
Chapter Six	45
Chapter Seven	53
Chapter Eight	59
Chapter Nine	64
Chapter Ten	82
Chapter Eleven	90
Chapter Twelve	97
Chapter Thirteen	108
Chapter Fourteen	113
Chapter Fifteen	122
Chapter Sixteen	128
Chapter Seventeen	135
Chapter Eighteen	155
Chapter Nineteen	160
Chapter Twenty	173
End Note	214

WINTER, 1891

"The man who comes sane and safe out of the hands of mad-doctors and warders… is very sane indeed."

My Experiences in a Lunatic Asylum, Herman Charles Merival

Prologue

The dreams had come again. He woke in a tangle of sheets, breathless, in the small hours of the morning. He prayed he hadn't screamed. After several minutes of waiting, he walked quietly to the table in the corner and splashed his face in a bowl of water. The flagstones were cold beneath his feet. Drying his face on the harsh, starched towel that hung upon a hook by the door, he sat for a moment on an old wooden chair. Rubbing his hands together for warmth, he waited for his heart to slow and his breathing to settle. Only then did he return to bed, pull the sheets over his head and attempt to sleep again.

His next awakening came, as usual, at six o'clock. The rasp of the door on its hinges was enough to rouse him. For a while he lay still, his eyes resolutely closed. A warder entered his room carrying a candle ahead of him. Walking to the window, he threw open the heavy curtains. It was to no avail, of course, for at this time of year there was no morning light to admit.

"Time to rise."

Bowman grunted in acknowledgement and buried his head deeper in his pillow.

"Inspection on the hour, as usual." The warder left the candle at his bedside and returned to the corridor, pausing only to turn up the gaslight directly outside the door.

Bowman swung his legs from the bed and stood to stretch. With his fingers at their full extent, he could touch the ceiling.

Still in his regulation nightwear, Bowman made his way along the corridor, a twist of used bedding bundled in his arms. As he joined the queue of dissolutes outside the bathing rooms, he let his eyes wander to each of their faces in turn. The cast-down eyes and grey, pasty skin spoke of nothing but despair. Some were soldiers from the African campaigns, he knew. Their twitches and groans gave them away. Each of the men deposited their sheets and nightshirts in a chute for washing as they reached the baths. The smell of sulphur pricked the air and, glancing up at the lamps, Bowman saw the walls and ceiling directly above the guttering flames were stained a ghastly, greasy black. Almost every other tile was missing or cracked. Despite the gas jets, he could plainly see his breath in the air around him. Several of his neighbours hopped from foot to foot or clapped their arms about them in a vain attempt to keep warm.

Being next in line, Bowman stripped where he stood and let his nightshirt and sheets slide down the chute. Stepping behind the tiled partition that hid the communal baths from view, Bowman felt a tap on his shoulder. Turning, he was greeted by a naked, grinning man.

"Fine day, ain't it, your Majesty?"

The manic gleam in the man's eye gave Bowman pause. He knew a response was immaterial. The man's face was framed with a haze of wild white hair but the eyes were alive with a childlike innocence. Bowman stepped into the bath and gasped. As ever, the temperature had been set just a few degrees below comfortable.

He had been trusted to use his own razor and strop for several days now, but still it felt a novelty to shave himself. Having walked back to his room in a freshly starched gown, he had dressed in regulation clothes from a locker outside his door; a collarless shirt, trousers with braces and a heavy, tweed jacket. His razor and a shaving mirror had been set in his room. Wetting the blade in the bowl, Bowman's eyes rose to see his reflection in the glass. He had certainly lost weight in the previous few months. Perhaps a stone or so. His skin was sallow, his moustache lifeless and wiry. His eyes were wide, the frown between them cutting deeper than he remembered. His hair lay limp on his head. The overall appearance was of a man some ten years older than his thirty-seven years. Bowman stood stock still in the silence, razor paused inches from his jaw, mourning for the man he would never be again. The breakfast bell jolted him back to the dreadful present and he rushed his shave, cursing as he nicked the skin on his neck.

The route to the refectory was interrupted by the queue for physical inspection. It was quick and perfunctory; a look inside the mouth and ears and a comb through the hair. The doctor peered down his prominent nose at Bowman, his head seeming to rest on the high wing collar of his shirt. The warders who assisted looked bored. Evidently free of ulcers or fleas, Bowman was let on his way and joined another ragged line to pass into the kitchens.

Despite the heat from the ovens and hobs that were already stewing meat for dinner, the room felt barely any warmer than the corridors outside. Having reached the head of the queue at last, Bowman was rewarded with a thick slice of bread smeared with lard and a cup of thin, steaming broth. Grateful for the warmth it afforded if nothing else, Bowman took the cup and cradled it in his hands. It was served by a large lady, her face flushed pink as a ham from her toil in the kitchen. Her apron was tied too tight about her fat waist and she would lift it now and then to wipe the beads of sweat from her wide brow. Meeting Bowman's eyes, the woman fixed him with a hard, deliberate stare. Bowman made his way to join his fellow diners at a trestle table, one of two that spanned the length of the hall. The noise by now was almost intolerable. The size of the room meant that every sound, no matter how small, was rendered substantial. Conversations and arguments were amplified. Shoes scuffed against the slate floor and echoed to the roof. The slamming of plates and scraping of benches joined the melee, so as to render the chance of any quiet conversation quite impossible.

As he lifted his cup to drink, Bowman became aware of a man opposite him attempting to raise his voice above the hubbub. Stabbing the air with a bony finger and jutting his lantern jaw before him, he commenced hurling the most inventive obscenities that Bowman had heard in some time. Holding up a hand, he attempted to quieten the man. Looking about him, he saw two or three warders roused from their torpor. The wild man was on his feet by now, tearing at his hair and thrashing wildly about him. His neighbours stood too, either to get as far away from him as possible or to egg him on. Bowman saw that some of the more sensitive souls were crying or cradling their heads in their hands. Yet more laughed. Upending his cup and spilling broth to the floor, the man now picked up his plate and sent it skidding the length of the table to roars of approval from his audience. Two of his fellows joined him in his ghastly performance, one to hold his arms by his side in an attempt to subdue him, the other to rub the remnants of his bread into his hair. Bowman sank back into his seat, wary. By now the warders had approached and had a hold of the man. His screams only increased as they pulled him to the floor, the crowd pressing forward for a better view. Bowman noticed the doctor who had given the inspections at the door had run in too, his coat tails flapping behind him. With his beaked nose and high collared shirt, he looked for all the world like a large, agitated stork.

One of the warders shouted into the maelstrom. “Take him out! Restrain him!”

The hall was in uproar. The man’s hysteria seemed to have spread like fire from table to table. Some had started fighting, others stood with their mouths agape or threw themselves beneath the tables for safety. Hair was pulled, punches thrown and cups spilled. Food was thrown about the room with abandon. Obscenities filled the air. Bowman kept to his chair and looked about him with caution. More warders had entered the hall and attempted to calm the crowd. Bowman saw them blowing on their whistles, but they were barely heard above the maelstrom.

“Return to your dormitories!” they shouted. “Return to your dormitories!”

Reasoning that removing the offender would help to quell the riot, they headed to help their fellows. Fighting their way through the ruckus, they lay their hands on the man wherever they could; his clothes, his limbs, his hair. A table was upended as they dragged him over the tiles to the door. One group of men had broken into song. Swiftly, Bowman took advantage of the moment and followed the warders in their wake, nimbly stepping into the path they left behind them. As he reached the door, he saw the old man who had spoken to him in the queue for the baths standing solemn and erect, chest puffed out and his hand raised in salute. Bowman acknowledged the gesture and slipped round the corner to the labyrinth beyond. Ahead of him, he saw the warders manhandling the deranged man towards the treatment rooms. Only months before it might well have been him. His mouth dried at the memory. His early weeks here had been marked by behaviour that swung alarmingly from hysteria to an opiate-induced fog of melancholy. Bowman knew the man would be administered a sedative and restrained for the rest of the day, either in his bed or in a bath with a sheet placed over him save for his shoulders and head. He would be assessed later that evening to see how he might then spend the night. With the noise of the riot receding behind him, Bowman turned off the main corridor to the dormitories.

At last, it was light. Bowman lay on the bed in his room. While he had been at breakfast, his sheets had been replaced. He knew that he had received preferential treatment in the past few weeks. The majority of his fellows languished in overcrowded dormitories with little or no privacy. They were noisy, unsettling places, as Bowman could testify. He had spent his first weeks in just such a place. Then, he had rarely slept due to the screams and shrieks that would punctuate the night. Often he would wake to find a stranger at his bedside, standing in eerie silence.

The regime consisted of rest and routine. Those that could be put to work were placed in the laundry or the kitchens. Bowman himself had been placed on the allotments over the summer, which seemed to him a form of treatment in itself. The soil between his fingers and the certainty of growth made him feel part of the world and its processes. Any excess from the crops he gathered was sent to help feed the great gorging monster of a city, barely nine miles away. London's appetite was insatiable. As he loaded sacks of potatoes and onions on to carts, Bowman had felt like a supplicant offering appeasement to a voracious god. Aside from the fresh vegetables, the food was nourishing enough but predictable. Stews and broth were the custom; in fact, anything that could be easily cooked in quantity was favoured by the kitchens.

Bowman was fortunate. His room was comfortable if sparse. Just a little further up his corridor there were rooms similar to his own in every respect but that they were padded, kept locked day and night. They were seldom used and only as a last resort for those who proved a danger to themselves or others. Bowman wondered if his companion from breakfast had been taken there.

As the light crept across the floor and up the walls to the ceiling, he could see clefts in the plaster above him. Cracked and rusted pipes leeched their ochre residue onto the walls. As Bowman sipped from his cup of malt liquor – another luxury he had recently been afforded – he let his mind drift. It was true he was feeling better every day, but he was scared of life on the outside. For the last six months, his life had been one of tedium. Excitement was mitigated and medicated against. Each day was much like the other, save for the gradual change in the seasons and the light at the window.

He imagined himself back in his parlour; the picture of the Emperor Nero askew above the fireplace, the battered chaise longue by the door. In his mind's eye, he lay there now, feet resting on a cushion, glass of Madeira in his hand. Looking to the chair by the fire where she would sit and sew, Bowman could see her slender hands at her needlework, her face inclined to him as she worked. The curve of her neck invited him, her skin alabaster. Anna. The very word seemed hollow now, devoid of meaning.

He heard the hooves again. Anna turned to look, surprise in her eyes. He dropped his glass and tried to call her name but the words froze. His heart beat hard against his chest. He couldn't move. And they were upon her. Bowman felt the blood fleck on his face. He opened his mouth to scream but heard a bell ring, long and loud. She lay in the road, shattered and twisted. And still the bell rang.

Bowman opened his eyes with a start and sat upright in his bed. His breathing came fast and there was sweat on his brow. He found he had been clutching at his sheets, his knuckles white. Looking to the open door, he again hoped he had made no noise. The bell was ringing for the airing courts. He rose from the bed and pulled the towel from its hook. Wiping the sweat from his face, he took a breath. His heart had settled. And the bell had stopped.

Bowman grabbed a regulation felt coat from a hook in the hall. Wrapping it about him, he joined the throng converging on the grounds. Most were herded to the airing courts; large, walled arenas laid to grass and shrubs where they could enjoy an hour's supervised exercise. The warders cursed the cold almost as much as they cursed the inmates. Looking about him, Bowman saw the grass was resplendent in a frosty rime. Each blade a crystal. Drawing his collar closer about his neck, he trod carefully away from the crowd, heading for the allotments where he had been given dispensation to work unwatched. There was little to do at this time of year. The ground was iron hard. Bowman busied himself in gathering fallen wood from the nearby cedars and yew trees in a bid to build a fire. The blaze would keep him warm and the ash would serve to feed the soil for the next year's crop. Looking about him he saw two or three others who, like himself, had earned the right to walk about the grounds alone. They kept their eyes down, Bowman noticed, as if in shame. After an hour, he was warm with his exertions. He stopped for breath and looked back at the building that had been his home, squinting into the low morning sun. Shielding his eyes with a hand, he tried to look at it afresh, as if for the first time.

Colney Hatch crouched low and solid against the horizon. It was a grey, squat building that sprawled east and west from a large central entrance flanked by a wide colonnade. To the right lay the female wing, to the left the male. A bell tower pierced the morning sky at its centre, crowned with a copper dome. Bowman knew that each of the thousand windows he could see from his vantage looked into surgeries and dormitories, dining rooms, visitors" rooms and treatment rooms. There were workshops, schoolrooms, a dairy and even a brewery. As well as being home to over a thousand patients, room was needed, too, for servants and staff, teachers, surgeons, warders and attendants, cooks and gardeners. A veritable town bustled within those high, forbidding walls. Craning his neck to the left, he saw a smudge of smoke rising from the dirty city on the horizon, a greasy smear in the sky. Much was made of the progress of industry these days, mused Bowman, but the greatest mysteries lay within these walls, those of the human heart and mind.

As he let his eyes wander back across the sprawling length of the building, Bowman saw an attendant approaching. Even from this distance and accounting for the hat and muffler the man wore against the cold, Bowman recognised him as the attendant once assigned to sleep in his dormitory. Dawkins was his name. Beyond that Bowman knew nothing of him, save he had a habit of grinding his teeth and calling out in his sleep.

"Bowman!" Bowman saw the man's breath twist about him as he approached. "Bowman! You're called to the board."

Bowman dropped his hand to his side and cleared his throat, nervously. "Thank you," he rasped, the cold air catching at his throat. He was suddenly aware that these were the first words he'd spoken all day.

The committee rooms stood at the very heart of the building, affording grand views of the grounds to the front and rear. Colney Hatch stood in seventy-five acres of farmland and formal gardens, now bereft of colour and foliage. As the superintendent stood looking out at the wide, sweeping drive to the front of the building, the trees stood bare and the gardens empty. He turned back into the room to face the poor unfortunate before him.

Ernest Wright was a young, unkempt man. His jacket was at least a size too big and his scrawny neck poked through a collar far too wide. His black, wiry hair defied all attempts to tame it and would, now and then, fall across his eyes. A protruding bottom lip gave him the look of a simpleton and his half-shaved face told the story of a man for whom there was never enough time. He sat with his hands between his knees, rocking to and fro, cutting a pitiful figure. It was the superintendent's duty to pass judgement upon Ernest Wright. Judgement, at least, on the state of his wits. With a sigh, he took his seat behind the long table that dominated the room. Looking up and down the line of chairs beside him, he saw the matron, the doctor, a clerk and the chaplain were all avoiding his gaze. Having delivered their evidence they sat, impassive or absently fingering the piles of notes before them.

The superintendent cleared his throat to break the silence. "Ernest Wright," he began, "I have considered the statements from those here present and listened to what you have to say. It is my duty to consider both what is best for you and for society at large with regard to your place in this hospital. The doctor has pronounced you physically fit which goes much in your favour, but it is to the matron that we must turn with regard to your mental health. It is she that has had the most contact with you over the past weeks of your stay, and so her words carry great weight. It concerns me to hear of your ongoing fits of violence." He noticed Wright's rocking increase in its regularity and adopted a conciliatory tone. "I am not apportioning blame, Ernest. I know that this is a symptom of your condition. I note that the frequency of your outbursts is decreasing, a fact that gives me hope that in but a few weeks more you might well take your place in the wider world."

Ernest Wright emitted a whimper. With a quivering hand, he replaced a strand of hair that had fallen over his eyes.

"Please, sir - " he began.

The superintendent straightened his necktie and nodded to the clerk. "It is my judgement that, pursuant to the powers invested in me by the Lunacy Act of Eighteen Hundred and Forty Five, you should be detained for a further three months and that you should undergo continued treatment for this time." A low sound had begun to emanate from the poor wretch before them. The matron flicked her eyes to the superintendent in alarm, while the chaplain shifted uneasily in his seat at the end of the row.

"You will be accompanied back to your dormitory," continued the superintendent bravely, "Where a more thorough timetable for your treatment will be presented to you."

Ernest had ceased his rocking, but now began to stamp his foot with such volume that it echoed around the room. A look of panic in his eyes, he emitted a desperate moan as he looked wildly about him. The superintendent caught the attention of the two warders at the door and they moved closer to their patient, arms outstretched to restrain him. Before they could reach him, however, Ernest was on his feet. With a scream, he picked up the chair and slammed it to the floor. Saliva flew from his mouth as he ranted, stamping on the shattered remains of his chair. The two men were upon him now and, together with the doctor, they bundled him from the room, the soles of his heavy boots leaving tracks on the parquet flooring. The clerk sprang from the desk to replace the shattered chair.

"That was unfortunate," murmured the superintendent.

The doctor dipped his head in agreement. "He'll need to be watched. He'll despair at his continued stay here."

Having placed a new chair in position, the clerk returned to his place at the desk. He made a note in a ledger that lay before him. "Will he require sedation?" he enquired.

"Almost certainly," replied the doctor, straightening his coat about him. The clerk made another note as a warder returned.

Looking down a list in front of him, the superintendent gestured absently with his hand. "George Bowman, please, Thomas."

The warder left with a curt nod as the matron leafed through her notes. The chaplain drew a watch from his pocket. "I had hoped to be finished by now," he muttered as he fixed a monocle at his right eye, the better to see his timepiece. "I have my duties."

"You have an appointment at your drinks cabinet." The superintendent cast the chaplain a look. "I'm sure you can last another hour."

The warder had appeared at last, with Bowman at his side.

"George Bowman," began the superintendent, "You may take a seat."

Bowman looked at each of them in turn as he sat. The young clerk was flushed with exertion. The doctor wiped his brow with a monogrammed handkerchief. The matron was her usual solid self. The chaplain seemed preoccupied, his hands shaking with an almost imperceptible tremor. Noticing Bowman's enquiring look, he slid them out of view beneath the desk. There was an atmosphere in the room, like a storm had passed.

The superintendent looked up from his notes and fixed Bowman with a benevolent smile. He suddenly felt very small on his chair.

"I understand," began the superintendent, "That you have been with us since May of this year?"

Bowman nodded.

"For clarity and the benefit of the clerk's records, would you mind speaking up?"

"That is correct," said Bowman. Hearing the length of his incarceration spoken aloud to him had taken him aback. Seven months.

"And do you understand the purpose of this board?"

"Yes."

The clerk scratched his response into his ledger.

The superintendent's voice took on a curious, sing-song cadence as he launched into a speech that Bowman had no doubt he had delivered a thousand times before.

"Having taken into consideration the evidence provided by the members of this board and, under the powers granted me as superintendent of this institution by the Lunacy Act of Eighteen Hundred and Forty Five, it is my place to decide whether to prolong your treatment or, having responded favourably to said treatment over the last seven months – " Bowman shuddered again at the words, "Discharge you back into public life. Do you understand?"

"I do." Bowman shifted uncomfortably in his seat.

The superintendent looked over his spectacles. "How have you found your treatment?"

Bowman paused to find the right word. "Beneficial," he said.

The superintendent narrowed his eyes, as if assessing the truth of the statement. "Excellent," he said finally. Taking his glasses from his nose, he turned to his right. "Doctor Taylor?"

The doctor coughed and shuffled his papers. "The patient was presented to us on the evening of the Nineteenth of May, Eighteen Hundred and Ninety One, following an incident that resulted in the unfortunate death of the patient's wife. Having been present at the incident, the patient was found to be at the mercy of an extreme melancholia." The doctor's voice was devoid of all feeling. He might as well, thought Bowman, have been reciting from the business pages of the Times newspaper. "The symptoms presented included a fearful delirium, fever and evident heaviness of heart. Over the next two days under our observation, he exhibited all the marks of a melancholy condition, namely; a deep, silent sadness together with a reticence to submit himself to treatment. The following four days were characterised by moody and sullen behaviour punctuated by episodes of belligerence bordering on the violent. Initial treatment comprised restraint, sedation, cold-water baths and solitary confinement. A course of leeches was prescribed to be placed upon the skull and a short programme of blisters to the base of the neck."

Bowman started in his seat. He had no memory of being the recipient of any such treatment. Perhaps, he mused, that was just as well.

"Within four weeks," the doctor continued, "improvements were seen and the patient was allowed to progress to the next stage of his treatment, namely; exercise, fresh air and manual activity. The patient learned to comply with his treatment and, from that point, his eventual recovery was assured." His report complete, the doctor sat back in his chair, satisfied he had discharged his duty. The baton then passed to the matron who held Bowman in a steely gaze. She gave her report without once looking down to the papers before her. Her voice was powerful and uncompromising. Bowman had learned she was not a lady to be trifled with.

"The patient," she began, "has benefitted from advantages during his term here. In recent weeks, allowances have been made due to his continued good behaviour and compliance, such that he has been allowed a private room and to walk unsupervised about the grounds." She cast an eye at the clerk. "I would wish it to be a matter of record that I strongly disapproved of such measures being taken. I believe that any deviation from the prescribed programme of treatment may prove unproductive. I understand that pressure was placed upon the superintendent from outside forces."

The matron was interrupted in her flow by an ill-tempered cough from the superintendent himself. Bowman's frown had deepened at the mention of "outside forces". He had been proven right in his suspicions. Far from his privileges being due to his improving behaviour, they had been granted due to interventions from beyond the hospital walls.

"The patient's night terrors are more infrequent and he has been taking food for some time. However, about the grounds and within the confines of the hospital building, it is rare to see him converse with his fellows. I should say that, before he is released from our care, I would wish to see him more sociable and able to navigate the complexities of discourse." Her declaration complete, the matron folded her arms across her not inconsiderable bosom.

"Would you have me talk of the weather?" Bowman's moustache twitched in agitation.

The superintendent attempted to wrestle back control of the proceedings. "Thank you, matron." Leaning forward on the desk, he gestured to the chaplain. "Father?"

Bowman noticed the chaplain's eyes snap open. Clearly taken by surprise, the wiry old man smoothed down his hair and shuffled through his papers. Clearing his throat to buy some time, he replaced his monocle and nodded sagely. "The patient has attended chapel each week for the last six weeks," he said at last, his voice slurred. With that, he sat back in his chair. Bowman had his suspicions the man was drunk.

Rolling his eyes, the superintendent looked back to Bowman. "Are you still visited by dreams?"

The question hung in the air. Bowman swallowed hard. "No."

"Louder, please," the clerk interjected, pen poised.

Bowman licked his lips and swallowed again. "No. I am not."

The clerk held his gaze for a while, then scratched his response into the ledger. He filled his pen at the inkwell as he wrote.

The superintendent rose from his seat and walked to the window behind him. The slope of the lawn below led his eye to the allotments and playing fields beyond. To his left and right he could see those still in the airing courts. A fight had broken out in one of them and, from his great height, the superintendent could see two or three warders running to calm the situation. Hands behind his back, he turned back into the room and took a breath.

"George Bowman," he began, "I have considered the statements from those here present and I have listened to what you have to say. It is my duty to consider both what is best for you and for society at large with regard to your place in this hospital. It is my judgement that you should be released from this place on probation. A notice will be sent immediately to the magistrate for his signature and your personal effects will be returned to you together with an allowance to aid you in your transition into public life."

"I'll need no allowance," Bowman asserted. "I have employment waiting."

"Then your employer shall be made aware of the following conditions. That if there be any recurrence of your condition, you shall be admitted for further treatment. Should you still be in good health after twelve weeks, you will be fully discharged and permitted to continue at large."

The matron made no attempt to disguise her disapproval, rolling her eyes to the ceiling and letting go a contemptuous sigh. The doctor folded away his papers as if satisfied while the chaplain woke with a start as his head rocked slowly to his chest.

Some two hours later, wearing clothes he hadn't seen for seven months and carrying a canvas bag of belongings that had been returned to him upon his release, Bowman stood outside the main door to the building. He looked about him for a final time. The grounds were quiet now, the patients returned to their wards. Walking down the long drive to the main gates, Bowman pulled on his gloves and wrapped his coat tighter about him. He jammed his hat on his head and swung his bag over his shoulder. Pausing at the gatehouse, he looked back at the long, low building that crouched behind him then turned his back on it forever. Slowly and with little ceremony, Detective Inspector

George Bowman swung the gates of the asylum shut behind him and focused his tired eyes hard upon the horizon.

I

A Gruesome Discovery

The stars stood out against the blackest of skies as the two lovers ran, hand in hand, over Westminster Bridge. St Stephen's Tower soared above their heads, the clock face a second moon in the firmament. The young girl laughed as they ran down the steps. Looking about her, she saw that all was still. The Thames lay before them, frozen almost the length of its foreshore. It was the first time in many years that the river had frozen this far downstream. Few people recalled the freeze of Eighteen Fourteen, the last time the Thames had frozen completely, but there persisted a collective memory of frost fairs, games on the ice and elephants walking on the frozen water. This year, a wide channel still flowed at the centre, but several feet worth of thick ice encroached from the bank for the whole of the river's length as far as the eye could see.

Few lights burned in the windows of the houses along the river. Occasional wisps of smoke ascended into the heavens, lending a grey black smudge to the pristine air. Beneath the bridge vagrants stood around a brazier, warming their hands on the coals and shuffling their feet in a vain attempt to keep warm. Somewhere, a lone dog barked.

Reaching the foreshore, the two youths paused to pull off their boots. Swinging a knapsack from his shoulders, the man pulled two pairs of skates from the bag and handed one to his sweetheart. Now it became a game to see who could pull them on first and tie the laces. Finishing before her lover, the girl laughed again and pulled his hat over his eyes.

"Hey!" he called in mock fury, a wide smile spreading across his frozen face.

"Catch as catch can!" she retorted, pushing her way off the foreshore and into the frozen reaches of the Thames. Straightening his hat, the young man watched her go, skimming across the ice like some graceful craft.

"Be careful in the middle!" he shouted after her, 'steer clear of the channel!"

Taking a deep, contented sigh, he reflected that his life might never be so sweet again. Then all was quiet. In reflective mood, he let his eyes wander from the river to the stars. The great constellation of Orion seemed to wink his approval at their adventure. A full moon held sway in the cloudless sky, giving light enough to see even at this late hour. And then he contemplated the ice below. The edges of the Thames stood frozen, tamed and implacable. Here at the bank, the water seemed still and quiet beneath the weight of ice, in stark contrast to the torrent at its centre. Time itself seemed frozen in the ice's grip. He felt he had an eternity. As if in defiance at the thought, the great bell in the tower started to chime. Midnight. Somewhere, a firework shrieked into the night leaving a trail behind it, comet-like. Standing unsteadily on his skates, he too pushed off onto the ice, cupping his hands about his mouth to call after his sweetheart.

"Hey, Sarah!" he called, "Happy New Year!"

Skidding to a halt some yards from the shore, he paused to hear her reply. Nothing. He called again.

"Sarah?"

Peering under the bridge the way she had gone, he saw nothing but the vagrants at their fire. One raised a half empty bottle to him in recognition of the New Year, while another bedded down on a pile of blankets and rags. Aside from this, he could discern no movement and hear no sound. Just as he was about to push off in pursuit, a scream pierced the still night air. It was unmistakeable.

"Sarah?"

The scream came again from beyond the bridge. Kicking ice behind him, he sped through the nearest arch. Beyond the span of the bridge, a figure resolved itself in the gloom. It was Sarah, he saw, kneeling on the ice by the shore, her face in her gloved hands.

"What is it? Are you hurt?" He skidded to a halt beside her, glittering shards of ice kicked up by his skates announcing his arrival. "I heard a scream."

Sarah took a hand from her face and pointed down into the ice. "Look!" she shrieked, visibly shaking now.

The young man followed her gaze to the ice, trying to peer deeper into the water below. "What is it? You had me so scared." Dropping to his knees beside her, he wiped at the frost with his hands. There in the ice where they knelt, like a fly trapped in amber, he could plainly discern the face of a young woman. Her sightless eyes gazed up at them, her mouth wide open in a silent scream.

"It's an obvious but unfortunate case of suicide." Inspector Ignatius Hicks of Scotland Yard stood upon an upturned crate he had found beside the river and declaimed from a lofty height to anyone who cared to listen. As it happened, the crowd was sizable for so early in the morning. They had been drawn by the sight of a team of men, stripped to their shirtsleeves despite the cold, sawing and chiselling their way through the ice near the shore. With occasional shouts and curses, they ordered more tools be brought from the cart they had pulled down to the river's edge. It was a curious spectacle in the harsh morning light, and one that attracted the attention of many on their way to work. Even the vagrants beneath Westminster Bridge had risen early to investigate.

The roofs and chimneys around them stood in sharp relief against a piercing blue sky where the rooks and pigeons wheeled. The sun, still low on the horizon, cast long shadows in the streets but even where it reached the ground unhindered, was of insufficient strength to offer any warmth.

Inspector Hicks was a large, bearded man muffled against the cold in a giant, calf length coat. He held a smoking pipe in a gloved hand the size of a large ham, and used it to punctuate his pronouncements as if this very action would lend them credulity. The motley gathering about him regarded him as nothing more than a circus turn.

Such was the scene that greeted Inspector George Bowman. His dark brows, jammed beneath a bowler hat, were knotted into a frown and his thin mouth was drawn down in an expression of concentration as he tried to keep his footing on the ice. The cold did not agree with him. Despite the application of several layers, a thick scarf and an extra muffler, Inspector Bowman felt frozen to his core. And he could no longer feel his feet.

"Happy New Year, sir."

He was joined, squinting into the sun, by Sergeant Anthony Graves, a man whose surname was quite at odds with his naturally cheery disposition. A curly mop of blond hair framed his handsome, youthful face and he seemed not to mind the cold at all. He wore no hat and no gloves.

Bowman grunted in reply and nodded across to the gangly young man and his pretty girlfriend who stood shivering by the river's edge. "Not for them, it isn't," he growled. "They found the body last night and raised the alarm. They just can't tear themselves away."

Graves followed his gaze. "Poor devils," he said. "I've ordered some hot soup for the men. I dare say they won't mind sharing it with them."

"I've never known it so cold," said Bowman, puffing on his hands in a futile attempt to restore feeling. "Will you take their statements?"

"I will. But I've no doubt Inspector Hicks has got the whole thing wrapped up by now."

Bowman could tell Graves felt awkward in his presence. It was there in the little sideways glances he had afforded him during their conversation. Finally, his tall companion cleared his throat.

"Are you feeling quite well, sir?"

Bowman felt the skin on his neck begin to burn beneath his scarf. "I am well, thank you."

It occurred to Bowman that this was the first time he had seen Sergeant Graves since the night of the incident. The mundanity of their conversation was a world away from their last meeting. Looking at Graves, Bowman could see that he had not changed a bit. His face still had the flush of youth, his eyes bright and inquisitive. For Bowman, however, a lifetime had passed. He felt he had aged ten years. Anthony Graves had seen it all. Indeed, he had held Bowman back as his wife lay trampled in the dirt. If he had been left alone to intervene as he had wished, Bowman would surely have died too. He had often wished it so.

"Well," Graves stammered, clearly eager to put an end to the exchange as quickly as he could, "It's nice to see you back, sir."

As they talked, the men had reached the little audience that surrounded Hicks and, seeing them approach, the bearded inspector broke off from his performance.

"Ah, Bowman, so glad you could join us again." The implication in Hicks' choice of words was harsh, thought Graves, and he winced at their cruelty. Unabashed, Hicks drew from his pipe then held it aloft in a dramatic fashion. "Listen and learn." Bowman rolled his eyes and looked down to his feet as Hicks continued, opening his arms wide in an expansive gesture. His great voice boomed over the crowd. He would, thought Inspector Bowman, have made an impressive actor.

"Imagine the scene," began Hicks, his eyes bright with the telling of his tale. "Two lovers meet in secret on Westminster Bridge, but theirs is a forbidden love. Perhaps their parents did not approve of their match. Perhaps it is a question of class." Bowman looked to Sergeant Graves who was very obviously trying to suppress a snigger at these outrageous assumptions. "And so a pact is made," continued the rotund inspector. "If they could not be together in life, then they shall be so in death. A final, tender kiss and they commit themselves to the Thames, taking with them the tragic sweetness of a forbidden love." The crescendo in his tale was enough to provoke a smattering of applause amongst some of the spectators. Incredibly, it seemed as if Hicks was about to take a bow. He stopped short of quite so theatrical a gesture however, and contented himself with a gentle nod of his head by way of thanks.

"But we have discovered only the woman's body. Where is that of her lover?" demanded Bowman as the noise subsided. The crowd turned as one to look at Hicks in anticipation of an answer.

"We've searched downstream and found nothing," added Graves.

"Then perhaps you should check upstream," Hicks boomed, proud of his response.

There was a flutter of movement from the crowd as the implications of his statement became clear. Even Hicks looked suddenly ill at ease.

"Are bodies now in the habit of floating against the stream?" teased Bowman, giving voice to the doubters around him. Keen to see how Hicks would react, the crowd swivelled in unison back to face him. The inspector cleared his throat to buy himself some time.

"Then I should have thought it was obvious to those of us who know the ways of love." This brought a spontaneous laugh from some in the crowd, a laugh that was quite lost on Hicks. As he warmed to his theme, he drew himself up to his full height and puffed out his not inconsiderable chest. "Her lover lost his stomach in the face of death. He watched his sweetheart fall but he couldn't jump. Thus, conscience makes cowards of us all."

This seemed to please the crowd, who turned to Bowman to hear his retort. "Then I shall look forward to him coming forward with his story. If he loved her so much, I doubt he could live with the guilt for long."

This strange performance was interrupted by a sudden shout from the team of workmen behind them. They had successfully cut through the ice and, with the aid of ropes and improvised pulleys, lifted out a large block that now rested on the frozen Thames. Around it, the men leaned on their picks and saws, wiping the sweat from their brows with their forearms. The team leader, a wiry old man with a flat cap and a drip of sweat suspended from his nose, called over to the knot of spectators by the shore.

"There is no body!"

"What?" roared Hicks.

"There is no body," he repeated. "Just a head. The rest was weeds and driftwood."

With that, Inspector Hicks turned back to his audience for a final flourish. "Aha!" he proclaimed without a trace of irony. "It's just as I said. Murder, plain and simple."

As Bowman made his way over reluctantly to examine the grisly discovery, the crowd began to disperse. Among them, quite unnoticed, was a barrel of a man dressed up against the cold in a cape and shawl. A scarf was pulled up high over his chin, but it was possible to see that he had bushy, greying whiskers that protruded from his cheeks, sweeping back over his ears. His skin was as brown as a nut. A pair of small, dark spectacles hid his hooded eyes from view as, unseen, he crept stealthily over the ice and away from the crowd.

II

The Fisherman's Tale

Joseph Morley cut a dashing figure in the tight-knit streets of Southwark. Resplendent in top hat and Astrakhan coat, he carefully placed his silver-tipped cane before him as he trod the slippery streets. Occasionally, he was torn between walking through the clean snow in the middle of the road and thus running the risk of an encounter with the odd cart or hansom cab, or keeping to the pavements which were already strewn with dirt and mud kicked up from the wheels and hooves of passing tradesmen and their horses. In consideration of his new handmade shoes and spats, he generally chose the former, although once or twice he was forced to make a quick retreat in the face of an oncoming cabbie. Beneath the brim of his hat, his greying temples betrayed his age. Aside from a set of fast developing jowls, he liked to think he could pass for forty five, particularly if he held in his stomach, but the reality was that he looked all of his fifty two years. Tipping his hat to the ladies who were out and about and cautioning them to mind their step, Morley rounded a corner into an open yard set back from the main road by a pair of wrought iron gates. On them, and on the side of the imposing red brick building ahead could be read the words, "Joseph Morley's Saw Mill". The sign never failed in its effect on the thickset man who stood and gazed up at its letters. Joseph Morley was inordinately proud of all he had achieved in his life. From humble beginnings in a house in Cheapside where his father worked as a tanner, he had worked his way up from the floor of the saw mill to the lofty position he now held, that of mill owner and manager. He had found the will to learn to read and write with the effect that by the time he was twenty, he was trusted to handle the mill's books and accounts. With an increase in wages came the opportunity to invest, which Morley did, and wisely. Money invested in the burgeoning tea trade paid handsome and regular dividends and so, in the fullness of time and with the help of a few friends at the bank (help not bought cheaply, mind) he had found himself, aged thirty five, in a position to buy outright the saw mill and all its equipment. As an employer he was determined to be firm but fair, mindful of his time as a young worker at the lathe. He was generally felt by all in the neighbourhood to be a right and proper gentleman, which pleased him greatly.

Pulling a great ring of keys from his coat pocket, Morley stepped carefully across the yard to the passage beside the mill. He liked to be the first to work, not least to wake the urchins who cleaned the saws and who slept for free on the factory floor. They would need, as usual, to be roused in good time before their work so they could avail themselves of a helping of soup from the workhouse across the road. It was an arrangement that Morley himself had secured, on the promise of an annual gift to the workhouse chapel.

As he walked unsteadily into the passage, blinking his eyes against the cold, there was a movement behind a stack of timber by the mill wall. A frantic, scuffling sound caught his attention and he stopped and held his breath.

"Who's there?" he demanded after a few moments of silence. "I'll have you know you're trespassing." Receiving no reply, Joseph Morley continued his progress up the alley. Somewhere a church bell tolled and the cries of early morning traders carried in the still air, mingling with the whistle of a train from the nearby railway. Another noise pulled him up short. It was closer this time, and ahead of him; a regular, rasping sound. Morley held his cane before him. "Well," he growled, "I shall beat you out like the common grouse."

Morley sidled up the passageway towards the source of the noise, waving his cane before him and steadying himself as he went with a hand on the wall to his side. There was a low, rumbling sound as a great pile of timber toppled and fell before him, narrowly missing Morley's head but making further progress impossible. He tried to back away but found his exit blocked by a man. He was shoeless but dressed in a threadbare coat and trousers with patches and holes at the knees. A greasy scarf hung around his neck and a weather beaten fisherman's cap was pulled down tight upon his head. Most repugnant of all, however, was the hideous, gap-toothed smile that was spread across his face like a wound. In his right hand, he carried a length of wire that he swung ominously before him.

"Get out of my way," snarled Morley, determined to outface the vermin. "I would advise you to step aside sir, or I cannot be held responsible for my actions." He held his cane aloft by the ferrule, its silver handle dancing perilously close to the villain's face. With a movement too swift for the eye to follow, the interloper grabbed the stick and pulled hard, sending Morley sprawling back through the alley. Struggling to regain his balance, he was about to break into a run when he felt a tightening at his throat. He instinctively drew his hand up to his neck, but it was too late. A burning pain could be felt at his collar, and he could taste blood at the back of his throat. With his eyes bulging and his faculties fading fast, Morley knew at once that the fellow was using the wire upon his neck. He felt hot breath in his ear as the killer leaned in to whisper.

"Down you go, my beauty."

Morley's legs buckled and he fell to his knees, the snow beneath him stained crimson from his gushing wound. All hope of screaming now was gone. He could barely catch his breath. The wire was pulled tight again and Morley felt his life bleeding away. As darkness overcame him, his assailant lowered him almost tenderly to the ground where he lay, face down, on the ice. And there, his fingers scratching involuntarily at the wall beside him, Joseph Morley died.

Isambard Fogg was quick and lithe, two qualities that served him well in his trade. Quick as a weasel he fell upon the body, his fingers searching through Morley's coat for anything of value. From an inside pocket he drew an expensive, handmade leather wallet monogrammed with the owner's initials. "A fisherman," hissed Fogg as he fingered through the notes inside, "That's all I am." He held a few up to the light, agog at his good fortune. "I reel in my catch, and then I gut it." He ripped Joseph Morley's wedding ring from his finger and released a golden pocket watch from its anchor on his richly embroidered waistcoat. Yanking at the silver buttons on his coat to pull them free, Fogg stopped with a sudden thought. "Fine clothes," he said, "They'll fetch me a pretty penny if I'm lucky." And so, working silently in the alley for fear of discovery, he proceeded to strip Morley's body of its more valuable clothing. All in all, he thought, the morning had been kind to him.

III

A Den Of Thieves

As the sun climbed higher into the brightening sky, a little of the ice which hung as icicles upon the tenement roofs of Southwark began to thaw. Dripping to the ground, they melted the snow and mud into a dirty slush as the city came to life. Private carriages and public omnibuses clattered through the narrow streets and alleys on the South Bank, and hawkers and traders set up their stalls amid the growing throng. Yards and workshops threw open their gates to workers and patrons alike and the air became heavy with the scent of smoke and horse dung.

Away from the bustle, in a grimy little room off a side street in Southwark, sat three dissolute men of ill repute, warming themselves by a fire. The choking smog that rose from the brazier in the corner of the room served to obscure their faces. The brazier was, aside from a few low stools and a pile of blankets in the corner, the only furniture in the little room. A cracked and dirty window gave out onto the narrow street beyond but admitted little light, so that it was difficult to discern one man from another in the gloom. The low ceiling was coated with a skein of tar from a thousand smouldering cheroots and the bare brick walls crumbled to dust upon being touched.

Jabez Kane sat closest to the fire, his swarthy appearance the result of successive layers of dirt and grime rather than any natural colouring. He picked at his teeth with a jagged blade and threw the last of his meagre breakfast into the flames. He was dressed in a motley collection of grimy clothes; hobnail boots, docker's overalls, a kerchief around his neck and a ring through his ear. He had stubbled cheeks, dark, impenetrable eyes and a hawk-like nose but, most grisly of all, was the wide and uneven scar that ran from his forehead, over his left eye and onto his cheek. Its origin was a thing of myth. No one had ever dared to ask. All that was certain was that Kane had had the scar for half a lifetime and, whatever it was that had caused it, had failed to turn him from a life of crime. As he stretched his feet towards the fire, he gave his neighbour a shove. Albert Hobbs was snoring. Hobbs, it seemed, could sleep through anything and was notoriously hard to rouse. Even in his awkward position, propped up hard against the wall, one leg folded under the other and his arms hanging at his side, it seemed as if Hobbs was enjoying a deep and rewarding sleep. His rounded chest wheezed and rattled as it rose and fell, and his throat and nose bubbled and popped as he snored.

"Hobbs!" Kane screeched, thumping him again for good measure. "Wake up or shut up!"

Hobbs stirred and swore at his companion, pulling the hat further down over his face in determined protest. "Let sleeping dogs lie," he drooled, lapsing again into a lazy doze.

"Careful Hobbs," came a voice from a darkened corner. Edmund Treacher had a ruddy face, the result of living an outdoor life. His hands were calloused and cracked, his clothes little more than a jumble of rags that afforded little protection from the cold outside. "They shoot dogs that live beyond their usefulness".

Treacher sat chuckling on his haunches, eating chestnuts from a bag. Periodically, he would throw the shells at the fire, not caring much if they struck his companions or fell short to litter the floor.

There was a rattle at the makeshift door that was little more than a wooden pallet, and Treacher rose to investigate. Peering through a crack to the street beyond, he gave a grunt of recognition. "It's Fogg," he announced, although the occupants of the room showed little or no reaction to the news. With an effort, Treacher levered the door open, scraping the bottom across the rough, uneven flagstones on the floor. The noise woke Hobbs who, his interest roused by the commotion, pulled his hat up over his face. Peering into the gloom, he wiped sleep from his eyes with the back of his hand and took a swig from the bottle of gin at his side.

"Here he is," said Kane turning his head to the visitor, "The organ grinder's monkey."

Hobbs laughed a low, abrasive cackle. “Looks like he’s got a little something for his master, too.” He leaned forward from the waist, the better to see the visitor and his wares. “Been busy have we?”

As Isambard Fogg squeezed in through the door he lowered the sack from his back, glad to relieve his shoulders of their heavy load. Rubbing his sore neck to ease the stiffness, he paused as his eyes adjusted themselves to the darkness of the grimy room.

“Trinkets,” he spluttered in the smog. “Trinkets and baubles, that’s all.”

As one, all eyes in the room turned to size him up. Fogg was much as he always was, save for two notable additions. On his feet, in stark contrast to the tattered hems of his filthy trousers, he wore a pair of exquisite handmade leather shoes complete with spats. Upon his head, a top hat was perched incongruously. The mood in the room shifted at once as Kane and Hobbs rocked on the floor, their laughter echoing around the cramped walls.

“Oh look, Hobbs, he’s a proper gentleman, so he is!” Kane was laughing hardest of all.

“I don’t think a gentleman would be seen with the likes of us, Kane,” said Hobbs, enjoying the joke. “P’raps he’s lost.”

“Fogg? Fogg, is that you?”

The low, booming voice had an immediate effect. The laughter stopped abruptly. Kane turned his face to the fire once more and Hobbs’ hat was pulled again over his eyes.

“Get your bones in ’ere where I can see ’em!”

As Treacher heaved the door closed behind him, Fogg swallowed hard. Throwing the bag back over his shoulder, he made his way to the tattered and greasy curtain that hung over a doorway to an adjoining room, the source of the imposing voice. Pausing to polish the toes of his brand new shoes on the backs of his legs, he stepped bravely through. As he disappeared from the room, the three remaining occupants glanced conspiratorially at each other, then threw back their heads once more in cruel, mocking laughter.

Beyond the curtain, Hardacre was sovereign. He sat, god-like, upon a grubby, moth-eaten chair before a grate festooned with candles. All around him, seemingly in every available space, lay the spoils of his profession glinting and glistening in the flickering flames. Silk scarves and handkerchiefs hung from the mantle, bags and sacks spilled their booty of coins and jewellery from low tables onto the floor. Stools and chairs were piled high with plates and silver salvers. Cutlery and kitchenware of the highest standard was strewn across the floor. Isambard Fogg knew this was Hardacre's domain and, as he shuffled through the curtain, his eyes fell instinctively to the floor in solemn reverence.

"Look at me, Fogg." Hardacre leaned forward on his chair, daring the wily vagrant to meet his gaze. Fogg looked up slowly, his eyes searching Hardacre's face for any sign of his mood. He had learned to look for tell-tale clues; a tightness in the mouth or a narrowing of the eyes to indicate displeasure, an incline of the head or an outstretched hand to denote compassion. This morning, thought Fogg as their eyes met, Hardacre was impossible to read. And this worried him greatly. Hardacre's barrel chest was thrust forward in defiance of the waistcoat buttons struggling to contain it. His hooded eyes looked down a bulbous nose at the sight before him and greying whiskers sprung from leathery, brown cheeks, reaching out like tendrils to spread back across his ears. "Where you been, Fogg?"

"Workin'." A hideous, toothless leer spread across Fogg's face as he recalled his encounter in the alley.

"What you got for me, then?"

Isambard Fogg swung the sack back down from his shoulder and let its contents spill to the floor; Joseph Morley's coat and handkerchief, waistcoat and trousers.

"Fine clothes," murmured Hardacre approvingly. "What else?"

Reaching inside his tattered coat, Fogg pulled Morley's wallet from a pocket. Daringly, he held the purse out to Hardacre, who snatched at it like a hungry dog might snatch at food.

"Good, Fogg, good. Currency." He flicked through its contents as Fogg stood at his feet, nodding and grinning in the half-light. This was going well. "What else?"

Fogg swallowed hard. Reaching into his trousers, he pulled Morley's watch from a hidden seam.

"Gonna keep that for yourself were you, Fogg?" Hardacre's voice was barely audible now, the threat implicit in its quietening tones.

Fogg struggled to find his words. "Forgot," he stammered, the smile disappearing from his face as he let the watch fall to the floor.

Hardacre leaned ominously to one side, reaching down beside his chair. Sitting back, king-like on his throne, he pulled a club from the folds of an old blanket and sat, resting it across his lap like a sceptre.

With a sudden hope of appeasement, Fogg reached up and snatched the top hat from his head. "Silk," he offered hopefully, as he threw the hat to the ground beside Morley's coat. "And these shoes, they're new." He hopped on one foot then the other as he removed each shoe and held them up in the gloom for Hardacre's inspection. He would have cut a comical figure, if his situation weren't becoming increasingly desperate. The atmosphere in the room had changed, and Fogg could feel it.

Fogg owed a lot to the despot in the chair. An orphan, he had been rescued from certain death on the streets by Hardacre who saw him as easy pickings. Fogg was already well versed in the ways of petty crime and Hardacre considered him a wise investment. So he had proved. In exchange for shelter and the protection of a criminal overlord, Fogg had risen to the challenge of becoming one of the best in his business. His unique quality was his ruthlessness. Fogg prided himself on never having shied away from inflicting harm in the pursuit of his booty. He took chances, and Hardacre rewarded men who took chances. Kane and Hobbs were mere hangers on by comparison, content to do just enough and no more for Hardacre's favours. The new man, Treacher, was still an unknown quantity. He had joined the gang in recent weeks and Fogg suspected he was soft. He returned each day with goods for Hardacre with never so much as a scratch upon him. Fogg guessed he was nothing more than an opportunist, snatching what he could through open doors and windows, never risking injury or discovery. However, as Fogg watched Hardacre swinging his club nonchalantly from one swarthy hand to the other, he got the distinct impression that he had done wrong, that perhaps this time the risk had not paid off.

"You've done well, Fogg," began Hardacre. "But not well enough." Fogg's eyes darted around the room like a trapped animal. He could run back the way he had come but the three men next door would surely catch him.

"I've just come from the Thames, Fogg," Hardacre continued, beating time on the palm of one hand with his cudgel. "Do you understand?"

"The Thames?" Fogg was sweating now, his heart beating fiercely against his chest.

"Do you remember the little job you did for me last week?"

Fogg remembered it well enough, and winced at the memory. "Yes," he whispered.

"Well, now. A couple of skaters found something in the ice last night."

"S-somethin' in the ice?" stammered Fogg, his mouth drying rapidly. He knew now what was to come, although he was not yet clear why. He had been on the receiving end of Hardacre's temper before, and did not relish the prospect of feeling it again. He braced himself for the inevitable onslaught.

"They found her head in the Thames, Fogg!" With a nimbleness that belied his size, Hardacre had sprung from his chair with a roar, raising the cudgel high above his head with his powerful hands. "They found her in the Thames!"

In the room next door, Treacher, Kane and Hobbs looked up as they heard the sound of wood crunching on bone from beyond the tattered greasy curtain to Hardacre's cell. Despite the unfolding horror, not one of them flinched a muscle in response.

Hardacre had fallen into a grisly rhythm now, punctuating each of his words with another blow to Fogg's unprotected head. "They – found – her – in – the – Thames!" The first blow had rendered Fogg unconscious and so he had fallen like a doll into an ungainly heap on the floor. Now each successive blow served only to compound his injuries, splitting his skull and eye sockets and matting his hair with blood and tissue. Hardacre's face was spattered crimson from the frenzy and, once or twice, he paused to wipe the blood from his cheek with a threadbare sleeve. Satisfied he had made his point, Hardacre stepped back, his whole body rising and falling in time with his frenzied breathing. Dropping back to rest after his titanic effort, he stumbled into his chair and sat sprawled, blinking sweat from his eyes and licking blood from his lips. "That'll learn you, Fogg," he whispered in triumph. "That'll learn you."

IV

The Thaw

"Ready when you are, Inspector Bowman." Doctor John Crane MRCS was a tall, elderly bird of a man who spoke with a refined Scottish burr. A pair of half moon spectacles perched precariously upon his nose and his hair was parted just above the ear then swept up over his head in an effort to disguise his balding pate. He wore an apron stained in reds and browns, the origins of which Inspector Bowman did not wish to consider.

Bowman had been waiting for an hour now, hat in hand, in the corridor at Charing Cross Hospital. The tiled walls echoed to the slightest noise and the gas lamps lit at regular intervals along the wall lent a sickly, yellow pallor to the very air. Strange, chemical smells escaped from every door, mixed with the odour of decay. The high windows of frosted glass were heavily barred against intrusion and allowed in little light. The corridor itself was below ground level, and the windows gave out onto the icy pavements around the hospital. Occasionally, Bowman had watched as disembodied feet walked carefully by, their owners completely unseen from the lower leg up. The whole impression was one of being a few feet closer to the flames of Hell itself. Inspector Bowman felt his palms moisten as he involuntarily lifted a hand to rub the back of his neck. He found himself searching for scars, any tell tale sign of his treatment. The doctor in Colney Hatch had mentioned blisters and the application of leeches. Did he bear a mark that all could see but him? He did not feel at all well. As Doctor Crane turned back into a room off the corridor, Bowman swallowed hard and followed him in.

Inside Crane's laboratory, the air was heavy with pungent steam. Condensation dripped from every surface. The countless bottles and vials that lined the walls were pricked with globules of water. There wasn't a shelf that was free of scientific vessels and instruments. Gas burners were arranged around the room on low wooden tables and, between them, culture dishes and large glass pitchers stood full of coloured liquids, powders and specimens. The tiled walls were hung with charts and diagrams, some of which made Bowman's stomach turn the more. Against the furthest wall, where Doctor Crane was busy donning elbow-high Indian rubber gloves, stood a stove. On its surface, a metal urn was balanced solidly on a frame above two gas jets that hissed and spat as they burned. The urn had a handle at each side and an ill-fitting lid.

"Thank you, Sergeant Graves, you may turn off the gas." Doctor Crane gestured with a bony finger to the dials arranged along the front of the stove, and the sergeant bent to turn them off. Bowman noticed that Graves seemed to be enjoying himself.

"You all right, inspector?" asked Graves, his youthful face beaming with a childlike excitement. "Feeling a bit queer?"

"No," swallowed Bowman. "I'm fine." His hand reached instinctively to his belly to calm his churning stomach. He noticed that Graves too was wearing a pair of protective gloves and had thrown a laboratory apron over his workaday clothes. The steam in the room had caused his blond locks to plaster themselves across his forehead. The heat had brought a flush to his cheeks. "You seem rather to be entering into the spirit of things," Bowman observed. By way of a reply, Graves offered him a conspiratorial wink. Bowman turned back to the doctor. "Is she – " he broke off. "Is it - "

"Thawed?" offered the doctor, looking over his glasses.

"Yes. Is it thawed?"

"It is not a procedure I would wish to rush, Inspector Bowman. It is imperative that the flesh remains intact. But yes, it is thawed. Sergeant Graves," snapped the doctor, "Might I have your assistance?"

The two men positioned themselves on either side of the urn and, with a look to each other to time their actions, plunged their hands into the water. After groping for a while to find purchase and with a look of careful concentration upon their faces, they lifted the head from the urn. Quite by chance, her face was turned towards Bowman as she rose. He could not but gasp as her eyes searched his. The jaw was slack and hung from its moorings so her mouth hung open in a silent, imploring scream. After holding the head over the urn to let the excess water drain, Graves and the doctor moved as one to deposit their load upon a wooden block with an unceremonious slop.

"Feeling a little uncomfortable, Inspector Bowman?" teased the doctor, removing his half-round spectacles to wipe them free of condensation on his apron.

Inspector Bowman's features looked more drawn than usual. His frown cut deep between his brows and his wide moustache twitched nervously at his lip. "No, Doctor Crane, not at all." Suddenly feeling the oppressive heat in the room, he removed his coat and bowler hat. Hanging them on a nail by the door, he turned back into the room and attempted to adopt a business-like air. Rolling up his sleeves as if he were preparing for nothing more extraordinary than writing a report to the commissioner, he bent down on his haunches and forced himself to look square on at the head on the block. He was sure she would have been a beauty in life. Her features seemed well proportioned, her little nose just slightly pointed up at the end.

"Well now," came the doctor's soft voice, "This should make your job a little easier." Both he and Sergeant Graves crouched down next to Bowman, the better to examine the object in front of them. Graves was the first to notice what the doctor was referring to.

"Her eyes are different colours."

Looking closely, Bowman could see he was right. The eyes were, indeed, of markedly different hues. The left was a clear, bright blue whilst the right was a deep exotic brown.

"It'll help in her identification, that's for sure." Bowman pulled a notebook and well-chewed pencil from his waistcoat pocket. "What might have caused it?"

"It's a natural occurrence, not brought about by any trauma. The blue eye lacks a pigment that accounts for the colour in the other. It could run in families, it could be entirely random. But perhaps only ten to fifteen ladies of her age would exhibit such a condition in the whole of London."

Bowman scratched in his notebook with the worn stub of his pencil, then turned his attention back to the physician in the apron. "Doctor Crane," he began, "Could you give me a description of the woman from what you have before you?"

Doctor Crane inched forward onto his knees and set his face closer to the specimen on the table. Bowman marvelled at the professional detachment the doctor employed in the course of his duties. To him, the head on the block was nothing more than a puzzle, an enigma to be unravelled. He glanced across to Sergeant Graves. His eyes were wide with wonder. Bowman envied his enthusiasm for, try as he might, he could summon nothing but revulsion for the spectacle before him.

"The head is of an average size and shape, so it would be no great leap of the imagination to assume she was of average stature. She was perhaps twenty five or thereabouts, certainly no younger than twenty." Crane felt around the head with his gloved hands. "There are no signs of trauma about the skull, which may or may not prove pertinent to your enquiries."

"Cause of death?"

"I should have thought that was obvious," said Graves to Bowman with a quizzical smile. "She had her head cut off."

"Ah, but that may have happened post mortem." The doctor looked at the blank faces before him, and offered a clarification. "After death."

"So we can't assume decapitation was the cause?" Bowman was looking thoughtful.

"It's impossible to verify. There is some bruising about the neck, maybe the result of earlier trauma."

"Strangulation?" offered Bowman.

"Possibly."

Sergeant Graves looked puzzled. "Why strangle someone, then cut off their head?"

Pointedly ignoring the inquiry, Doctor Crane continued with his examination. "Otherwise, the tissue is remarkably well preserved. I should say she had not been in the water above six hours."

"But that part of the river has been frozen these past three days." Graves had a look of concentration on his face that was almost endearing.

"Then she entered the water some six hours before the freeze."

"That would be December the Twenty Ninth." Bowman wrote the date in his notebook.

"Then you have your date of death, at least," ventured the doctor in his soft Scottish lilt. "If not the exact time."

Bowman felt some progress had been made, but was eager to learn more. "Anything else?"

Doctor Crane was unnervingly still for a moment before suddenly reaching forward to cup the head in his hands. As a veterinarian might examine a horse, he first pulled down the lower eyelids with a finger then, with his thumb, prised the lower jaw gently open. "Her teeth are all present, but they're in rather poor order."

"Is that significant?"

"It would, together with a yellowing of the eyes, indicate she had led a healthy life until her later years, when she was not in the best of health."

Looking further into the mouth was impossible with the head in its present position, so the doctor tilted it back at an angle. "Could you hold the head in this position please, sergeant?" Sergeant Graves moved around the back of the table to oblige the doctor and put a hand either side of the head to steady it. Reaching into the mouth with his fingers, the doctor made a discovery. "Ah," he said quietly, "The tongue has been removed." As Bowman scratched at his notebook, the doctor continued. "Just before the frenulum." Looking around him, he noticed he was confronted with blank looks once more. "It's the ligament which anchors the tongue to the bottom of the mouth. I should imagine the tongue was pulled forward, thus," he put his fingers perilously close to his own mouth, then mimed pulling his tongue forward over his lower teeth. "Then severed with one cut." He made a swooping movement with his other hand, as if cutting his own tongue off with a knife. "The cut is a clean one." He stared hard at the tips of his gloves. "Now, what's this?" Opening her mouth wider still, he angled the head into the sparse light thrown from the gas lamps on the wall. "There's something trapped at the back of the throat." He reached back in between the teeth and pulled out a rich, muddy substance that he rubbed between a forefinger and thumb.

"Earth?" suggested Sergeant Graves from his lofty position behind the table, but Doctor Crane was peering back into the mouth.

"It's packed tightly at the back of the throat."

"It's red in colour. Is it clay?" Inspector Bowman slid his pencil behind an ear and looked closer as the doctor coaxed more of the muddy substance from the depths of the unfortunate woman's throat. He rubbed it again between his fingers and held it to his nose, looking for all the world as if he were taking a pinch of snuff or smelling a fine cigar. Then he turned his beady eyes on Bowman.

"You must draw your own conclusions, inspector," he said, "but those are the facts as I see them presented before me."

V

Precious Cargo

Treacher was getting restless. Hobbs and Kane had fallen back into their stupor following the commotion behind the curtain. Jabez Kane had reached for his opium pipe and now, leaning back upon a pile of rags, fell into oblivion as he drew upon it intermittently. Albert Hobbs snored against the wall by the brazier. Treacher knew he'd not move much further for the rest of the morning. In fact, in the three weeks he'd been part of Hardacre's gang, Treacher had seen little of the behaviour that had earned these men their reputation as two of the most reviled villains this side of the Thames. Perhaps, he reasoned, they were marking time, waiting for the circumstances to come right before embarking upon their latest criminal pursuit. Or perhaps they were waiting for Hardacre's word. In the meantime, they were happy enough to while away their time in this dark, dank cell, smoking opium, sleeping or drinking. Every other day or so, they would rouse themselves from their torpor enough to go out for food but, on the occasions Treacher followed them, he saw neither of them attempt anything untoward. He was, frankly, disappointed. Screwing up the now empty bag of chestnuts, he threw the paper into the brazier. He was getting worried about Fogg. Several minutes had passed now since the noises from behind the curtain and Fogg had yet to reappear. Treacher knew that to have moved to help Fogg would have been hopeless. He would surely have been stopped by Kane and Hobbs and most likely have found himself out on the street with a solid beating for his pains. And so he had waited. He had never seen beyond the curtain into Hardacre's domain. He had never been called in and had never dared make use of his companions" incapacity to pry when they were asleep. Treacher knew not to rock the boat in a situation such as this.

His patience was rewarded with a pulling back of the curtain at the doorway as Hardacre threw what looked to be a bundle of bloodied rags to the floor by the brazier. Upon closer inspection,

Treacher saw that it was Fogg, and he was not in a good way. Blood was caked on his skull and hair, his face was bloated and bruised. His eye sockets shone black and his jaw and nose were crooked. As Treacher leaned closer, he could see Fogg's chest rising and falling with shallow, desperate breaths but no sound at all escaped his open mouth.

"Will someone take this bag of bones and dump it in the Thames!"

Hardacre's voice was enough to rouse Hobbs from his sleep. He opened a lazy eye, annoyed at the interruption. "Aye," he mumbled as he shifted to a more comfortable position. "Throw him in the Thames, along with the other turds." With that, he fell again into his slumber with a lazy cackle. Jabez Kane, his mind filled with opium-fuelled fantasies, stared unseeing at his companion, but even he in his addled state allowed an uneven smile to spread across his face. Fogg had got his just deserts, that was all.

As Hardacre lumbered back into his room to gather Fogg's spoils from the floor, Treacher sprung into action. He carefully wrapped Fogg's shattered body as best he could in the few oily blankets he could find on the floor around him, then lifted him up and over a shoulder. Steadying himself against a sooty wall, Treacher carefully picked his way across the room with his load then, pulling the makeshift door away from its frame, stepped gratefully out into the cold, bright glare of the morning sun.

The passing crowds on Blackfriars Road seemed unconcerned at the sight of Treacher and his grisly load slipping in the mire that had started to accumulate on the side of the road. Had Hardacre been watching, he would have seen Treacher step out onto the highway but then, instead of turning right to Upper Ground and the Thames embankment where he had been instructed to throw Fogg, turning left towards Stamford Street. It had never been Treacher's intention to follow Hardacre's orders. Such insubordination would have ordinarily led to a severe beating at the gang master's hand but, in this instance, it didn't matter. Treacher had no intention of facing Hardacre and his gang again. At least, not alone. He quickened his gait as he got within striking distance of his final destination. The crowds were pressing against him as he cut into the side streets and made his way through Paris Garden and Meymott Street onto Waterloo Road. The busiest thoroughfare this side of the river, it was a throng of carts and carriages. Stalls had been set beside the road selling everything from flowers to fish. The scents which greeted Treacher's nostrils swung between the exotic and the repugnant. Twice he was pushed into the road by the shoulder of a careless passer by, and had to steady himself and adjust his load before continuing, just turning away in time from an oncoming dray about its business. Omnibuses clattered past, painted brightly in their company livery, bells ringing. The horses kicked dirt and sludge into Treacher's path but he set his face into a mask of grim determination. With Fogg's body seeming to gain in weight with every step, he was glad to reach the corner of Mepham Street and York Road. He raised his eyes to read the sign above the building before him; "Waterloo Station".

Surrounded by slums and ramshackle stalls, the terminal's many entrances were an indication of the haphazard nature of the station within. Around the Central Station from which departing trains left the city southwards, were a network of platforms given incongruous names; the Cyprus Station for suburban lines and the Khartoum Station for services to Windsor and the west. Each station had its own ticket office and concourse, and these were home to as disparate a collection of London life as any visitor was likely to see. Beggars and vagrants took their chances with the hoi polloi of London society, bankers from the suburbs spilled out from the platforms, traders sold food of uncertain origin and quality and, everywhere, the air was thick with the cries and shouts of a thousand people. The screech of a whistle would periodically announce the arrival of another service. The acrid smell of steam hung in the cavernous space beneath the roof. It was into this cacophony that Treacher stepped, his already ruddy face red from the effort of his journey. Despite the cold, beads of sweat stood out on his brow as he paused to undo the buttons on his ragged coat. Stopping beneath the great clock at the station's heart, he lowered Fogg's body from his shoulder and laid him gently on the ground. As he did so, he heard a sound escape from Fogg's blood-caked lips, the first such noise he had made since his beating. "Don't worry, Fogg," Treacher breathed in his ear, "You're quite safe now." Reaching into his waistcoat, Treacher's fingers sought out a hidden pocket. Pulling out a silver whistle, he held it to his lips and blew, long and loud.

The effect in the station was immediate. Even in the hubbub of the concourse, the shrill, piercing whistle could be heard from one side of the station to the other. Passers by broke their stride, twisting their heads to look around and discover the source of the noise. Stray dogs pricked up their ears, whining in reply. A mess of startled pigeons made for the roof. Treacher let the whistle drop. Through the stillness came the sound of running feet as two young constables approached, smart in their uniform; top hat and tails. Treacher fumbled for his papers; official documents which denoted his position in the Metropolitan Police Force.

"Inspector Edmund Treacher," he said by way of introduction.

The taller, fresher faced of the two men nodded in response. "Constable Baker," he said, "This is Constable Roache." Treacher noticed that Roache, who looked the older of the two, was out of breath.

"Constable Baker, help me carry this man to a hansom, and Roache, tell Sergeant Williams to meet me at Bow Street in one hour. I've no doubt you'll find him lunching at the Criterion. See if you can tear him away."

With a curt nod, Constable Roache turned on his heels and ran back to the main entrance of the station, mopping his brow with his sleeve. As Constable Baker bent over to help lift Fogg, Treacher lent over again to whisper in his ear. "It's all right son, we'll soon have you shipshape." Fogg murmured something in response, his eyes opening briefly to blink in the light. "What was that?" Treacher put his ear closer to Fogg's mouth, the better to hear his response. Propping himself up painfully on one elbow, Isambard Fogg pushed his face closer to the inspector's, his mouth set in an expression of resolve. With a great, rattling breath, Fogg drew upon all his remaining strength to deliver his response, and spat squarely in Treacher's face. Chuckling painfully to himself, his head rolled back as he sunk once more into oblivion.

VI

A Deal With The Devil

In the time that Bowman and Graves had eaten their lunch, the sky had turned. Grey clouds that had lain brooding on the horizon now advanced across the expanse of blue, plunging the city into a sudden gloom. With a subtle rise in the temperature the softest snow had begun to melt and, as they stepped from The Silver Cross Inn, the two men found themselves walking in a cold, slushy mess. Inspector Bowman had sat aghast for the previous half an hour, watching as Graves devoured his steak and kidney pie almost whole. His appetite, it seemed, had been quite unaffected by the events in the Charing Cross laboratory.

"Not eating, sir?" Graves had enquired through a mouthful of pastry.

Bowman had looked down at his own bowl of rustic pie and pushed it away, reaching for his tankard to take a draft of ale.

"I'm not hungry."

"Then, do you mind?" Not waiting for a reply, Graves had reached over to Bowman's bowl and pulled it towards him. Bowman had waved his assent and watched as Graves scraped the last of his food onto his own plate. He frequently envied Graves' ability to wander through life untouched by the horrors around him. He had a childlike exuberance for his work quite at odds with Bowman's more measured approach. Bowman's brows were knotted into their usual, deep frown as he thought over the morning's events and considered how best to proceed. Wiping the porter from his moustache, Bowman turned to Graves as he embarked upon his second pie.

"It's about time we made this investigation official, Graves. Could I charge you with a visit to the commissioner after your pie? If you wouldn't mind turning your attention to the paperwork, I'd be grateful."

Bowman had noticed the disappointment in Graves' eyes, but his colleague recovered quickly enough.

"Of course," he had spluttered. "I suppose someone's got to do it. What are your plans for the case?"

"We need to identify the young lady as a matter of urgency."

Graves had washed a particularly stubborn piece of gristle down with a swig from his ale, then wiped his mouth with the back of his coat sleeve. "At least Doctor Crane was of some help. The eyes will be the clincher, I'm sure."

"I'd also like you to check the inventory for the last three days, see who we've had banged up since the twenty-ninth. Might as well start discounting everyone we can. You'll need to get onto Bow Street, too."

"Will do," the young sergeant had replied, cheerily. He would rather have been out and about with Inspector Bowman, but at least an afternoon in the office at Scotland Yard meant he would be warm. "And what about you?"

Bowman had stared down into his tankard, swilling the dregs of his porter as he thought. "I'm off to make a deal with the Devil".

After settling up the bill, the two men had gone their separate ways, Bowman turning up his collar as he turned right onto The Strand, Graves whistling gaily as he made his way back towards Northumberland Avenue and the imposing building that was Scotland Yard. The streets were a mess. The passing of successive cartwheels had served to stir the snow and ice in with the dirt and manure of the road. Several times, Bowman's coat was splattered with mushy detritus by a passing cab, the driver neither knowing nor caring that he was the cause of the inspector's muttered oaths. The lamps burned again in the half-light. Ahead of him, Bowman could see the lamplighters at work on their ladders, igniting the gas in the lanterns with their tapers. It was barely past noon, but already the daylight was retreating fast. Bowman glanced up at the glowering clouds as he arrived at his destination. Stepping off the main road and knocking the sludge off his shoes by the door, Inspector Bowman pushed open the door to the offices of the London Evening Standard, and stepped warily inside.

Jack Watkins was a ferret of a man. Tall, thin, with a long, bewhiskered face and a fine head of red hair, he sat at his desk tapping out a rhythm on his typewriter. The stump of a cigar was clamped tight in his teeth. If he had noticed that it was periodically dropping ash onto his waistcoat as he smoked, Watkins certainly showed no sign of caring. His fingertips and trim moustache were stained a sickly yellow, the legacy of a lifetime as a smoker. His office was on the second floor, and his window afforded a fine view of the comings and goings on The Strand below. Around the room, shelves groaned with books, atlases and newspapers. Not an inch of space was left unadorned. Tables and maps lined the walls and even the floor was strewn with books. Watkins sat at his desk in his shirtsleeves. A single lamp burned next to him and this, together with the fire burning in the grate behind him, was sufficient to light the room. He had barked a sharp "Come!" at Bowman's knock, and now the inspector stood, awaiting an audience with the editor of the city's most influential daily newspaper. His patience wearing thin, Bowman tore a page from his notebook and slid it over the desk into Watkins' field of vision.

"Watkins, I'd like this in The Standard tonight." Bowman stood awaiting an answer, toying with his hat in his hands. He knew the game Watkins was playing, and wasn't going to give him the pleasure of rising to the bait. The editor of The Evening Standard didn't even raise his eyes, indeed he gave no indication of even being aware of Bowman's presence in the room, but carried on mechanically tapping at his typewriter. His cigar tip glowed a fierce orange as he took another draw. Bowman fought back the urge to cough as he was enveloped in the choking smoke. Rolling his eyes to the ceiling, he saw that it was stained an unhealthy, brownish-yellow colour and he couldn't help but wonder at the state of the editor's lungs. He had seen enough dead bodies opened up to know the damage wrought by many things considered harmless, tobacco chief among them. For this very reason, Bowman had forsworn tobacco with the zeal of an evangelist, but couldn't help coming into contact with it in the course of his professional duties.

Sensing that Watkins was content to play his game for as long as it pleased him, Bowman tried a different tack.

"It is a matter of urgency and great importance. I thought it warranted an expert hand." His remark had the desired effect. At once, Watkins stopped typing, his lean, yellow fingers poised in the air above the keys as if he had been captured in a photographic portrait.

"Flattery is a useful device, is it not Inspector Bowman?" Taking the cigar from his teeth, he crushed it in an already overflowing ashtray upon his desk and held the note under the lamp, the better to read its contents. "A woman in the Thames?" Watkins' eyebrows rose almost comically upon his forehead as he read the details of the case or, at least, those details that Inspector Bowman was willing to divulge at this moment. "And you want me to run this this evening, you say?" Bowman gave a shallow nod. Watkins, knowing all the cards were in his hands, threw himself back in his chair and crossed his feet nonchalantly on his desk. There were other chairs in his office, but not once during the course of the interview would he offer Inspector Bowman a seat. This too, was all part of his game. He sucked air in through his teeth as he contemplated Bowman's request. "It won't be easy. We go to press at four o'clock."

Bowman's thin lips rose into a wry smirk that almost passed for a smile. "I'm sure you'll manage," he said in a measured tone.

Watkins swung his legs back down from their elevated position and, pushing his chair back from the desk, got up and walked to the window. He stood staring at the street below, his hands clasped behind his back like a general inspecting the field of battle. "Look at them, inspector. Hundreds upon thousands of them pass my window every week."

Bowman stood his ground. If the price to be paid for Watkins' cooperation was to be held a veritable hostage and lectured to for a while, then so be it.

"They're vulnerable," continued Watkins. "All of them. They unwittingly place themselves in harm's way at every step. Pickpockets, murderers, rapists and thieves may pass among them quite unnoticed, until they strike. Then they cry out as one,

"Who will protect us? Where were the police? How can these dreadful things happen?" No one understands, you see, what Scotland Yard actually does." He turned back into the room. "Forgive me, inspector, but to a lot of people on that street, you and your Metropolitan Police Force are an irrelevance. If only they understood."

Bowman held his nerve. He was beginning to realise where Watkins was heading.

"If only they could see you work," continued Watkins, warming to his theme. "They would understand that you are their servants, dedicated to keeping them safe. If they knew the nature of your duties, how you toil in their interests, I am certain you would win their respect. Each and every one of them would look at you, Inspector Bowman, and your men in a new light."

Bowman looked pointedly at the clock on the wall and cleared his throat. "Watkins, what exactly are you suggesting?"

Sure that he had Bowman in his sights, Watkins walked back from the window to sit again in his studded leather chair. Resting his elbows on the desk, he turned his eyes to meet the inspector's in an unblinking gaze.

"Let me in, Inspector Bowman. Let The Evening Standard be the people's eyes and ears in the Force. Let me follow your investigation into this woman in the Thames from the inside, and I'll make sure that Scotland Yard is given the chance to shine."

"What use is that to Scotland Yard?" asked Bowman, his features set into an attitude of quiet defiance. Watkins took another cigar from a box at his side and struck a match. Puffing vigorously at the cigar as he lit it, he quickly filled the air with its pungent smoke.

"I realise you're in a difficult position." Watkins blew on the match to extinguish the flame. "You are the public's servant and their master. You must both police them and answer to them; a difficult line to tread. Here is an opportunity to show them how you tread that line. How you spend their money wisely in upholding the law of the land. An opportunity to show them you are professionals, not amateurs, and that you are far from irrelevant."

Now it was Bowman's turn to pause. A lot of what Watkins had said was true. The public was still loath to trust the fledgling police force, many considering them a drain on public resources. Bowman had heard the word "amateur" levelled at him and his fellow officers many times before. Perhaps Watkins was right. Perhaps Scotland Yard should take the lead, show the public what they do. Justify themselves.

"What do you propose?" Bowman sighed.

Watkins moved in for the kill. "If you were prepared to grant me unparalleled access to your investigation, and exclusive rights to the story - "

"Subject to approval, of course," interjected Bowman.

"Approval is a word I cannot bear, Inspector Bowman," retorted the editor. "For my taste, it is a little too close to censorship. If my terms are unacceptable to you, then I would not wish to take up any more of your time."

Watkins' fingers clattered over the typewriter once more as he returned to his work, refusing to acknowledge Inspector Bowman's continued presence in the room. Now it was Bowman's turn to play his hand. Reaching forwards to the desk, he clutched at the paper upon which Watkins typed, and tore it from the mechanism. Now he had his attention once more, the inspector leaned over the desk to meet Watkins' gaze.

"We both know that you need me as much as I need you. Your circulation is falling. I'm sure you could do with a little scandal to liven up your front pages. If you were to play fair by me Watkins, and give me final approval before you print, then I am willing to grant you access to my investigation. You will answer to either my colleague, Sergeant Graves, or myself. And you shall know only what we think you should know. Is that understood? I don't want you prying into matters that do not concern you or your readership."

Watkins considered this for a while. As he stood to face the inspector, man to man, a wide smile spread across his face, displaying an uneven row of yellow-brown teeth. He held out one hand to seal the bargain, and clapped another across Bowman's shoulder with a strength that belied his wiry frame.

"I must be going soft," he said as he shook Bowman's hand, "It's a pleasure doing business with you, inspector."

Bowman shifted uncomfortably where he stood. He had had little choice, but he felt uneasy with the deal he had just struck. Still, he reasoned, as long as Watkins was kept on a tight rein he couldn't wreak too much damage. Who knows, it might even do the Force some good."Excellent," he said. "But steer clear of Ignatius Hicks."

"A condition?" queried Watkins, his eyebrows rising high upon his head.

"Only the one. Inspector Hicks would be only too pleased to offer you his unconsidered opinions. I would rather you didn't ask for them."

Watkins made a mental note, then took up Bowman's scrap of paper once more. "These are all the details you have, inspector?"

Bowman turned at the door, placing his hat on his head in readiness for the cold outside. "At present, yes. The detail of the eyes is most telling, of course. Is there any chance of including a likeness? The head is being held by Doctor John Crane at Charing Cross. I told him to expect you."

Watkins was taken by surprise at this extra nugget of information. "The head?" he enquired.

"It was severed at the neck," replied Bowman reluctantly. He was wary of giving away too much information but it was obvious that, if Watkins was going to include a portrait from life, he would find out sooner or later. "I would rather we kept the more grisly details to ourselves."

Watkins thought. He had always prided himself on his investigative instinct, and something told him this was a story that deserved special attention. It would do no harm to his profile or his career prospects if this story led to a rise in circulation. Ordinarily, he would have despatched the staff recorder to draw the likeness but, in this instance, he felt it would do no harm to go himself. In fact, it would do no harm at all if he were to take this story entirely upon his own shoulders. That way, he could bask in the glory alone as the readership grew.

"Well," he said, moving to the coat stand by the door, "I'd hate to keep the doctor waiting."

As Bowman turned to follow, the door suddenly burst open before him, and in poked Sergeant Graves' shining face. He was panting heavily from having run up the stairs two at a time in his enthusiasm to share his news.

"Ah, Inspector Bowman, glad you're still here."

Bowman raised an eyebrow. "I thought you were opening the case with the commissioner?"

"I got as far as Trafalgar Square," panted Graves, "When I was stopped by a runner from the Yard. There's been a garrotting in Southwark, thought you might like to come along."

Bowman shook his head. "No thank you, Graves. I'll head back to the Yard myself. I have some thinking to do."

As Bowman skulked out the door, Graves turned to Watkins with a wink.

"It's all go today, isn't it?"

VII

Interrogation

Bow Street Police Station was an imposing building, the subject of many recent renovations. It presented a grand façade to the outside world, all Palladian pillars and columns, its many windows reflecting the grey, broiling clouds above. It was home to 'E' Division of the Metropolitan Police and, exactly sixty years earlier, had been the site of London's first ever Police Office. Now, it often drew crowds as prisoners were transported by Black Maria, a large, black, horse-drawn prison van, from the cells to court or even more sensationally, to the gallows at Newgate.

Deep within the bowels of Bow Street, Isambard Fogg lay on a bed in a police cell. Despite his wounds having been cleaned, he still looked a sorry state. Both his eyes were swollen and shone a lustrous purple-black. His nose was spread across his face and a cheek was cracked. His hair was plastered down upon his head. Clots of blood peeled from his scalp. There was little furniture in the cell aside from a ledge beneath the high, barred window that served for a seat and Fogg's bed, a soiled mattress on a cold metal frame. Next to this, there was a bucket and a rickety stool.

"He looks like a simpleton, and not long for this world, neither." Sergeant Williams' broad Welsh vowels sang out along the rows of cells beneath the station. Williams had a pockmarked face and wide, brown eyes. A full set of whiskers graced his cheeks and his hair was swept back from a widow's peak. Inspector Treacher stood alongside him, now in smarter clothes, his hands deep in his pockets. The row of cells was set back from a short subterranean corridor, separated from the main thoroughfare by vertical bars and doors, giving the attendant officers an unbroken view of the felons inside.

Today, three of the six cells were occupied but, aside from the occasional cough or grunt, the inmates were quiet.

“You goin” in, then?” Williams turned to Treacher, scratching his chin with his stubby fingers. Treacher nodded and Williams fumbled with the keys on his belt. Unlocking the door and swinging it slowly open, the sergeant stepped aside as Treacher approached the prone figure on the bed.

“Can you hear me, Fogg? It’s me, Treacher. You remember me from the den, don’t you?”

Fogg opened a painful eye and began to writhe on his mattress.

“Can you hear me, Fogg?” Treacher crouched next to him and tugged gently on his sleeve.

“A fisherman,” Fogg rasped. “That’s all I am.”

Behind the bars, closing the door after Treacher, Sergeant Williams threw back his head and laughed. “Any the wiser now, are you?”

Treacher called over his shoulder, bristling at Williams’ levity. “He’s lost a lot of blood, that’s all. He’s delirious.” He turned his head back to the wretched heap beside him. “Fogg, do you know where you are?”

Isambard Fogg tried to lift his head from the mattress, his throat rattling with the effort. “Heaven?” he whispered through a mouth caked with blood.

“No, Fogg,” said Treacher sadly. “Not in Heaven.”

Fogg pulled his knees up to his chest, clasping his stomach in agony. A sudden panic overcame him. “Then I am in Hell!” he wailed, his eyes brimming with salty tears.

Treacher reached out to calm him as he writhed in pain, speaking now in hushed tones to dispel his fear. “No Fogg, not in Hell neither.”

Williams cackled from behind the bars. “Not yet, at any rate.” Pulling a pipe nonchalantly from his pocket, he began to pack it with tobacco from a leather pouch. Ignoring the remark, Treacher continued.

“Fogg, you are safe. You are in the cells at Bow Street.”

Fogg looked around him, his eyes as wide as he could prise them. “Peelers?” he stuttered in alarm.

"He's more afraid of us than of the Devil himself," observed the sergeant in the corridor wryly, tamping down his tobacco with a thumb.

Treacher leaned forward and cradled Fogg's head in his hands. "I am Inspector Edmund Treacher. I brought you here from Hardacre's den. Fogg, he hurt you."

Fogg squinted into Treacher's face, as if trying to make sense of the image. Slowly a look of recognition dawned. "I remember," he gasped.

"Good. Now Fogg, if you help us, we can help you. How long have you known Jabez Kane?"

"Kane?" spluttered Fogg, his breathing laboured. "What d'you want to know about Kane? I'll not see him hanged."

"We suspect him of many things, Fogg, but he's slippery. We can't get anything on him. I infiltrated the gang to catch him, but I swear he knew. He did nothing but spend his days with his pipe. We need evidence, Fogg. Something to pin on him. You owe him nothing, Fogg."

Fogg's eyes were rolling back into his head as he tried to stay conscious. He grasped Treacher's lapels as if his very life depended on it. Suddenly, he seemed to muster his strength. His breathing settled and his eyes became clear. He drew himself closer to Treacher's face and with a tremendous effort he formed his words, each taking a whole breath to propel them from his drying mouth. "What – will – become – of – me?"

Treacher looked around at Sergeant Williams and, with a look, cautioned him to say nothing. "Fogg," he began, "Where did you get those clothes? The ones you brought to Hardacre?"

Fogg released his hold on Treacher's coat and sunk back into his bed. "Found 'em," he lied.

"Well," continued Treacher, "We found something this morning too, Fogg. We found a gentleman's body in Southwark. The sort of gentleman that would wear such clothes as you 'found'. What do you know of that?"

"A man might swing for such a murder, Fogg," Sergeant Williams added from the door. "But we can spare you if you tell us all you know of your friend, Jabez Kane."

At this interjection, Isambard Fogg took a deep breath and erupted into a horrible, dry, painful laugh. "He ain't no friend of mine. Hardacre's the one. He looks out for me."

Treacher rose from his crouched position and began to pace the cell, rapidly losing patience. He had spent many long, uncomfortable hours in that blasted den trying to get something on Kane and he saw Fogg as his last, best hope for information. "Hardacre's no friend of yours, Fogg. He beat you," he exclaimed. "He wanted you in the river!"

Fogg began to descend once more into his delirium. "I've done nothing but good for him," he cried, plaintively. "He meant no harm by his beating."

Treacher knew his time was short. Fogg's injuries were beyond repair and it was only a matter of time before they got the better of him. He sprang to Fogg's side once more and, sitting on the ramshackle stool beside the bed, raised his voice in desperation. "What do you know of Jabez Kane?"

Fogg's head was limp now, a cold sweat breaking out upon his brow. His fevered state had the effect of loosening his tongue and, like a body of water as the flood gates lift, the words came pouring forth. "He killed that peeler at Blackfriars, made him swallow his own tongue. He told me." Treacher looked again to Sergeant Williams, but could see that he had already fumbled for his notebook and pencil and was scratching feverishly at the pages.

"Grayson." Treacher had known Grayson well enough. A man who'd spent his whole life in service, Sergeant Grayson was as good a policeman as any in the Force. He had been attacked one night whilst off duty, and his body had been found in the gutter. "I hope you're getting this Sergeant Williams."

"Of course," replied Williams sharply, without lifting his eyes from his notebook.

"There was a family in Shoreditch," Fogg continued. "Kane was caught liftin" their silver. The guv'nor chased him off but he came back. Slit their throats and torched the place."

"Curtain Road," offered Sergeant Williams to Treacher's blank look. "I remember the blaze." He returned to his notes, scratching his pencil on the paper in earnest. Meanwhile, Fogg was fading fast. His whole body was twitching now, his hands grasping at the air and his back arching painfully from the bed.

"And then," he gabbled, "The sack. There was a sack."

Williams stopped writing and looked up. "Sack?" he said in his soft Welsh brogue. "What sack?"

Fogg was silent now, his eyes staring into space as if beholding some vision quite unseen to Treacher. He reached for the air with an outstretched hand, seeming to clutch at something that hung before him.

"What is it Fogg?" asked Treacher softly, aware that he didn't have long. "What do you remember?"

Fogg was crying again now, the tears coming full and fat to his eyes before rolling down his blood encrusted cheek. "I had to bury it... but it was so heavy. I had to see... had to see." His chest rising and falling rapidly, Fogg started to hyperventilate. Treacher cupped his head between his hands to try and still him, and shouted into his face.

"Tell us, Fogg. What did you see? What did Kane do?"

Fogg's hands gripped the frame of the bed, as if he were trying to keep himself from flying off. His head rolled frantically from side to side. Spittle and blood foamed at his lips. Slowly, he found the strength to speak again, each word seemingly summoned from the deep recesses of Fogg's mind with a colossal effort. "He cut off her head."

Treacher and Williams shared a look, the sergeant's pencil poised.

"What?" Treacher barked, desperate that Fogg should give him something more. "Who? Kane? What did he do, Fogg? What did he do?"

Evidently summoning up the last of his strength, Fogg lifted his upper body clean off the bed and looked straight at the inspector with a look that shook him to his very core. "He cut off her head!" he screamed. Then, with a strange smile playing over his face, Isambard Fogg fell slowly back onto the mattress and was still.

Treacher reached out from his stool beside the bed and felt for a pulse in Fogg's neck. He turned to Williams, disappointment in his face. He wasn't sure Isambard Fogg had given him enough. "He's dead," he said.

Sergeant Williams took a puff from his pipe and regarded the wretch on the bed from behind the smoke that curled about his face. "Well, Fogg," he said plainly, smoothing his whiskers down across his cheeks, "It seems you escaped the hangman's noose after all."

VIII

Plans Are Hatched

Detective Inspector Bowman liked his office. As he stood at one of the four great windows that overlooked the city from the top floor of the newly built Scotland Yard, he felt he could reach straight out to any point in London with his fingertips. From the grand government buildings of Whitehall to the slums across the river on the South Bank, Bowman had made it his business to know London as intimately as one might know a friend; its back streets and alleys, its wide streets and squares. To aid him in this, one entire wall of his wood panelled office had been given over to the display of a large map of the city, a circle drawn on it to indicate the areas over which he and his division had jurisdiction. It was a very wide circle. On his desk behind him where he stood, hands clasped behind his back, lay a single sheet of paper. Written in a flowery hand, Bowman's own, was a quote from the Met's first commissioner, Sir Richard Mayne. It served both as a reminder to Bowman of his duties to the public, and as a riposte to the likes of Jack Watkins who thought little of the Force and their efforts to keep the streets of London safe from criminals. "The primary object of an efficient police is the prevention of crime," it read. "The next, that of detection and punishment of offenders if crime is committed. To these ends all the efforts of the police must be directed." Bowman took the time to read the motto every day and took special note of the last sentence, even going to the trouble of underlining it in a heavy pen to highlight its importance; "The protection of life and property, the preservation of public tranquillity, and the absence of crime, will alone prove whether those efforts have been successful."

Bowman was troubled. To have two murders reported in a day was unusual. Even given the fact that the head had lain frozen in the Thames for perhaps three days, the timing bothered him. Despite the preconceptions of the public, crime was still a relatively rare event on the streets of London, murder even more so. There were perhaps a hundred murders a year in the city, and that number had been falling for years. Various press campaigns highlighting the dangers of walking the streets had put fear in the hearts of many, but Bowman knew that, statistically at least, the Met was winning. Which was why the report of two such violent crimes so hard on each other's heels was causing him so much consternation. As he turned back into the room, his eye fell instinctively to the latter half of Sir Richard Mayne's statement; "The protection of life and property, the preservation of public tranquillity, and the absence of crime, will alone prove whether those efforts have been successful." Today, Bowman was not so sure they had been.

A knock at the heavy oak door served to lift Bowman from his reverie.

"Come!" he barked.

The door swung open to admit Sergeant Williams, resplendent in regulation police cape and top hat. His knee high boots left little pools of water on the floor where he trod, and a sheen of mist had settled as glistening drops upon his face.

"I must say, Inspector Bowman, I envy you your view," he remarked as he removed his damp hat and placed it on Bowman's desk.

"It's not much of a view at the moment," answered Bowman. "Not with this fog. How is life at Bow Street?"

Bowman rather liked Sergeant Williams. He had had the pleasure of his company many times before during the course of various investigations and he relished his plain speaking and dry, mordant wit. He could think of no finer man to have on his side in a tough spot.

"It's enough to keep a man busy," Williams replied. "Of course, we don't live in such luxury there." There was a twinkle in his eye as he spoke. Bowman was happy to accept the jibe. He motioned the bluff Welshman to join him at his desk and the two men sat.

"What can I do for you, Sergeant Williams?"

Williams shifted in his seat and leaned forward to the inspector. "I have some information for you," he began. "If it proves of use, I would ask you to consider a proposition."

Bowman leaned back in his chair and let his eyes wander to the ceiling. He sighed. He'd had quite enough of deals and propositions for one day but perhaps he would give the sergeant the benefit of the doubt for now. His eyes fell back to Williams. "Go on," he said, tentatively.

"It concerns your lady in the lake," smiled Williams, his eyes shining, mischievously.

Bowman winced at the analogy, the truth was about as far from the sergeant's romantic allusion as it was possible to get. "Oh yes?"

Sergeant Williams had reached into an inside pocket and pulled out his familiar pipe and tobacco pouch. Pulling at the shreds with his portly fingers, Williams filled the bowl with tobacco as he talked. "We've been trying something new over at Bow Street. Inspector Treacher calls it "infiltration". He has, for the past three weeks or so, lived the life of a vagrant in a criminal cell. We've been hoping to gather evidence on a certain Jabez Kane and his gang master, Jeb Hardacre." He pulled a matchbook from another pocket and paused to light his pipe. "This morning, Inspector Treacher captured a vagrant, one Isambard Fogg, and brought him to the cells for questioning. We think he pointed the finger at Jabez Kane with regard to your woman in the Thames."

"Jabez Kane," mused Bowman, his hands clasped together in front of him. "I'm not familiar with the name."

"That's no surprise, inspector," said Williams between puffs. "He's slippery. We suspect him of a dozen crimes but we've got nothing on him. Hence Inspector Treacher's drastic actions."

Inspector Bowman rose again, as much to get out of the direct path of Williams' choking pipe smoke as anything else. Walking once more to the window, he turned to face the room, leaning on the sill. "And your proposition?"

Williams gestured with his pipe. "We strike at this man's lair. Tonight. As well as Kane himself, we know the leader of the outfit to be a pimp and a thief and suspect him of a murder or two to boot." Williams' Welsh accent was all the stronger now as he spoke in low, conspiratorial tones. "It's a close call, and we're not sure if we can trust the words of a fellow criminal, but Treacher thinks we've got enough to warrant it."

As he absently parted his wide moustache with a thumb and finger, Bowman thought this through. If this Isambard Fogg really had identified the man responsible for the head in the river, this was too good an opportunity to miss. It would steal a march on Jack Watkins, too. How useful it would be to have the case sewn up before The Evening Standard could get involved. However, something troubled him. Was the word of a criminal really to be trusted? Before he gave the matter any more thought, Bowman thought it might be prudent to speak personally with the man in the cells at Bow Street. "Is this man Fogg still in your cells?"

By way of reply, Williams pulled a pocket watch from his cape. "He is for now," he said, glancing at the watch face. "And shall be for the next quarter of an hour."

Bowman's eyebrows rose in surprise. "You're letting him go?"

"In a manner of speaking, yes," A smile played over Williams' wide face. "He's dead. And he's to be collected at five o'the clock by the coroner." Williams shook his heavy head in mock exasperation. "Death in custody, you see."

Bowman sighed in response.

"The commissioner has given me the authority to take Constable Evan from 'H' division, two inspectors from the Yard and Treacher," Williams continued, pushing his chair away from the desk to stand up. Stamping the feeling back into his still cold feet, he walked to the map on Bowman's wall and pointed with the stem of his pipe. "We're to meet under the clock at Waterloo Station at seven o'the clock and proceed from there to Southwark where Hardacre has his lodgings." He tapped his pipe at the exact location of Hardacre's den.

Bowman turned to look at the encroaching fog from the window. The street below was lost in a swirling, impenetrable mist, the light from the lamps now only visible as a sickly yellow smudge. It wasn't the perfect night to effect an ambush. "Well," he said, "You can count on Sergeant Graves if you want him."

"Thank you," said Williams, reaching for his hat on the desk. "I shall find him on the way out."

"And I'll have Inspector Crouch meet you at Bow Street in an hour," continued Bowman as Williams turned to leave the room. "He's a capable man, fearless too. You might need him."

Williams had reached the door by now, and paused with his hand on the handle. "That won't be necessary," he said with meaning.

Bowman looked up, "Oh?"

"No," said the sergeant as he opened the door to step through. "The commissioner suggested you might come along yourself."

With that, Sergeant Williams walked from the room, pausing only to shut the door behind him.

IX

The Ambush

The fog was thickest where the land was low. The streets of Primrose Hill lay at the bottom of a bowl into which the fog seemed to pour like a viscous soup. Despite the half moon spectacles balanced upon her nose, Patricia Bessom could barely see five yards ahead of her as she made her way over the railway line back to her modest lodgings on Chalk Farm Road. She was a middle-aged frump of a woman, but she had a kindly face that lit up with a smile when she chose to show it. A large, wide-brimmed hat was pinned to her greying, curly hair. A voluminous coat added to her considerable bulk as she shuffled carefully through the streets. She was governess to two children of a wealthy family on the hill. She had chosen not to live in. The master of the house was of sufficient funds and valued Mrs Bessom's qualities so highly, that he was happy to pay for her rent in a small set of rooms just fifteen minutes" walk away in order to secure her services. The arrangement suited Mrs Bessom perfectly. She loved all children, and her current charges were exceptionally well behaved, but she relished the opportunity to come home each night and have her own few things about her.

As she rounded the corner to her house, Mrs Bessom was pleased to see a familiar figure emerge beneath a halo of lamplight. Martin Quigley was an engaging Irish youth half her age who ran a paper stall. Instinctively a matronly figure, Mrs Bessom had come to regard Quigley, with his engaging smile and easy good looks, as the son she had never had. She always looked forward to their early evening encounters.

"Good evening, Martin," she offered as she neared his stand. It was no more than a wooden box piled high with bundles of newspapers tied with string. Quigley was happy for the diversion. The evening had been quiet. In the cold and the fog, people generally hurried home, their heads buried deep in their scarves. Thcy had no inclination to converse, let alone to stop and buy an evening paper. The large piles of newspapers by Quigley's side stood testament to his lack of custom.

"Ah, Mrs Bessom, good evening to you." Swinging his cap from his head, he bowed low as if he were in conversation with the Queen herself. Mrs Bessom blushed at the gesture.

"Oh, get away with you now," she laughed. "A woman could get ideas above her station at such behaviour."

Quigley held a rolled up newspaper out to her, the tips of his fingers poking through his threadbare gloves. "Will you take a Standard?"

"I will, thank you Martin," giggled Mrs Bessom as she reached for her purse. "And a pearl of that fine Irish wisdom to see me safely home, if you'd be so kind as to oblige me."

Quigley rubbed his handsome jaw with his hand and thought, his lively eyes sparkling in the lamplight. "How's this for you? Never be fooled by a kiss, and never be kissed by a fool." To Mrs Bessom's surprise and evident delight, Quigley clutched at her glove as she passed over her change and kissed her playfully on the back of her hand.

"Well, it seems I have been!" she laughed. "Oh, to be young again!" She withdrew her hand slowly, perhaps more slowly than was seemly. "Martin Quigley, you're a tonic on these winter days, you really are."

"Happy New Year, Mrs Bessom." Quigley passed her newspaper and took her change, dropping the coins into a leather pouch around his waist. His eyes narrowed as Mrs Bessom walked away, the fog enveloping her like a shroud as her footsteps echoed off the smart townhouses by the road. Jamming the stub of a cigarette in his mouth, Martin Quigley's cheery expression fell as if he had removed a mask. He swore beneath his breath at the cold and knelt to cut through the string on another bundle of unsold newspapers with an old, rusty blade.

The grand clock suspended from the vaulted roof of Waterloo's Central Platform chimed seven. As the roosting pigeons took wing in fright, the crack of their wings echoed into the vast space below. Beneath the clock, on two benches arranged to face each other over an open stretch of flagstones worn smooth under a million boots, sat a disparate group of Scotland Yarders. At Sergeant Williams' command, they had each of them assumed disguises, some perhaps more successful than others in their ability to deceive. On the bench directly beneath the ornate clock sat Inspector Bowman. He looked ill at ease in an old knee length coat and a pair of grimy hobnail boots. His face was smeared with soot and his hair and moustache were greased flat against his head and face. Not entirely convinced by the wisdom of the enterprise, Bowman shifted uncertainly on his seat. As the clock struck the first of its seven chimes, Sergeant Graves walked over to the bench to join him. He wore a shapeless, black, felt hat that fell over his eyes. An unlit clay pipe was clenched between his teeth. His eyes met Bowman's as he gave a nod of acknowledgement and unfolded a grubby newspaper from under his arm. On the bench opposite, sat Treacher and Williams. Inspector Treacher was shelling nuts from a bag and had a full, fake beard attached to his chin. A dishevelled hat and neckerchief gave him the air of a rather bohemian artist, and his eyes darted from left to right as a great throng of bustling commuters made their way between the two benches, on their way to catch their trains. A tattered knapsack hung on his back. At Treacher's side sat Sergeant Williams, his beard full of sawdust and a patch over one eye. He wore a baggy pair of workman's overalls under a great ex-army coat. Incongruously - and almost comically - a hook extended from his left coat sleeve in place of his hand. Behind them both stood a younger man. He looked no more than twenty five years old and had a fresh open face, on which his feelings could be easily read. He was obviously uncomfortable, due both to the strange company in which he found himself, and the expectation of the ordeal ahead. He wore a station porter's uniform that Sergeant Williams had requisitioned for him from a rather disgruntled London and South Western Railway employee.

"That's Constable Evan," breathed Sergeant Graves into Bowman's ear. "He's been afforded the post of lookout. He's a bit green and we wouldn't want to see him hurt."

Bowman cast his eyes over the young man and could tell that he was anxious. “Then he’s the luckiest man among us. This could get very messy indeed.”

“Williams seems to have thought of everything,” continued Graves. “These disguises should buy us some time if we’re spotted.”

As Graves finished, the clock above them ceased its tolling for the hour. In a predetermined sequence, the men on the benches rose to their feet. With no more than a cursory glance to young Constable Evan, Sergeant Williams ambled through the crowd to the main exit on Waterloo Road. Picking his way through the throng, Evan endeavoured to keep the sergeant in his sights as he followed at a discreet distance, then darted to the left towards a different exit. This would ensure that, as they all emerged onto the street outside, Evan would be a hundred yards or so ahead of the group. Inspector Treacher made for an exit on the station’s north side, affecting, noticed Bowman, an exaggerated nonchalance as he skirted round the mass of commuters. He looked to Sergeant Graves who, with no more than a nod, started out for yet another exit near the Cyprus Station. Bowman rose to his feet and straightened his coat about him. To his mind, the little group had looked ridiculous, but he had to admit as he looked about him, that they looked far from out of place among the detritus of London society that seethed around him. Walking just a few paces apart, Bowman and Graves barely turned a head as they left the station and slipped out into the night.

The one thing Sergeant Williams hadn’t taken into account, was the fog. In the time that the motley group had gathered beneath the clock and waited for the hour to chime, it had taken hold of the city streets and smothered them of life and light. As the small party walked gingerly through the streets, it became apparent that keeping each other in plain sight was going to prove impossible.

“Blimey,” ventured Graves as Bowman caught up to him. “This came down quickly. Just about puts the kibosh on things, I’d say.”

Bowman had to agree. With a shake of his head, he reflected how the all-enveloping fog had made their disguises redundant. And he suddenly felt all the more ridiculous.

"We can barely see the other side of the street," continued Graves, peering through the mist to the opposite pavement where he hoped Williams and Treacher were keeping pace with them.

Bowman trained his eyes directly in front of him, and could just make out a ghostly figure, crowned with the peak of a porter's hat. "I can just see Constable Evan," he said.

"Can you make out his hands?" enquired Graves, his usually cheerful face knotted into an expression of intense concentration.

"Yes," replied Bowman. "Just about. They're in his pockets by his side."

"Watch him carefully, Bowman. If he takes his hands from his pockets, there's trouble."

This was a prearranged signal agreed with Sergeant Williams before the enterprise began, though Bowman thought the sight of Constable Evan running back towards them would have been a more obvious and probably more likely sign that all was not well.

As they rounded the corner from The Cut onto Blackfriars Road heading north, Inspector Bowman suddenly felt an impact at his shoulder. Almost blind in the fog, he gave a cry as he swung round, reaching out instinctively for something to prevent his falling to the grimy pavement. He was greeted by a loud, high pitched shriek which left his ears ringing, and immediately brought his colleagues to his side. Looking down, Bowman could see that he had hold of a mop of curly, red hair. Beneath that, a pair of blue eyes stared up at him from a dirty, soot-smeared face.

"Hey! Get your filthy hands off me!"

As the urchin started to kick at Bowman's shins, Sergeant Graves took hold of him by the lapels of his threadbare coat and shook him to be quiet.

"Get off me! I wasn't meaning no harm!"

For a small boy he could make a lot of noise, thought Bowman. Too much noise. He looked around as best he could, trying to see if anyone else had noticed the commotion, but it was impossible to make out anything in such conditions.

"Just ran into you, like," continued the ruffian. "Couldn't see you, could I?"

"Quiet lad," hissed Bowman, worried now that the whole operation was in jeopardy. He placed a hand over the boy's mouth in an effort to quieten him, but even then he continued to shout.

"Ow!" squirmed the boy. "Come on mister, let me go! You're hurting."

Bowman thought on balance it was better to let him go. He couldn't risk drawing any more attention to himself and his colleagues. As he released his hold, the boy paused to spit at Bowman's feet before running off to be consumed by the fog, his footsteps echoing off the filthy tenement walls around them.

Graves plunged his hands deep into the pockets of his coat as he watched him go. "The whole of Southwark will probably hear of us in the next five minutes," he said, shaking his head.

Inspector Treacher was at his side by now, looking anxiously around him for any signs of further unexpected activity. "Well," he began, "We're in too far now. What do you think, Sergeant Williams?"

As one, the men swung round to face the sergeant to find his gaze was directed into the fog behind them.

"I think," he said, stroking at his beard in an anxious gesture, "We've lost Constable Evan."

As the other men turned to follow his gaze, they peered into the curtain of impenetrable fog for any sign of their young lookout. Constable Evan was, indeed, nowhere to be seen.

Patricia Bessom hummed absently to herself as she rounded the corner into Chalk Farm Road and made her way carefully through the fog to the smart townhouse at the end. She had been lucky enough to secure herself two rooms on the first floor of this well maintained building, helped no doubt by an excellent reference from her employer which had endeared him to Mrs

Bessom all the more. She felt safe on the first floor, too. In more clement weather, the bay window in her front room gave her an almost panoramic view of the street below. Today, it was all she could do to see the path just three steps ahead of her. Reaching the end of her ditty, Mrs Bessom allowed herself a little giggle as she pushed at the gate to her gravelled path. Locating her keys in a pocket, she picked a piece of loose holly from the wreath which still hung on her front door, pushed it open and stepped inside.

Back on the streets of Southwark, there had been a tense discussion as to the best course of action. Bowman knew they would have to look for Evan but, once he was recovered, he was in favour of abandoning the exercise. He was in no doubt that the boy would have raised the alarm and that, in just a few minutes, Hardacre and his gang would disappear into the fog-shrouded streets of the South Bank to evade capture. Treacher and Williams, however, felt they had invested too much to give up the chase.

"I spent three weeks squatting in their filth," protested Treacher. "I'm not turning back now. If we're quick we could still catch them."

Bowman had sympathy with Treacher's position and so agreed that the ambush should continue.

"Evan knew the route to Hardacre's den," interjected Graves with cheery optimism. "We've no reason to think he's come into any difficulty." He glanced at each of the men in turn. "If we continue on, no doubt we'll find him."

And so it was agreed that the men should carry on in pursuit of their quarry, with the hope of finding Constable Evan in the meantime. Now, Inspector Treacher took the lead. Bowman, Graves and Williams, rattled by the incident with the ginger-haired boy, had decided there was safety in numbers. They followed in a group a few yards behind, each of them keeping as good a look out as they could for any further trouble. Denied his sense of sight, Bowman found he relied increasingly upon his ears to tell him of his surroundings. The sound of their footsteps resounding off the walls told him whether the road was wide or narrow, and so he was able to make an educated guess as to where on the route they were. He was relieved to hear no other sound but their own boots. The local residents had evidently decided that, in the face of such weather, the best course of action was to stay indoors. In that moment, Bowman wished he could join them. The small rooms he had in Hampstead now seemed a long way away, and he yearned to be sitting by the fire, a lamp lit in the window and a glass of Madeira in his hand.

Bowman's train of thought was brought to a sudden halt. Williams had paused at a crossroads and was peering from one direction to the next, as if lost. Having removed his false hook some time ago, reasoning that no one could see him anyway, he held up his hand to slow the party behind him. They were with him in moments, and Bowman could see the sergeant was anxious.

"What is it?" whispered Graves as he looked out into the fog.

"Shh!" commanded Williams and he cupped a hand to his ear.

If Inspector Bowman held his breath, he discovered he could hear it too. A quick, rhythmical pounding on the flagstones. The sweat pricked at Bowman's eyes as his blood ran cold. Hooves. He could hear the clatter of hooves. He couldn't move. His vision, impaired already by the fog, became confused and there came a ringing in his ears. His heart beat in time with the thump of the approaching horses as he felt himself lose balance. Shifting his weight to correct the feeling, he pressed his gloved hands hard against his temples. Time collapsed and he was back on the street with Anna. A flash of bridle caught his eye and he twisted his head to where he knew she was. Too late. She lay twisted on the ground, her blood mingling with the dirt. And now he was restrained. Opening his mouth to scream, no sound came. Sergeant Graves had him by the arms, pulling him back from the careening carriage that sped past them, its driver slumped over the reins. Graves was calling. "No, sir! It's too late!" As if breaking a spell, the words reverberated around the tenement walls and Bowman was drawn back to the here and now.

"Sir!" Graves had him gingerly by the sleeve. "Someone's coming."

Bowman fought to steady his legs. Not hooves, but footsteps. His breath returned.

"Sir?" Graves was peering at him through the fog, his usually open features clouded with concern.

"Yes, but from where?" answered Williams, his Welsh brogue all the stronger with the tension he felt.

His wits restored for now, Bowman looked about him. It seemed only Graves had noticed his momentary confusion. Williams had a point. In this fog, it was impossible to tell from which direction the sound was coming. It echoed off the tall buildings that bore down upon them and seemed to come from everywhere at once. His eyes still on Bowman, Graves was the first to formulate a plan.

"There are four roads joining here," he began. "And four of us. Treacher, you take Fordham Street to the north, Williams, you south. Bowman, you look back the way we came, and I'll stand here facing west. That way, we'll catch the beggar wherever he comes from."

They barely had the time to take their positions when the man was upon them, flying into Bowman like a wild animal. The force of the impact threw him to the ground and they writhed in the street, a mess of arms and legs, while the others came to Bowman's rescue. Williams threw himself on top of the two grappling forms on the ground, and attempted to take a hold of Bowman's assailant.

"Hold him," yelled Bowman, his fists flailing uselessly against his unknown attacker.

Treacher stood back and drew his revolver. He waved it in a futile gesture, unable to discern between the two figures before him. "Police!" he yelled, "Let go, and show yourself!"

Williams and Graves had a good hold on him now, and they dragged the assailant off Bowman's body onto the muddy street beside him. They held him with his arms behind his back, face down in the mud. As Bowman stood, rubbing a painful elbow and knee with his hand, he knelt to pick something up from the road.

"Let him go, Sergeant Williams," he said with an odd, calm note in his voice.

"What?" roared Williams, fired up from the thrill of the chase.

"It's Constable Evan." Bowman held up a porter's hat which, until just a few moments ago had been jammed tight on Evan's head. "Let him go."

At this, Evan himself piped up from the dirt. "Sergeant Williams sir, it's me, Evan. You're hurting."

Exchanging looks of exasperation, Williams and Treacher hauled the scared young man to his feet. Sergeant Williams brushed him down as best he could, whilst Treacher straightened the knapsack on his own back.

"Evan, what on Earth got into you?" rasped Treacher into his ear. "If that young urchin didn't wake the whole neighbourhood, you sure as hell did."

Bowman could see that Evan was white with fear. His hands trembled uncontrollably and his eyes darted from left to right as he spoke.

"I got as far as the end of the alley here before I realised you weren't behind me. I decided to double back and see if I didn't run into you before long."

Williams gave a sardonic laugh. "You certainly did that, sonny."

"Sorry, sir. I'm afraid that, what with the fog and all, I took a fright. I got completely lost. Didn't know where I was. I must have run in circles." Evan was scratching at his head, trying to make sense of it all. Inspector Bowman stepped towards him and put a hand on his shoulder.

"Constable Evan," he said, looking the young man in the eye, "The last thing we need now is a jittery youth among us. Are you well enough to carry on?"

Evan swallowed hard, then nodded his head. "I think so sir, yes."

"Then walk behind us, Constable, and try to keep an eye out." Bowman clapped Evan on the shoulder to try and steady his nerves, then turned to Graves as the young constable made his way to the back of the group. "Keep him out of harm's way, Graves. We need him for numbers, but don't give him more than he can handle." Graves nodded in understanding and, taking Evan's hat from the inspector, joined the youth who was now shuffling his feet nervously a few paces behind. At a signal the little group continued on their way, passing off the main roads and into the fogbound alleys and passageways of Southwark.

As they plunged deeper into London's dark heart, Bowman felt the atmosphere itself changing around him. The smell of human squalor rose into the air to mingle with the fog and sulphur from the nearby brickworks. Bowman could taste the air, and resisted the urge to cough as it caught him in the back of the throat. The ground was harder going now. The sleet and snow was mixed with other debris, harder to identify, but soft and giving under foot. Piles of rags and rubbish were gathered beside the buildings and in the roads, making it difficult to find the space to walk. More than once, Inspector Treacher led them on minor detours to avoid the makeshift barricades. Then, as they rounded the corner into a small close, Treacher stopped.

Bowman squinted into the yellowing mist around them. Tall, forbidding buildings rose high on either side and, ahead of them, a windowless wall soared up into the fog, its top completely obscured so that it could have risen for miles. Bowman suddenly felt uneasy. He had a sense that the buildings were closing in on him, bearing down to crush him to the floor. Shaking his head to clear it, he glanced at Treacher for instructions. The inspector took the kerchief from his neck to wipe the moisture from his forehead, then gestured with a finger to a small corner of the building to his right. There, propped up against the brickwork, was a heavy wooden pallet, the door to Hardacre's den. Treacher pulled the knapsack from his back and, reaching in, produced a small lantern. Pulling a book of matches from his pocket, he carefully lit the lantern and raised a thumb to signal his readiness. The little group shuffled into formation. Sergeant Williams stood forward and placed a hand on the door to signal his intent, while Bowman and Treacher drew their revolvers from their pockets in anticipation. Constable Evan, at a nod from Bowman, stood to one side to look back down the alley, his eyes squinting into the smog for any sign of activity. When Sergeant Williams was sure he had his companions' attention, he put a shoulder to the ramshackle door and pushed.

Having climbed the stairs to her rooms, Mrs Bessom paused for breath before heading into the small communal kitchen. Turning up the lamp on the wall, she placed her bags on the table and set about lighting the stove. She placed a battered and dented kettle to boil, then poured herself a glass of sherry to help keep out the cold. Moving back onto the landing, she proceeded to shed her coat and hang it, with her hat and scarf, on one of the many hooks fixed there. She could tell from the other empty hooks that she was alone in the house for the evening. She busied herself at the grate in her small living room and, having built a handsome fire, settled in her favourite armchair to reflect upon her day.

The air was rent with the sound of splitting wood as Williams put his whole weight against the pallet, and it gave way into the room behind. Treading over the shattered debris, Williams was first in the room, Inspector Treacher following hard on his heels. He held his lantern high to light the room. Graves and Bowman poured in after, the inspector's revolver scanning the room for signs of movement.

"Hold hard or we'll shoot!" yelled Bowman, his hobnailed boots struggling to find purchase on the splintered wood beneath.

"Make yourself plain!" added Treacher, swinging the lantern before him. "We're armed!"

Bowman and Graves moved further into the room as the dust settled, Bowman kicking over the piles of rags and papers that littered the floor.

"Nothing," breathed Graves, his voice hoarse from the exertion. "They've flown the nest." Treacher motioned him to be quiet and, catching Bowman's eye, gestured to the greasy curtain that separated the room from Hardacre's cell. Bowman took up position beside it, his revolver levelled at head height in front of him. Inspector Treacher reached up to the curtain and, with a look to Bowman, tore it down in one movement, charging into the room beyond. Bowman followed at once, his body tensed for action. As Treacher held his lantern high, turning circles in the room to light each corner, Bowman could see the cell was empty.

"It's clear!" Treacher yelled back to Graves and Williams in the main room, a note of incredulity in his voice. Pocketing his revolver once more, Bowman emerged back through the curtain, Treacher following close behind, despondent.

"They've gone," he said, the disappointment plain in his demeanour. "And with them the evidence." He raised his eyes to meet Williams', who shook his head sadly at the news.

"Then it's all come to nought," said the sergeant.

For a while, the four men stood with their eyes to the floor, dejected and confused. Williams lent back to rest upon something harsh and metallic, then sprang back up with alarm. The brazier. The sergeant turned and put a hand cautiously over the coals.

"The brazier's cold," he said to no one in particular.

His interest piqued, Bowman walked to the corner of the room where Williams stood, kicking at a pile of scraps in his way. He reached out and picked up a coal from the brazier.

"And wet," he observed.

There was a movement at the door that caused each man to tense suddenly where he stood. Constable Evan trod carefully through the hole in the wall, holding a hand in front of his face to shield his eyes from the glow of Treacher's lamp.

"Too late?" he stammered, nervously.

"They must have got word," replied Treacher.

"Must have been the boy, then," said Evan. He had clearly been ill at ease outside and seemed to relax visibly as he sidled further into the room. "He must have raised the alarm."

"The enterprise was doomed from the moment we ran into him," offered Williams. He looked up to meet Bowman's gaze. Neither of them had the heart to tell Evan that his own behaviour might well have been as much to blame.

"Still," grumbled Bowman, "They can't be long gone. The brazier's wet but this coal still has some warmth in it." He threw the coal to the floor and wiped a sooty hand on his coat.

Evan looked suddenly terrified that the search for the villains was about to start all over again. "But, the fog," he spluttered. "They could be anywhere by now and it would be impossible to find them."

Bowman smoothed down his moustache with a finger. "Just a moment." As his eyes narrowed, the assembled party turned as one to face him. "If you got word of an ambush, and wanted to get out quick, would you take time to throw water over the fire?"

"Possibly," said Treacher slowly, swinging his lantern to where the brazier stood in the corner.

"But surely you'd be more concerned with getting out in a hurry," Bowman retorted. "Unless..." Bowman's eyes dropped to the brazier's feet. Squatting on his haunches, his great coat trailing in the grease behind him, he grabbed Treacher's lamp from him and traced a line across the floor where the brazier had been dragged through the dirt and straw.

"The brazier has been moved. That's why they cooled it," he mused aloud. "Treacher, you didn't notice the brazier was in a different position?"

"I thought nothing of it," shrugged Treacher from the shadows.

Bowman traced the lines in the dirt where the brazier's feet had been dragged and stood, pointing at a flagstone in the centre of the room. Even in the gloom, it was possible to see it had been recently disturbed. It was ill fitting and its sides and corners were chipped. Bowman put a finger to his lips to call for silence in the room, drew his revolver from his pocket and motioned to Williams to lift the flagstone from its place in the floor. As the sergeant knelt to lever up the slab, Graves stepped forward to help him lift it to one side with some effort. Once removed, it revealed a deep, dark hole in the floor.

Having warmed herself satisfactorily, Mrs Bessom headed back to the kitchen to prepare her supper. Reaching into the bag she had left upon the table, she felt for the cold meat and potatoes she had bought on her way home and stretched up to a shelf above the window to feel for a pan. The last of the water from the kettle would serve to boil the vegetables. As they cooked, she turned again to her bag to retrieve her copy of The Evening Standard, smiling at the memory of the ever-cheerful Martin Quigley. Taking a quick nibble from the smoked ham on her plate, Mrs Bessom flicked through the pages absentmindedly before turning the paper over for a more in-depth investigation. The headline on the front page gave her pause; 'A GRUESOME DISCOVERY'.

"Come on out and make yourself known!" shouted Treacher into the hole. There was no reply. Resigned, Bowman took the lantern from Treacher and, with a look to Graves and the other men in the room to make sure they were ready, launched himself into the darkness below.

The party in the room heard the soles of Bowman's boots slap against the floor in the cellar below, then a scuffling noise as he regained his balance. The lamp cast an eerie glow back up the hatch, illuminating the pit as if it were some furnace. For a while there was silence and Inspector Treacher tightened his grip on his revolver in anticipation. Then, Inspector Bowman's voice echoed into the room.

"The booty's here, all right," he called as his head popped up through the hole in the floor. "But not a soul to be found." Graves knelt to help his fellow inspector up as Bowman continued. "Inspector Treacher, perhaps we should arrange to have an inventory made of everything that's down there. We might be able to return some of it to its rightful owners."

"Then tonight hasn't been a complete disaster," offered the ever-optimistic Sergeant Graves, his face beaming in the lamplight.

Bowman was brushing down his coat and trousers. "Agreed. Though where they've got to is anyone's guess."

"Too fly for you, eh?" A new voice echoed off the soot and tobacco stained walls. It was a voice Inspector Treacher knew well. As the party turned as one to face the door, two men stood illuminated by Treacher's lantern. One was Jabez Kane. As a grisly smile spread over his dark and swarthy face, the scar that ran down from his forehead to his cheek creased into a deeper fissure. What startled the attendant officers most, however, was the sight of Constable Evan being held against Kane's chest by an arm about his shoulders. A jagged blade was at his throat.

Shaking her head at the depravity of it all, Patricia Bessom turned from her Evening Standard to retrieve a little mustard from a jar. Spooning it onto her plate next to the ham, she prodded the potatoes with a fork as they rolled in the pan of boiling water. Five more minutes, she guessed, and her supper would be ready. Turning her attention back to the article, she couldn't help but feel a thrill at the more salacious details. A body discovered in the ice. A young woman in need of identification. Holding the paper closer to the flickering lamplight, Mrs Bessom slid her spectacles to the end of her nose, the better to peer over them. There, just below the article was a drawing, a likeness of the young lady found in the river, and alongside that were printed the words, "Most curious of all are the young lady's eyes, each being of a different colour to the other". Mrs Bessom looked long and hard at the picture, her mouth opening in a silent expression of alarm. Releasing the paper in horror, her eyes grew wide in fear. It was a face she knew well. "Oh, Lord," she exclaimed, her hands flying involuntarily to her face. "Mary!"

"Where the Devil did you spring from?" demanded Graves, somewhat redundantly. It was plain to Bowman that Kane had jumped on the young man's back after slipping in through the door behind him. Evan's eyes rolled in fear and his breathing was quick and shallow. He pulled at Kane's arm with both hands but it was plain that he was no match for his assailant. Kane kept the blade at Evan's throat.

"All right, Evan," soothed Treacher, keeping his voice calm and level as he addressed the young constable. "Easy does it, there's a good lad."

"There's a voice I know," rasped Jabez Kane peering into the gloom. "And a face to match it, too. Got word to the peelers, did you Treacher?"

"It's much worse than that, Kane. I would advise you to put down that blade and come quietly. There are many more of us than you, as you can see."

"And we're armed, too," offered Sergeant Williams, stepping into the meagre light thrown into the room by the lantern.

Kane looked from him back to Treacher, tightening his grip about Evan's throat. "A peeler yerself, are you? I knew there was something queer about you. Lucky we got word that you was on your way."

"Then why did you come back?" Treacher was inching ever closer now, cautioning Inspector Bowman to keep his distance with a glance. Both he and Bowman had their revolvers trained on Kane, but it would be difficult to get a clear shot with Constable Evan in their sights.

"I came back for my prize. A little momento of your visit, if you like." Kane began backing towards the door, dragging the young constable with him for security. "Can't get your shot though, can ya?" he leered at Bowman and Treacher. "Wouldn't risk putting a bullet into one of yer own now, would ya?"

Bowman took a tighter grip on his revolver, eager to reassure Evan that the situation was under control. "It's all right, Constable," he said, his voice loaded with tension despite his wish to reassure.

Kane's smile grew broader, the scar on his cheek creasing deeper into his face. "Constable, eh?" he cackled hideously. "Well then, got meself a nice young chicken, haven't I?" With his free hand, he smoothed down the hair on the constable's head, pressing his lips closer to Evan's ear. "Don't struggle, chicken. Don't ruffle yer feathers."

Evan was plainly at tipping point. His mouth opened and closed in quivering, silent speech and his eyes stood out in terror. His pale skin was pricked with beads of sweat. His whole body had begun to shake involuntarily. As the young constable was pulled through the door to the alley beyond, Inspector Bowman became aware that Evan was now looking directly at him, his imploring gaze seeming to bore directly into his skull. Whatever the outcome of this particular incident, the inspector knew that look would haunt him for years to come. Evan raised a pleading hand towards Bowman as a word formed on his lips. "Sir," he gasped, swallowing furiously in his panic.

With a flick of his wrist, Jabez Kane let Evan drop to the rubbish-strewn floor, using the movement as a distraction during which to make good his escape. His feet scuffing against the flagstones, he ran through the doorway to the alley beyond. He pulled the ragged door off its hinges as he did so and threw it back into the room behind him as he fled.

"Evan!" shouted Williams as he ran to the prone figure on the floor.

Treacher and Bowman grappled with the door, heaving it out into the alley then giving chase as best they could. Their feet struggled to find purchase on the greasy floor. Inspector Bowman let loose a shot, the blast echoing off the confining walls around them, but both inspectors knew it was in vain. Skidding to a halt on the wet cobbles, Bowman put a hand on Treacher's shoulder to steady himself. He shook his head in dismay. "We'll do more harm than good in this fog."

As Bowman and Treacher stepped back into the gloom of Hardacre's den, they found Graves and Williams on the floor at Evan's side. The constable's head was cradled in Graves' lap while Williams held a piece of rag, now soaked in blood, firmly at his neck. The young man's eyes were open but staring, lifeless, at the ceiling. Graves looked up and met the inspector's gaze.

"We've lost him, sir. Evan is dead."

X

Night Thoughts

This time, Bowman was flying. Beneath him, the bustle of London life squeezed its way through the narrowing streets. He knew he would appear at any moment, just around the furthest corner. This was how it had always been. He had a theory that all his life had led him here. Every decision he had taken, every choice he had made had ended with him at this corner at this moment. The moment Anna had died. It was a theory they had tried to dispel at Colney Hatch. Much of his treatment had been to quash this heavy, hopeless malaise. The medication, the relentless discipline, the cold baths had all been with the intent to shock him into the present from the fearful past. Bowman daren"t admit to anyone that they had failed.

He was closer to the ground now, only a few feet from the grimy flagstones. He fancied he could smell the hides from the tanning factory across the way. All around him there was bustle. Street urchins jostled with traders and hawkers. Beggars and vagrants skulked beneath the railway arches, hiding from the glare of the low, May sun. Businessmen, smart in their frock coats, cleared a path with a swing of a silver-tipped cane. Bowman noticed they were moving at half speed, swinging their sticks like scythes through grass. Looking about him, he saw everything had slowed. The throng pressed past him as if waist-high in water. A bone thrown for a dog described a leisurely arc through the air. Cruelly, Bowman realised, events were to play out in front of him more slowly than ever before.

Rising to the rooftops now, he saw Anna rounding the corner from Whitechapel. Her face obscured by her bonnet, her purposeful stride gave her away. At such slow speed, it seemed for a moment that Bowman might avert the catastrophe to come, that he might swoop like an angel to persuade her from her course, that she might look up to see him and falter in her step. But it was not to be. From his lofty height, Bowman could hear the clatter of hooves on the flagstones and he knew that Anna would surely die. Again.

As he was held above the scene, he suddenly felt a pressure on his chest. A swift tug seemed to pull him through time and space. He was at home now, seemingly suspended from the ceiling of his rooms in Hampstead. Below him, playing out that morning's conversation like actors in a play, he could see himself and Anna.

"Must you go?" she was imploring. "I had hoped you might accompany me to the refuge."

"I am called for, Anna."

"By whom?"

"Williams has need of men to put an end to a case. He has this past fortnight been close to bringing an end to a case of slavery. A troupe of hawkers in Whitechapel has been abducting children, sending them north to the industrial cities for fodder. Well-to-do children sometimes, not just urchins."

"Ah," Anna breathed, smoothing Bowman's habitual frown with a gloved finger. "So now the toffs are angry and the case must be solved." There was a look of gentle reproach in her eyes but Bowman forgave her easily, as he forgave her all things. He knew he was being teased.

"It is good work, Anna. Children will be saved."

Anna dipped her head. "Then, who am I to stand in your way, Detective Inspector George Bowman?" She pronounced his name slowly, deliberately and quietly. In the spaces between each word, she rose up on her toes to plant the softest of kisses on his lips. From his vantage above, Bowman felt the kisses again as if freshly planted, but this time each was like a little ache.

Anna was moving to the door now. "Well, I shall be in Whitechapel, too. Perhaps, when you have saved the world from blight, you might pass by the Women's Refuge to walk me home?"

Bowman felt the urge to reach down, to shout, to hold her back and prevent her from leaving, but he felt pinned to the ceiling like a butterfly to cork.

"I will do that," he heard himself say, his words distant.

Anna had been justly proud of her work at the refuge. She had grown up around Blackfriars, the only child to a respectable clerk, and had often seen women whom her father had named "fallen" on her walks about the Embankment. At first she had not known what he had meant. Conversation about them was forbidden, particularly at the table. With a click of her tongue and a shake of her head, her mother had let it be known that such a dialogue was not welcome at dinner. In what way were they fallen, she had mused as a child. Had they lost their footing on the pavement? In truth, they were often seen to lie prone by the roadside, their petticoats spread about them. If they had indeed fallen, why did no one help them up? In her later youth, Anna came to understand. Far from being appalled at these unfortunate women, she felt sadness at their plight and a sharp pang of guilt that she enjoyed the comforts of a prosperous home while they did not. She learned that these women were in the employ of unscrupulous men. That it was they who profited from their work. Anna felt helpless in the face of their destitution. Soon, however, she had befriended one of them.

Anna had found a little employment at her father's office and would often pass a woman called Joan on her walk to work. After a day filing accounts she would engage with her in conversation on the way back home. She was young, Anna discovered, only a year older than herself. Joan hoped to find a man to look after her, she had said, a man to give her the love denied her by her family. Over the summer months Anna learned to look forward to these shared moments and she fancied Joan did, too. She even dared to hope that she was being of some practical help. And then, one day, Joan was gone.

Anna had noticed her failing health as the dreary autumn days had shortened. She would often find her slumped against the roadside with nothing but a threadbare shawl to keep her warm. Still, Anna knew, she plied her trade. Her pimp demanded payment. Without it, he could withdraw the protection he offered. Such meagre protection. Noticing Joan's absence that day, Anna took it upon herself to investigate. Walking nearer to the Thames than she ought on such dark nights, she sought other women who might know of Joan's whereabouts. Eventually, she found someone with the information she dreaded. Joan had indeed been taken sick. So sick in fact, that her master - how Anna had blanched at the word - had taken it upon himself to remove her from the market. Bad for business, he had apparently said. She'd been removed from her spot and taken to the slums and back alleys of Blackfriars. There she had been left to die and rot, propped up against a filthy tenement wall with no hope of discovery or salvation. The news had taken Anna aback. Her eyes had been opened to a world of misery such as she hoped she would never see. Her solemn oath then, had been to fight for these wretched drabs. If they were indeed, as her father would have it, fallen women, then she would reach out a hand to lift them up. She knew of the fledgling Women's Refuge in Hanbury Street, founded by the Booths and their Salvation Army. After a perfunctory interview, she was engaged to serve hot, sweet tea at the entrance to any wretch that found themselves upon the porch. Upon payment of a penny, any woman of desperate means could find herself fed, watered, cleaned and with a safe bed for the night. The building's plain, austere exterior belied the potential for transformation contained within, a thought that pleased Anna greatly as she stepped from the kerb to cross the road. And then she froze.

To Bowman, time had become tangible. He could touch it, feel it. His coat tails were suspended about him. He circled Anna like a bee at a flower. As she stood frozen, mid-step before him, he became aware of the scene in every detail; from the detached eyelash that rested upon her nose, to the dog that slavered in the gutter behind him. From the vagrant suspended mid-fall as he ran from a fish-seller, to the steam that was captured as in a picture, rising from the locomotive on the bridge. He was everywhere at once, aware of all things. Next, a thin whistle sounded in his ears and, with a whoosh, Bowman was observing himself. Half a mile or so away, there he stood with a revolver in his hand. He had just loosed the shot that would change his life forever.

Bowman had been called by Sergeant Williams to provide some fire power if needed. Detective inspectors were allowed to carry arms, and Williams had a thought things might take a turn for the worse. He had been right. Inspector Bowman and Graves had joined the sergeant off Baker's Row, just in time to catch the villains at work. Williams had intercepted certain of the gang's communications and, as a result, had lain in wait with his colleagues across from the workhouse. The rogues had plans to abduct more children. It was a profitable business. With industry booming in the north, manpower was in short supply. Far cheaper and more productive to employ urchins from the streets of London. Within days, the little wretches would find themselves beneath the looms that spun imported cotton into fine clothes worn by the ladies of the city. They would lose fingers and limbs as they fought to maintain the machines or free an obstruction. They could be worked to exhaustion, and even sometimes death, and no one would raise their voice in protest. No one would miss them. Now, Williams lay in wait across the road. Before him, a line of waifs was waiting to be admitted to the workhouse. Easy prey, mused Bowman as he crouched beside the sergeant, weapon drawn. Graves shifted his weight behind them. He had held his position for so long, he was starting to lose the feeling in his legs.

"Here they come," Williams hissed, his eye on the black cab that had rounded the corner. "Be ready now."

The carriage came thundering at speed, the horses' hooves kicking up dirt behind them. The wheels rattled on the road as it slowed. Williams fought against every urge to make himself known. He knew he had to wait. To catch these rogues would be prize enough, but to catch them in the act would be enough to see them hang. With a hand held high to gesture that Graves and Bowman should keep their positions, he watched as the brougham careened closer to the kerb. The door was opened and a man hung from the carriage, his arm outstretched. As the driver cracked the whip from where he sat, a scarf wrapped around his face to thwart identification, his passenger simply leaned out and plucked one of the unfortunate wretches from the line. Kicking and screaming, the boy was pulled inside the carriage and the door slammed shut. Now, Williams pounced. As the carriage sped away, scattering pedestrians before it, the sergeant gave chase. Bowman and Graves were at his heels.

"Halt!" screamed Williams, his Welsh brogue all the stronger in his desperation. "Stop that carriage!" The brougham sped on regardless, increasing in speed as it readied to turn the corner into Old Montague Street. Williams knew that if it completed the turn, all would be lost. Which is why he had invited Inspector Bowman. With a nod to his colleague, Williams stepped out of the line of fire. Bowman pulled the revolver from his coat and steadied it at his arm's length. His view down the street was clear. Thankfully, the speeding carriage had cleared a way down the road. Passers by picked themselves up from where they had fallen, surprised by the commotion and the oncoming carriage. Others shouted their admonishments after the driver. Somewhere a baby cried. As the brougham turned at the junction, Bowman finally had a clear view of the driver. He loosed his shot. And time stopped again.

Bowman was keenly aware of the bullet as it hung suspended before him, the air around it bent out of shape. Halted on its inexorable journey, it was all lethal potential. Following its trajectory, Bowman was now at the carriage. The driver was frozen like a figure of wax, leaning forward with his hands gripped tightly at the reins. As time resumed, there was a crack. The bullet passed clean through the carriage canopy. The driver slumped forward, a hand clutching at his left side. The bullet had made its home in the man's internal viscera, passing first through his spine then into his heart and left lung. The bullet had claimed its first life. It was about, quite accidentally, to claim another.

From his vantage, Williams saw the carriage careen into Queen Street. "Quick!" he barked, rubbing the sweat from his eyes with his hands. "That road loops round back onto Hanbury Street. We can catch it where is emerges, by the Sally Army refuge."

Bowman's heart quickened at the thought. Surely, Anna would be inside by now. He calmed himself in the certain knowledge that she would be safe. The three policemen were running at full pelt now, Williams blowing hard on his whistle to summon any uniformed help that might be nearby. A mob of pigeons took flight before them. People shouted after the three detectives in the confusion. As they neared the refuge, Bowman could hear the clatter of hooves from round the corner. He knew by their sound that the horses were out of control. Their hooves slid on the cobbles as the brougham hove into view, lurching at a precarious angle as it rounded the bend back onto Hanbury Street. Then Bowman saw her.

Anna was just yards in front of the carriage, directly in its way. Cruelly, time sped up. Bowman had relived this moment again and again, both sleeping and awake. Sometimes, events had lengthened such that he had the time to save her. Other times, she had been a step or two behind or in front and, crucially, had stepped clear of the carriage's fearful path. This time, there was no chance to intervene. It was all too quick. He opened his mouth to call her name in warning, but the horses were already upon her. Their hooves fell upon her body, and Bowman saw her sucked beneath the wheels. There was no time for her to scream. As the carriage thundered on, Bowman slowed his step. His face fell slack. Everything slipped away. He viewed the scene as if through a lens. Sounds collided. Coming to a halt, he felt the spatter of her blood on his face. He had to reach her. As if from a distance, Bowman saw himself step into the carriage's path. Then there were arms around him.

"No, sir!" Graves held him tight about the shoulders, but Bowman struggled against him. He had to help her. "It's too late!" Graves breathed in his ear. And Bowman knew it would always be too late. The bullet he had fired could never be recalled.

He was falling. He woke with a start. His heart thumped against his chest and he felt blood in his palms where he had clenched his fists too tight. Fighting his erratic breath, Bowman rose from his chair. With an almighty effort of will, he forced himself into the here and now. It was not a place he cared to be.

It held nothing for him now. Falling against the mantle, Bowman took a hold of the portrait that stood there. Anna smiled from the picture, her almond eyes seeking those of her husband beyond the glass. His fingers traced the outline of her hair as it tumbled across her shoulders. He noticed a tremor in his hand. With a deep, shattering sigh, Bowman replaced the frame on the mantle and shuffled his way to an empty, fitful bed.

XI

An Identification

Scotland Yard was impressive. Solid and inscrutable, the newly completed red brick building stood, fortress-like, on the north bank of the Thames. The louring sky reflected in its windows afforded it a forbidding air as Mrs Bessom pulled up outside in a hansom cab. Craning her neck through the window, she allowed her eyes to be drawn up to the full height of the building where tall, square chimneys stood to attention on the roof.

She stepped gingerly from the footplate, placing each foot in turn carefully on the slippery kerb. Steadying herself against the woodwork of the cab, she turned to give her fare to the driver, tipping as handsomely as her modest wages would allow. The morning was overcast and, although the city had been spared any more falls of snow, the roads and pavements were treacherous. What ice there was had been churned into a brown, slippery mess. Looking around her, Mrs Bessom saw that the blanket of fog that had covered the city like a shroud the night before had condensed out of the air. It lay on the fences and lampposts in a watery skein. The river behind her was in the midst of a thaw. The channel running through its middle now flowed with some force. It grew wider with every passing hour as the ice retreated. As the day progressed, Mrs Bessom had no doubt there would be floods somewhere. Making her way down a side street to the main entrance, she could not but be impressed by the imposing solidity of the building. Half way up, the grey brick course gave way to a brighter red that stood out in cheery relief against the melting drifts of snow that lay in the shadier corners.

The head had been discovered not two hundred yards beneath him. It was an irony not lost on Inspector Bowman as he gazed from the window in his office over the Thames below. It felt to Bowman that the head was taunting him, mocking. He realised the importance of solving such a high profile crime, both to his reputation and to that of the fledgling Metropolitan Police Force. He knew the morning papers were already full of the news, courtesy of Jack Watkins and his ilk, but he also knew this was an opportunity for Scotland Yard to prove itself. As he absently smoothed his moustache with his fingers, he mused upon Sir Richard Mayne's statement. "The primary object of an efficient police is the prevention of crime. The next, that of detection and punishment." He had singularly failed upon the first point. The unfortunate woman had fallen victim to one of the most heinous crimes Bowman could remember. He shuddered to imagine what sort of character the perpetrator might posses. If he had failed upon the first point however, Bowman was determined to succeed upon the second. The offender must be detected and punished. Preferably in as public a manner as possible. As he turned from the window to sit at his desk, there was a knock at the door.

"Enter," Bowman barked.

The heavy door swung open with a creak to admit Sergeant Graves. Bowman could tell at a glance that Graves had none of his usual chirpiness about him. Bowman gestured to the chair opposite and the young man sat with a heavy sigh.

"Good morning, Sergeant Graves," Bowman offered.

Graves lifted the hat from his head. Bowman noticed he knocked the moisture from its brim with perhaps more force than was necessary. "No sir, it is not a good morning. I have just spent an hour with Sergeant Williams from Bow Street trying to offer such solace as I could to a distraught young lady."

Bowman couldn't help but feel Graves' discomfort. The young sergeant usually took events in his stride, sometimes eerily so, but this morning's business had taken a heavy toll. Graves toyed with the hat in his hands, turning it this way and that in his state of agitation.

"One who has just heard," he continued, "that her fiancée has been murdered in the course of performing his duty as a constable."

The words hit Bowman hard. He rose from his seat and made his way to the window, his back to Graves so his face might not be seen. As his hand fell to his side, however, he was suddenly aware that the tremor had returned. Bowman gripped his hand with the other to try and disguise the motion, but still his suspicions were roused that Graves had noticed. As he turned back into the room, the young sergeant averted his gaze just a little too quickly. Bowman slipped his shaking hand into a pocket, willing it to be still.

"Constable Evan was to be married?" he asked, barely audible.

Graves took a breath. "He was. To a Miss Jane Carmichael. A sweeter creature I have yet to meet. We tried to offer the lady such comfort as we could but – " His voice trailed off and his eyes rested on the desk, immobile. Sensing Graves' distress, Bowman turned.

"I'm sure you acquitted yourselves admirably, Sergeant Graves. It's a nasty business, of that there is no doubt."

Graves was drawn out of himself at the remark. "Me and some of the lads are talking of a fund, Inspector Bowman. To help provide for Miss Carmichael."

The men were interrupted in their thoughts by a further knock at the door. At Bowman's command it opened to admit a rather large lady, clad in layers of fur and wool as protection against the bitter cold. Her face flushed with the effort of climbing so many stairs, she pulled her gloves from her hands and surveyed the room. Even through her exertions, she could tell that she had somehow come upon a sombre scene. The wood panelled room seemed heavy with grief and she wondered for a moment just what conversation she had interrupted. Her keen eye sized up the two men before her; the taller one wearing a coat, slumped in a chair, toying nervously with a hat, the other by the window, a heavy moustache accentuating a doleful expression.

"Inspector Bowman?" she enquired.

"And this is Sergeant Anthony Graves." The man at the window gestured to the seated figure with an open hand. "Can we be of assistance?"

Graves sprang to his feet, almost glad of the interruption. Offering his chair to the lady, he found himself the recipient of several scarves, gloves and a hat as she sat, composing herself.

Reaching into her bag, she pulled a copy of The Evening Standard from its depths and placed it on the table, smoothing the paper with something approaching careful ceremony. Bowman could see a tear rise at her eye as she began.

"I know her, sir. The girl they found in the river."

Graves flicked his eyes to Bowman as he acknowledged the remark. "You know her?"

"Yes, sir. Her name is Mary Henderson."

Bowman moved to the lady to console her. "Please, Mrs - "

"Mrs Patricia Bessom, sir."

"Would you have a brandy, Mrs Bessom?"

Mrs Bessom looked between the two men. "Thank you, inspector. I can't pretend I don't need it."

As Bowman continued, Graves moved to the ornate bureau beneath Bowman's map of London and poured a small brandy from a glass decanter.

"You're certain you know the girl, Mrs Bessom?" Bowman sat himself on the corner of his desk.

Mrs Bessom took the glass gratefully from Sergeant Graves and took small sips of brandy. The effect was to firstly fortify her against the cold that still clung about her, and secondly to calm her ragged nerves.

"As certain as I can be from the picture and the description." Placing the glass on the table in front of her, she leaned forward and peered over her spectacles, the better to read the pertinent passage. ""'Most remarkable are the poor woman's eyes which are of different colours; one blue, the other brown." It cannot be anyone else."

At a look from Bowman, Sergeant Graves took a notebook from his pocket and proceeded to scratch at it with the stub of a pencil.

"A Miss Mary Henderson, you say?"

Mrs Bessom nodded as she folded the newspaper in front of her. The likeness staring out from the front page had unnerved her.

"How did you know her?" continued Bowman. "Was she family?"

"No, inspector, not family." Mrs Bessom's lip began to quiver at the thought. "Though she might well have been."

Mrs Bessom had kept her grief in check the whole morning but now, in the company of these two men, it somehow overcame her. The tears sprang readily from her eyes as, reaching into a pocket of her dress for a handkerchief, she surrendered to her sorrow.

"Oh sir," she continued, lifting her spectacles from her nose to wipe her eyes, "I knew her from a little girl." She paused to compose herself.

"I'm sorry Mrs Bessom, but I'm afraid I must press you."

With a deep breath of resolve, Mrs Bessom began again. "I am a housekeeper by trade, and have been for over thirty years, thirteen of them with the Henderson family at St John's Wood."

From the corner of his eye, Bowman could see Sergeant Graves making careful note of the salient facts, his brows knitted in concentration.

"Mary is," Mrs Bessom stopped to correct herself, "*Was* their only child. The father was a doctor, a rather austere man who, in my opinion, paid rather more attention to his patients than his own daughter. Her mother was the quiet type, fragile you might say."

Bowman nodded in understanding. "You were in their employment for thirteen years, you say?"

"Almost to the day. I began my work there on Mary's third birthday and I left just a few days short of her sixteenth."

Graves looked up from his notepad. "When was that?"

"Some four years ago, Sergeant Graves."

Graves looked to the ceiling, as if seeking inspiration there. "Then Mary would now be twenty years old." He looked to Bowman. "That tallies with Doctor Crane's estimate."

Bowman let that sink in. This was beginning to look like a very positive identification. For the first time in his professional life, Bowman found himself thanking the heavens for Jack Watkins. "Where might the Henderson family be now?" he asked.

Calm at last, Mrs Bessom pushed the handkerchief back into the folds of her dress. "To my knowledge sir, they live in the same house to this day. The doctor has a surgery there."

Before Bowman could respond, there came the noise of approaching heavy feet outside his office. In a moment more, as a shutter might fly open in the face of a great wind, so Bowman's door was flung aside to admit a force of nature no less unpredictable. The unexpected visitor tore the pipe from his mouth and bellowed into the room.

"Grab your coat and waders, Bowman!"

Bowman moved to quieten the man. "Inspector Hicks, what on - "

Ignatius Hicks thrust his great bearded chin at the inspector, using his pipe to punctuate his words as he spoke. "The Thames has just delivered us more of its secrets." With a flick of his eyes, Bowman drew Inspector Hicks' attention to the lady in the chair, a flicker of his heavy brows cautioning him to not disclose too much.

Bowman continued, carefully. "Where?"

With a smile, Hicks paused. More than loving an audience, he loved playing an audience. His innate sense of drama told him he had the attention of everyone in the room, and he relished the moment. "Chelsea Embankment," he boomed with a flourish of his pipe, each word carefully enunciated and separated by a pregnant pause such as an actor would use at the theatre. Hicks clamped his pipe back in his teeth in triumph and set his mouth in a wide, self-satisfied smile.

Bowman turned to the lady in the chair. "Mrs Bessom, would you excuse me? I should like to take that address from you in a moment." Mrs Bessom nodded her assent and began to gather the newspaper from the desk. Bowman turned on his heel, suddenly galvanised into action. "Sergeant Graves could you please accompany the inspector to Chelsea and prevent him from jumping to too many conclusions?"

With a knowing look, Graves jammed his hat back on his head. He functioned best when he was being of practical use and, after this morning's solemn duties, clearly relished the prospect of being back in the fray. Bowman stopped the two men at the door as they bustled from the office.

"And Inspector Hicks?"

The mountain of man that was Ignatius Hicks turned slowly in the doorframe.

"The next time you find a closed door between us, would you do me the courtesy of knocking on it first?" Hicks let a puff of noxious smoke escape his lips by way of a reply. Bowman blinked furiously against the effects of the fug and rather pointedly cleared his throat. "Sergeant Graves, take whatever you find to Doctor Crane at Charing Cross. I should like a report from you in two hours."

With a sharp nod of assent, Graves bundled Inspector Hicks through the door, closing it behind him with a rolling of his eyes. Bowman took a breath to clear his lungs, then turned back into the room to face a bemused Mrs Bessom.

"Now, Mrs Bessom," he said, walking again to his side of the desk. "The address, if you please."

XII

Complications

The passage leading to Jeb Hardacre's squalid slum was no less imposing by day than by night. The road was strewn with rags and paper, some of which may have concealed a sleeping urchin or two, and was crowded on both sides by tall tenements. The damp walls rose high enough to block the sun from view such that, even on the hottest day, they dripped with rivulets of water. The greasy brickwork crumbled to the touch and unknown moulds competed for space on the mortar. Other than the rats that ran between the piles of human detritus that littered the pavements, at this early hour there were no signs of life in the alley. The streets beyond were awakening to another day. The cries of the sellers and hawkers echoed through the streets and plumes of smoke and steam rose into the sky as the factories and mills heaved into life.

At the entrance to the alley stood a squat, hooded figure, scanning the rooftops as if in anticipation of some new arrival. Sure enough, there, standing out in sharp relief against the pale morning sun, a spectre appeared. Moving stealthily between the chimneys, jumping now and then between the gutters, the apparition seemed to flutter in the wind as it made its way with well-practiced movements to the alley below. Shinning down a drainpipe, it finally coalesced into the figure of a small, red haired boy, short for his age and dressed in rags. His face was grimy with soot and his hands and nails were calloused and gnarled. The hooded man turned to acknowledge him, slowly removing his cowl to reveal the nut-brown, bewhiskered face of Jeb Hardacre. Hardacre caught the young boy in his steely gaze.

"So?" he asked.

The boy shook his head. "Nuffink, Mr 'Ardacre."

Hardacre took a step forward and, for the first time, the boy could see he was hiding something under the folds of his ragged cape.

"Nothing? You're sure?"

“As sure as I’m standin’ ’ere, sir. It’s all clear. I stayed for a while and saw nuffink untoward.”

Reaching into his pockets, Hardacre swung his cape aside and revealed a cudgel tied to his belt. Straining in the early morning light, the boy could plainly see it was stained with blood and hair. He swallowed hard. Hardacre was not a man to be crossed, he knew that. He had done his job well, but still he shuddered to think how things might have gone had it been otherwise.

Pulling his hand from a pocket, Hardacre tousled the boy’s hair playfully with the other. “Thomas Crowley, you’re a wily one and no mistake. And as you’ve done right by me, so I will do right by you.” Hardacre opened his fist to reveal a shiny, silver coin.

“Wh-what is it?” stammered young Tom Crowley, his eyes wide with wonder.

“The most valuable coin in the world,” Hardacre chuckled. “A Dutch guilder, boy. From Holland.” Hardacre knew it was as good as worthless on the streets of London, but it looked pretty enough as he turned it in his fingers. “Go on, boy. Take it.”

Gingerly, the boy reached out to take his prize. In all his little life, Thomas Crowley had never yet reached into the jaws of a crocodile, nor put his hand into the lion’s maw but, as he snatched the coin from Hardacre’s hand, he fancied he had a taste of a danger just as keen. He looked up into the wide, brown face that hovered menacingly above him. “Will you take me there one day, sir? To ’Olland?”

Hardacre squatted on his haunches and stared long and hard into the boy’s enquiring eyes. Such innocence, he thought.

“That I will, son. That I will.” Hardacre flicked his eyes up to the roofs, a signal that Tom knew well. His audience was at an end. With a curt nod and something approaching a salute, the boy turned on his heels and leapt with feline grace to the drainpipe, the gutter and finally to the chimneys above. “If you live that long,” Hardacre added with a macabre chuckle. The boy picked his way with certainty, almost dancing along the tiles and balustrades. He moved with a confidence that could only belong to a citizen of another, higher world. Hardacre watched him go then stood and turned back down the alley. Kicking the filth at his feet and swinging the cudgel at his belt almost playfully, he made his way back to his den that, thanks to the boy, he knew to be unguarded.

A sizable crowd had gathered by the river at Chelsea Embankment. The Thames was flowing with some force again now, the ice all but gone save by the reeds and weed that grew on the banks. It never ceased to amaze Sergeant Graves just how quickly a crowd could gather. It could not have been above twenty minutes since the alarm was raised but already there were all manner of people present. Tradespeople and bankers, housewives and businessmen, all stamped their feet against the cold as they gossiped and theorised as to what this latest discovery might mean. Curiosity, mused Graves, was a great leveller.

The object of their fascination lay partially buried in the mud of the north bank. To the obvious delight of the onlookers, a tangle of sackcloth and limbs had been discovered protruding from the mire. What held their fascination the most, however, was the small, delicate hand that rose from the sod. Where the mud had been washed away a pale, almost translucent skin had been revealed. The bystanders had already agreed it was the hand of a woman or a young child, but what drew them most was the sight of the index finger, uncurled from the fist and pointing eerily, accusingly towards the heavens.

As Sergeant Graves and Inspector Hicks made their way carefully through the mud, Graves noticed that Jack Watkins was already on the scene, notebook in hand. The ever-present cigar encircled his head with a wreath of smoke, a tangle of red hair plastering his forehead beneath a hat that seemed at least a size too small. Graves rolled his eyes in exasperation. No doubt Watkins had already interviewed certain of the crowd. He could practically see that evening's Standard headline written all over Watkins' smug features.

"Ah, gentlemen," Watkins began at their approach, raising his voice against the sound of the wheeling gulls above. "How goes the investigation?"

Before Graves could respond, Hicks broke in. “Not well. We botched an ambush last night and it cost us dear.”

It takes a lot to stop Ignatius Hicks in full flow, but Graves managed it with a sharp jab to the ribs with his elbow. “I think that’ll do, Inspector Hicks,” he cautioned.

Watkins’ interest was piqued. With an arching of an eyebrow, he leered closer to Hicks, pencil at the ready. “Oh? How so?”

Ever grateful for an attentive ear, Hicks ploughed on, seemingly oblivious to Graves’ warning glances. “We lost one of our most promising constables to a madman’s blade, that’s how so. What was his name, Graves?”

Graves answered quietly, the previous night’s events still fresh. “Constable Evan.”

“Evans, yes, that’s it.” Pulling himself up to his full height, Inspector Hicks summoned all the gravitas at his disposal to deliver his verdict on the whole sorry affair. “He was a great loss to the force,” he announced with something approaching feeling.

Watkins could scent blood. “And the ambush,” he needled, licking his pencil in a curiously rodent-like movement, “How exactly did it go wrong?”

Hicks could barely disguise his delight at being asked his opinion. “It was a botch from start to finish,” he declaimed, now raising his voice for the whole crowd to hear. “Now, if I had been in command - ”

Graves had heard enough. Stepping between the two men, he led Watkins away towards the discovery in the mud. “Might we turn to more urgent matters, Watkins? I hope you have left all as it was found?”

“Of course, Sergeant Graves. I wouldn’t dream of disturbing the evidence.”

Pushing aside several of the onlookers, Graves squatted with Watkins at his side, heedless of his coat tails trailing in the mud. “So, what do we have?”

Watkins, stung by Graves’ earlier reluctance to talk, responded with a surly nod to the pile of limbs and cloth. “Take a look for yourself, Sergeant Graves.”

As Graves peered closer, Inspector Hicks came sliding up behind them. The crowd sniggered as his boots struggled for purchase against the mud. They would consider their morning complete if they were lucky enough to see a Scotland Yarder fall flat on his backside. Hicks denied them the pleasure, however, by throwing his arms wide to steady himself.

"It is just as I said," he began. "I knew the body would turn up sooner rather than later."

Ignoring him, Graves turned his face to the newspaper man at his side, blinking against the early morning sun which now glinted off the surface of the Thames. "Who found her?"

Watkins consulted his notebook. "A young boy. Timothy Wilkes. Lives in the slums close by."

Inspector Hicks had put a hand on Graves' shoulder to steady himself. "Any distinguishing marks?" he boomed, craning for a better view.

Watkins turned to him, rubbing his chin thoughtfully. "I should have thought the fact that she was without a head would be distinguishing enough."

Those of the crowd who stood the nearest to the scene broke into laughter at this. Even Graves, though he was well aware of the gravity of the situation, couldn't help but smirk. Keen to re-establish the authority that he could feel ebbing away as quick as the Thames tide, Hicks cleared his throat pretentiously.

"I would urge you, Mr Watkins," he began, thrusting his smoking pipe in Watkins' direction, "To exercise caution in your summarising. We wouldn't want to jump to any conclusions now, would we?"

This last was said, noticed Graves, without a trace of irony. Choosing not to engage the blustering inspector still further, however, Graves let the comment pass. He stooped again and removed a glove to take a handful of mud. Rubbing it between his fingers, he could plainly see it was of a dark, red colour. The same colour as he had seen in Doctor Crane's laboratory just the day before, packed hard into the unfortunate woman's mouth.

"It's from the brewery over the way there," offered Jack Watkins, pointing to a large brick building on the south bank. It stood, solid and squat against the horizon, steam belching from one of three tall chimneys that pierced the sky like needles. "They discharge their waste directly into the Thames."

Graves raised an eyebrow.

"I've been conducting some enquiries of my own," continued Watkins. He clasped his lapels with mock authority. "Perhaps I'll make an inspector yet."

Sergeant Graves stood to get a better view of the building. "I was of the impression that Inspector Bowman had given you licence to observe our investigations Mr Watkins, not to start one of your own."

Following Watkins' gaze, he could discern a reddish-brown slick in the water, emanating from the brewery. Was it reasonable to assume the head had once been buried here with the body? Had it somehow made its way downstream?

Hicks was resentful of Watkins' deductions. "Of course, there is still the matter of her identity," he began, "You are no nearer to - "

"It's a Miss Mary Henderson," Graves interjected. "A young lady from St John's Wood." Hicks stood, puffing his cheeks in exasperation. Graves turned to face him. "I believe Inspector Bowman is to inform the family in person this morning."

St John's Wood was an area of London as far removed from the slums in which Bowman had spent the previous evening as was possible to imagine. Home to the prosperous, professional classes, it was a leafy, spacious suburb of wide streets, private gardens and squares. Immaculate townhouses stood proudly in their own, well-tended grounds.

As the hansom cab rattled away, Inspector George Bowman was left standing before a house of grand proportions. Set back from the road by a neat front garden, Fifty-Five, Acacia Road stood elegant and tall, its smooth facade punctuated by high sash windows. The house was painted a cheery yellow, which felt most at odds with the grim news the inspector had to deliver. Bowman pulled a pocket watch from his waistcoat as he crossed the road. It was already near midday. He could only hope somebody would be in beyond the domestic servants.

Climbing the stone steps to the front door, Bowman removed his hat, smoothing his moustache and hair in his reflection in a large, brass plaque fixed to the wall beneath the bell-push. "Doctor Joshua Henderson, MRCS", it proclaimed, portentously. Clearing his throat in the hope it would clear his nerves, Bowman pressed the button long and hard. He heard the bell ring throughout the house. As he waited for an answer, he turned to view the street below.

A wide boulevard lined with bare elm trees, Acacia Road was a busy enough thoroughfare. Traps and carriages rattled past with regularity and well dressed ladies and gentlemen bustled this way and that on important business. A lone street seller stood across the way; a young, pleasant-faced lady with a tray of muffins. She rewarded her customers, Bowman noticed, with a pretty smile and a twinkle in her eye. Feeling a sudden pang of hunger, the inspector resolved to try her wares once his interview was over.

The door behind him swung open and Bowman turned to face an elderly footman. He was stooped and frail and looked out on the world through a pair of pale, rheumy eyes. His thin face rested on a starched collar, his pale skin contrasting sharply with the black coat of his uniform. Not a hair was out of place. The man stared down at Bowman with the air of one tolerating a mild nuisance.

"Yes?" he enquired, simply. His voice was high and had a weary tone.

Bowman cleared his throat again. "I wish to speak with Doctor Henderson."

There was a pause as the footman's gaze fell to Bowman's feet. The inspector knew he was being sized up and appraised. An Englishman's home is his castle indeed, thought Bowman, and this man is a worthy sentry.

"Could you tell me if he is at home?"

The footman fixed Bowman with a watery gaze. "I could. And who might you be?"

Bowman resisted the urge to clear his throat again and reached into his pocket. Feeling like a naughty schoolchild in his headmaster's study, he pulled some identification documents from his wallet, pressing them flat into the footman's skeletal hands.

"My name is Bowman. Detective Inspector George Bowman." He swallowed hard. "From Scotland Yard."

The footman cast his eyes across the paper in his hand, seemingly scrutinising every letter. Finally he looked up, the smile that appeared on his face revealing a row of haphazard teeth.

"Forgive me, inspector, my name is Pollard." Bowman returned the paper to his wallet as the footman continued. "Doctor Henderson is a busy man. He is a surgeon of some note and it is a common belief among the poor that he will turn his hand to any pox or blight that is presented to him."

Bowman gave a polite laugh.

"I am his first line of defence, if you will," said Pollard, leaning in.

Bowman peered beyond the footman into the hall for further signs of life. "I am not here to seek medical assistance." He looked back at the old man before him. "After all, it would not do to trouble a doctor with matters of health."

At that, Pollard's smile faded as quickly as it had appeared. "If you were not an officer of the law, inspector, I would turn you away for that remark."

The inside of Fifty Five, Acacia Road was no less grand than the outside. Bowman had an eye for quality and saw it everywhere he looked. From the Persian rug on the parquet floor to the water colours on the walls, it was obvious that Dr Henderson was doing very well indeed. The subjects of the paintings had a nautical bent, from ships at sea to depictions of foreign lands. Artefacts were arranged in cabinets; stuffed birds and animals, maps and trinkets. Inspector Bowman recognised scientific instruments such as one might find on a ship; astrolabes and compasses, sextants and telescopes. As he was shown into the drawing room by a rather terse Pollard, his eye was drawn first to the ornate candelabra that dominated the room, then to the large picture of a formidable nautical vessel on the wall above the fireplace. Warming himself by the fire, he took the time to examine it further. It seemed an impressive enough ship with four sturdy masts festooned with sails, billowed by the wind. There were painted figures working the ropes and, by their scale, Bowman estimated the ship was perhaps a hundred feet long. Dramatically, the artist had pictured the ship in a storm. An angry, louring sky pressed down on the swell of the sea, the ship broaching waves twenty feet high. Bowman heard footsteps at the door, and turned to face a rather austere man with a curiously ageless face. His greying temples and lines about the face spoke of a man in his middle sixties, but his clear, blue eyes danced with a keen agility redolent of one much younger.

"Ah, the Nimrod. A fine ship if ever there was one." Henderson's voice was low and sonorous. A kindly voice much used to offering comfort, Bowman thought. He was in his shirtsleeves and waistcoat, a silver armband at each elbow.

"A frigate?" Bowman offered.

"Schooner."

Henderson allowed himself a smile at Bowman's blank look. Entering the room, he gestured that the inspector should join him in one of the comfortable, wing-backed chairs at either side of the fire.

"You've never been to sea, inspector?"

"Never." As Bowman sat, he noticed Henderson's hands and nails were meticulously clean.

"Spent my finest years there as a young doctor. Ship's surgeon on the Nimrod."

Bowman could not hide his surprise. That such a slight figure might serve in such an environment as depicted in the picture seemed hardly credible.

"Three long years that made a man of me. And a competent surgeon, too."

Bowman felt suddenly incongruous in such refined surroundings. A clock ticked gently on the mantel. The room was bathed in light from the midday sun, admitted by the large bay window that overlooked the road. The high ceiling afforded the room a great sense of openness, despite the rich and plentiful furnishings. A chaise longue stood beneath the window, a large day bed was positioned beneath another nautical painting, this time of a much older vessel, and a writing table and chair stood on another rich Persian rug to the other side.

"My man Pollard said you were quite the persistent sort at the door."

Bowman's attention was drawn back to the figure in the chair opposite. The doctor presented himself as a very contained sort of man. Perhaps that's what people expected of their doctor.

"I doubt you hot footed it from the Yard to gossip of ships and seafaring."

Bowman felt the atmosphere in the room thicken. The clock seemed to tick ever louder as he loosened his collar in preparation for delivering his news. Why on Earth hadn't he sent Sergeant Graves? Because, after the morning the young sergeant had had, it simply wouldn't have been fair. To ask a man to deliver two pieces of bad news in one day would be beyond the pale. Besides, Graves was the sort who revived in fresh air. A morning at Chelsea Embankment would have done him good.

"I'm afraid I have some bad news." Bowman suddenly felt very hot.

Doctor Henderson leaned in closer, his fingers tightening slightly on his knees. "Good Lord, really?"

Bowman could feel his heart pounding against his chest now and his mouth was dry. "I should tell you plainly sir, that your daughter, Mary, is dead."

Henderson's eyes widened at the news, and his jaw dropped. Used to observing people under such conditions, Bowman felt there was something more about the doctor's expression that eluded him. What was it? Surprise at the news, or surprise that she had been found?

"She was found yesterday in the Thames," he continued, "In circumstances that indicate foul play."

Doctor Henderson rose in silence and placed a hand on the mantel to steady himself. "But this is terrible."

"I'm sorry."

The doctor took a breath that seemed to calm his nerves. "So am I, Inspector Bowman, most sorry indeed. I fear you have been the subject of a misguided prank."

Bowman's brows knitted together in confusion. Rather dramatically, Doctor Henderson turned from the fireplace to face him.

"I do not have a daughter."

XIII

Progress Thwarted

A fire had been made from wooden pallets just a few feet from the entrance to the den. Hardacre recognised a few of the men huddled round it as he passed. He grunted and nodded at the one or two who raised their eyes to greet him. As he picked his way to the entrance, he saw the door lying smashed on the floor. Hardacre knew that, given just a few minutes more, it might very well have made it onto the fire behind him. Standing framed in the doorway, Hardacre noticed a slick of blood in the filth beneath his feet. Looking about the dingy room, his eyes slowly acclimatised to the gloom.

"Kane?" he rasped, kneeling for a lantern from the floor. Striking a match to light it, he held it high to illuminate the room. The atmosphere was such that the light seemed to barely penetrate more than a couple of feet. Hardacre moved to the centre of the room and located the loose flagstone with the toe of his boot. He stamped on it hard, calling louder now.

"Kane! You there?"

Cursing, Hardacre knelt to lift the stone, placing the lantern carefully amidst the rubbish on the floor. With an effort, he slid the stone across the floor, revealing the entrance to the cellar beneath. With a look about him to see that no one had followed, Hardacre lowered himself carefully through the hole into the gloom beneath.

Feeling the ground beneath his feet, Hardacre took a moment to steady himself before reaching up to retrieve his lantern. Last night had been disastrous, he mused, but he might yet win the day. If he could get away with his booty, or at least a good part of it, he could set up just a few streets away and never be found. He had found it easy enough to melt away into London's backstreets before, and he could do it again if the need arose. Muttering to himself as he ran his options through his head, he turned to survey the cellar, to be met by a wholly unexpected sight.

"So, the spider returns to his web. Welcome home, Jeb Hardacre."

Lifting the lantern higher, Hardacre studied the face that appeared before him.

"There was just too much to leave behind wasn't there?" Inspector Treacher looked cleaner than when Hardacre had last seen him. His face was clean-shaven and his hair had been cut, but he was still recognisable as the man who had lived in Hardacre's den for the last several weeks. Most disconcertingly, Hardacre noticed the man had a revolver levelled at his chest.

"You," he grunted.

Treacher gave a nod of greeting. "Inspector Treacher, Bow Street."

"Filth, eh?" Hardacre could barely disguise his contempt. "Well, you looked the sort. I was told this place was clear."

Even in the low light afforded by the lamp, Hardacre could tell Treacher was smiling.

"The small boy with the red hair?" he chuckled, "I don't know what you promised him, Hardacre, but it wasn't enough."

So, young Thomas Crowley was a snitch. He'd pay, thought Hardacre. No matter if they hanged him, he had ways of punishing those who let him down. Isambard Fogg had found that to his cost, and so one day would Thomas Crowley.

"And what'll you do with me now, filth?"

Inspector Edmund Treacher reached forward to take the lantern from Hardacre's great hands. Lifting it high, he peered into the gang master's fearsome face.

"Well now," he said. "That's rather up to you, isn't it?"

The journey back to Scotland Yard found Bowman in a disconsolate mood. As the wide boulevards of St John's Wood gave way to the meandering alleyways of Mayfair and Victoria, Bowman stared from the cab at the blur of the outside world. He let his mind wander over the last few minutes of his interview with Doctor Henderson.

"Are you certain?" the inspector had asked ridiculously, regretting it almost as soon as the words had left his mouth.

"That I don't have a daughter?" Henderson had replied, his steel blue eyes barely concealing his amusement at the question. "As certain as any man can be."

Bowman had squirmed awkwardly in his seat.

"But, Mrs Bessom - " he had begun.

"A drunkard, Inspector Bowman," Henderson had concluded by way of explanation. "And nothing more." He had sighed in an expression of weary resignation. "Dismissal was my only option. I should imagine that this is some ill-advised attempt at revenge."

In the pregnant pause that had followed, Bowman felt Henderson's eyes boring into his head. The ticking of the infernal clock on the mantel grew ever louder. Eventually, Bowman had found his voice again.

"I am very sorry," he had offered.

Doctor Henderson, he could tell now, had enjoyed Bowman's discomfort as he called Pollard to show him to the front door.

"Not at all, inspector. I can only apologise that I can't be of further assistance. Now, if you would excuse me, I have the good fortune to be a very busy man."

Pollard had seen him out with a look even haughtier than that which he had used to welcome him. Now, as his cab passed through Constitution Hill, Bowman could only hope that Doctor Henderson was not the sort to speak directly to the press or, as no doubt a man with connections in high places, the sort to file an official complaint with Scotland Yard. Bowman's mind ran through the morning's events again and again. He had slipped up badly, that much was clear, but there was something that troubled him more. As he had been shown from Doctor Henderson's residence, he was sure he had heard something from an upstairs room. Something that had sounded for all the world to Bowman like a woman crying. At the edge of the park, Bowman ordered the driver to bring the cab to a halt. He alighted to continue his journey on foot, making good use of the fresh January air to clear his thoughts.

Sergeant Williams had had no compunction about throwing Hardacre in the darkest, dampest cell beneath Bow Street police station. With nothing but a bench and a bucket for company, Hardacre had stood motionless as Williams sat watching from a stool beyond the bars. A single lamp on the table beside him was the only light source in the gloom. Williams was writing in a notebook with a small pencil attached with string. Keeping his eyes cast down, he could almost sense Hardacre's shoulders rising and falling slowly beneath his great coat in his cell. As Williams wrote, a low growl began deep in Hardacre's throat and then, in full cry, he turned and threw himself at the cell door. Gripping the bars like a caged bear, he threw his whole weight against them and roared in frustration. Great beads of spit flew from his mouth.

"What's the charge, filth?" he snarled, shaking the door on its hinges for good measure. "You can't hold me without a charge. That much I know."

Williams declined to look up from his work and replied with an affected and well-practised nonchalance. "I'm compiling a list that will be presented to you in good time." He continued scratching at his notepad.

"A list?" With a final rattle of the bars, Hardacre turned back into his cell, kicking the empty slops bucket in his rage.

With a sigh, Williams put down his pencil and stood to stretch his legs. "In the three weeks Inspector Treacher was a part of your company Hardacre, he heard gossip enough to compile a list of charges as long as the Devil's arm."

Hardacre still had his back to him. "You'd rely on the words of villains and gypsies?" he rasped, "You can't hang a man on gossip alone, filth." With that, he spat on the filthy straw at his feet.

"Isambard Fogg will be enough." Williams leaned against the wall near Hardacre's cell. He was wise enough to keep out of reach, but positioned himself close enough to gauge the gang master's reactions. "He died in that very cell across the way. If you care to look, you may still see his blood on the straw."

Hardacre turned with a sneer of disdain. "Fogg?" He gave a hollow laugh. "Vermin! You might as well charge me for stepping on a rat in the alley."

"Then there's the matter of a woman's head found yesterday in the Thames," continued Williams in measured tones. "Inspector Bowman suspects one of your acquaintance and no doubt believes, as I do, that you had a hand in it, too." With a studied indifference, Williams sauntered back to his stool, picked up his pencil and continued his work. "All in all, I think you'll find we've got enough to be going on with."

Hardacre launched himself at the door again, his great paw swiping ineffectually for the sergeant on his stool. With a final, angry push at the bars, he turned once more and sat on the up-turned bucket in his cell. Minutes passed in silence until, once he was sure Williams' attention was on his work, Hardacre slowly fingered a jewel set into a ring on his finger. With a barely discernible flick, the jewel was removed to reveal a tiny white pill beneath. With a strange smile playing over his lips, Hardacre tipped the pill into his other hand. Slowly, silently and unobtrusively, he raised it to his mouth.

XIV

A Chink In His Armour

The brief walk having done nothing to clear his mind after all, Inspector Bowman was in no better mood as he passed under the arch at the entrance to Scotland Yard and climbed the steps to the door. As usual, the lobby was a hive of activity. Police sergeants and constables struggled to contain their charges or walked briskly this way and that to deliver evidence and paperwork to one of a seemingly endless number of offices. Bowman nodded in acknowledgment as he caught the eye of one or two other inspectors he knew, and made his way to the front desk. Women and men of uncertain professions and abodes sat on benches that lined the walls. In one corner, Bowman could see a drunkard rolling about the tiled floor, moaning in his delirium. As his footsteps echoed about the cavernous space, his eye caught that of a fresh-faced young lady dressed in black. She was taller than average, slim-waisted and elegantly poised. Her head was inclined slightly in an expression of friendly interest, and Bowman couldn't help but return a smile.

"Good afternoon, Inspector Bowman."

The voice belonged to Matthews, the young duty sergeant who stood behind his desk like a sentry at his post. His hair was parted neatly in the middle and plastered down with pomade upon his head. He was clean-shaven and Bowman noticed the buttons on his uniform seemed to shine just that little bit brighter than any others in the room.

"Matthews, were you on duty here this morning?" Bowman leaned his elbow on Matthews' desk.

"Yes sir, since five o'clock, sir. And a brisk morning it's been, too." Matthews nodded down to his logbook that Bowman could see included many fresh entries for the day.

"Do you remember sending a Mrs Patricia Bessom to my office?"

Tracing down a column of entries with his finger, Matthews located the name the inspector had given him. "Ah yes, Mrs Bessom. Large lady. I do indeed remember sir, at five and twenty past nine to be precise. It's all down here."

Bowman strained to read the entry upside down. "Including her address?"

Matthews swallowed a little uncomfortably. "She declined to leave it with me, sir. To be honest she seemed a little nervous, and I didn't like to press her for it."

Bowman let his elbow drop. "Well, you should have." The duty sergeant held his gaze. "In future, Matthews, I want full particulars to be taken before anyone has access to my office."

"That's not standard procedure, sir," blustered Matthews.

"Hang procedure!" The note in Bowman's voice was enough to silence the room, and Matthews was suddenly aware that all eyes were upon them. Even the drunk in the corner was now giving Bowman his full attention. The detective inspector swallowed hard. The thought occurred to him that there were many in the room who may have heard of his incarceration at Colney Hatch. How far along the ranks had the rumour spread? Did Matthews know? Accusatory eyes glared across the room. There was insinuation in every look. Bowman felt his hand begin to quiver involuntarily. He held it in the fist of his other hand, squeezing it hard. The young sergeant shuffled nervously from foot to foot behind his desk.

"I'm sorry, Matthews," Bowman offered. "I didn't mean to embarrass you."

"It's not I who should be embarrassed by such behaviour, sir." Matthews had regained his composure quickly and turned his attention back to his log book, a gesture that was intended to put an end to the affair.

Looking around him, Inspector Bowman again caught sight of the young lady in black, now sitting on a bench beneath a large, barred window which gave out onto the busy street beyond. Almost instinctively, he removed his hat to smooth down his hair.

"Matthews?"

"Yes, sir?" Matthews declined to raise his nose from the book.

"Who is the young lady beneath the window? With the umbrella?"

Reluctantly, Matthews followed Bowman's gaze across the room. The young lady, now very much aware that she was the focus of attention, looked demurely away. The officious duty sergeant made a point of consulting the book on his desk before replying.

"A Miss Elizabeth Morley sir," he replied. "She's the daughter of the garrotting on the South Bank yesterday. Come to claim some belongings from Sergeant Graves." At last, he raised his eyes to Bowman. "I neglected to get her address."

Bowman offered him a conciliatory look. "No matter, Matthews. Thank you."

Matthews returned to his business with an almost indiscernible smile as Bowman crossed the room. As he neared the woman on the bench, she raised her eyes to meet his and he slowed his step. The smile that played across her delicate features seemed to light the room, or at least the corner in which she sat. She raised her eyebrows expectantly as the inspector approached. Bowman resisted the urge to clear his throat.

"Miss Morley? May I be of assistance?"

Elizabeth Morley stood and smoothed her dress about her.

"Sergeant Graves?" she enquired.

"I am Detective Inspector Bowman. I'm afraid my colleague is busy on other duties."

Elizabeth flashed another smile, and Bowman could swear she looked him up and down.

"Then, Detective Inspector Bowman, you will have to do."

Inspector Treacher examined the paper before him. Torn from Williams' notepad, it included a very thorough list of charges that might be brought against the man in cell number nine.

"Very good, Sergeant Williams."

Williams drew deep on his pipe, the smoke hanging lazily in the cold as he acknowledged the inspector's praise.

Treacher looked up. "The magistrate will be pleased at this."

His Welsh accent becoming more pronounced in his excitement, the sergeant placed a heavy hand on Treacher's shoulder. "There's enough work here to keep him busy until the next New Year." A broad smile spread across his wide, pock-marked face.

"There is that," Treacher beamed in satisfaction.

"And more besides if we can find the evidence."

Treacher nodded, his eyes twinkling knowingly. "There's always evidence, sergeant. It's just a question of looking - "

Treacher broke off as the sound of a heavy thump came from Hardacre's cell. As he spun round on his heels, Treacher stuffed the paper into his pocket. A stifled cry reached his ears and he shared a startled look with Sergeant Williams. Motioning him to unlock the door, Treacher manhandled the sergeant closer to the cell, following directly behind him, lantern in hand. Williams fumbled for the keys on his belt and quickly unlocked the door.

"Careful now," Treacher cautioned, holding the lantern higher to help illuminate the scene. "Easy does it, Williams."

The sergeant was inside now, and approached Hardacre's prone body with care. He had seemingly fallen where had sat, brooding on his upturned bucket. He was lying, sprawled on the floor at Williams' feet with not a sound coming from him.

"Hardacre?" he entreated. "We've got your number, Hardacre. If you're trying something - "

Williams knelt slowly to shake the man gently by the shoulders. When there came no response, he shook harder, eventually rocking him with such force that Hardacre rolled over onto his back. His heavy arms came to rest ungainly by his side.

"Is he - " Treacher hardly had time to finish before Williams had placed his head on Hardacre's chest, listening for any signs of life. His exasperation rising, he held one lifeless hand by the wrist to feel for a pulse then placed an ear at the prone man's mouth. Nothing. Letting Hardacre's hand fall lifeless to the floor, Williams stood and rubbed his hand across his face. He turned to Treacher who stood motionless by the door, a look of bemusement across his face.

"This is turning into one of those weeks," he said.

The properties room at Scotland Yard was tucked away at the back of the building. Inspector Bowman led Elizabeth Morley through the maze of corridors, slowing his pace to let her keep up. After some small talk concerning the weather, an easy silence fell between them as they walked. Bowman fumbled for the key in his pocket and swung the door open for Elizabeth. She gave a gasp at the sight that greeted her, and involuntarily put her hand to her throat in what Bowman considered a most beguiling gesture. The room was filled, from floor to ceiling, with sturdy wooden shelves arranged so as to make cramped walkways up and down its length. Each shelf groaned with wooden boxes, trays and cartons and these in turn were full to their brims with documents and personal effects. As Bowman led her through this warren of wood, Elizabeth noticed that each shelf was tagged alphabetically. Furthermore, every box or tray was marked with smaller labels giving tantalising details as to what might lay within. As she passed, she craned her neck to read a few; 'Anderson, W, Theft in Knightsbridge', 'Chelsea Nov 14th, Goods Recovered', 'Chesterton, B, Personal Effects'. Elizabeth caught her breath again.

"But this is awful!" she exclaimed.

Inspector Bowman was fetching a ladder from a corner. "I beg your pardon, miss?"

"Do each of these boxes represent a death? A murder like my father's?" Elizabeth looked around her, wide eyed.

"This is where we store lost property," Bowman informed her as he set his ladder at a particular shelf. "Recovered goods from stolen hauls and, yes, clothing and properties of the unfortunate deceased."

Quite unexpectedly, Elizabeth gave a little laugh. "The unfortunate deceased?" She lifted her hand to her throat again, but this time in a gesture of mock distress. "How grim."

Bowman had seen such odd behaviour before. He had often noticed how, under circumstances such as this, the mind sought refuge in frivolity. Once, he had delivered the news of a young boy's accidental death to his mother. Quite unexpectedly, she had not broken down into tears as Bowman would have expected, but rocked back on her chair and laughed. Her reaction had seemed an indication of guilt to the young Inspector Bowman. He soon realised that, rather than confront harsh reality, the poor woman's mind had instead decided to treat the whole thing as a joke; a jape dreamed up by her husband as a tease. Even at the funeral she wore a knowing grin, as if she were in on the charade and sure that her son would present himself at any moment. He would have to tread carefully with Miss Elizabeth Morley.

"Miss Morley," he began quietly, "Have you seen your father?"

Elizabeth looked him squarely in the eye, a look of puzzlement on her face. "Of course. I identified the body at the scene."

Bowman paused. "Then you will know that he did not die a peaceful death."

Elizabeth cocked her head. "But he is at rest now." Heeding Bowman's expression, she laid a hand upon his arm. "You are concerned for me, I can tell, inspector. You no doubt find my manner somewhat frivolous."

Bowman could feel his temperature rising beneath his collar. "I know that grief can manifest itself - "

"Grief?" Elizabeth interjected. "Piffle! Why grieve for a man in Paradise?" She withdrew her hand now and wagged her finger at Bowman in admonishment. "No. If I grieve at all I do so for myself." She broke Bowman's gaze and looked away, suddenly tearful. "For having lost so wonderful a father."

"I am sorry," Bowman began as Elizabeth reached into her sleeve for a plain, cotton handkerchief. "Please forgive my impertinence."

Elizabeth dismissed the remark with a wave of her hand. "Death is all around us, inspector," she sniffed through her handkerchief. "You, above all others, should know that." Bowman's heart quickened. Was she alluding to Anna? Elizabeth Morley was clearly a woman of the world and most certainly a keen follower of the news. Bowman's story had been expounded upon in great detail by the newspapers at the time. If she had read it, Bowman was certain she would remember it. Having calmed herself, Elizabeth let a smile play over her lips.

"Father lived life to the full, and died a quick death. There is little to grieve in that."

Nodding in understanding, Bowman climbed the rungs of the ladder to the very topmost shelf above him. There, he located a box marked 'Morley, J, Southwark' and pulled it free from its place. Stepping carefully off the ladder with his load, Bowman led his companion to a rickety trestle table, seemingly the only clear space in the room. Motes of dust danced in the watery light afforded by the two tall windows above the table as the inspector began to empty the wooden box of its contents.

"We managed to recover his cane and purse, some papers and clothing - and this."

Bowman handed Elizabeth a rather plain looking, gold plated locket, no bigger than the size of his thumbnail. It was threaded on a thin, gold chain and had been found on the ground near Morley's body. Perhaps his assailant had neglected to notice it as it fell from Morley's throat in the attack, or had thought it too easily identified to warrant thieving for sale later. Elizabeth let it rest in the palm of her slender hand.

"My mother gave him this before she died. It contains a likeness of her. See?" With a deft movement of her fingers, she had flicked the locket open. The case opened on a small, delicate hinge to reveal a tiny portrait of a woman. Though clearly older than Elizabeth, Bowman could plainly discern a familial resemblance. There was something in the way the subject held her head, the same inquisitive eyes and subtle cleft in the chin.

"Quite beautiful." Bowman was alarmed to hear the words escape from his lips, seemingly unbidden.

"Yes, she was," Elizabeth replied quietly. Had she glanced up in that moment, she would have been puzzled to see that Inspector Bowman wasn't looking at the locket at all. "I like to think I have inherited all her best qualities."

Bowman felt helpless, entirely unable to tear his eyes away from Elizabeth's face. There was something in the way the light fell upon her that struck him as familiar. "From the likeness, I should say that you have."

Again, Elizabeth wiped away a tear and Bowman suddenly felt a wave of compassion engulf him. "Miss Morley," he offered, carefully, "it may be a comfort to know that the villain who killed your father was himself murdered by an accomplice."

Elizabeth at last lifted her gaze, snapping the locket shut in her hand. "I can see no comfort in the death of one criminal at the hands of another, Inspector Bowman. Only sadness."

There was a pause. Bowman felt the full glare of her eyes as she studied the inspector's face in detail. He could feel himself, for the second time that day, being sized up. It was not a comfortable feeling.

"You are not a happy man, are you, inspector?" said Elizabeth at last.

"Miss Morley, I - "

Elizabeth shook her head as if to clear a thought. "I'm sorry. I did not mean to be so bold."

In the silence that followed, Bowman picked up the now empty box and tore the label from its face. He was about to return it to a pile of similarly empty cartons in the corner when he was stopped by Elizabeth's hand, again on his arm. This time he could feel the pressure of her grip through his coat. Turning to face her, he saw her eyes were now alive with curiosity. Whether it was a curiosity about him, he had yet to discern.

"Tell me, inspector," Elizabeth began, breathlessly, "What do you know of the Spiritualist movement?"

The remark caught Bowman off guard. "Well, I have heard of it, of course, but not enough to reach a judgement." He couldn't help but laugh at her strange outburst. "Miss Morley, if you'll forgive me. You are rather - " he searched for the word quite deliberately. "Unpredictable."

"I know," she said.

As they turned back towards the door, Elizabeth now carrying her father's cane and having secreted his other effects in her bag, Bowman found himself charmed by the creature beside him. She seemed at once both demure and impetuous.

"You see," Elizabeth continued as they reached the door, "I believe fervently in the Supernatural. I am sure with all my heart that the spirit world exists as surely as does our own. Given this, I cannot be sad at the death of my father. Rather, I rejoice that he is reunited with my mother, and that they both await me in the spirit realm."

"I see," replied Bowman, seeing her out first and locking the door behind them. As they walked back through the twisting corridors to the reception hall, it felt for all the world as if they were enjoying a Sunday stroll in the park.

"I don't believe you do, inspector," his companion teased. "Not fully." As they reached the lobby, Bowman was pleased to feel Elizabeth withdrawing her arm from his. As pleasant as the experience had been, he thought it inappropriate to be seen in public, arm in arm with a strange young lady still in mourning for the loss of her father. There was another feeling, too. One with which Bowman was all too familiar. Guilt. Even now he could feel Sergeant Matthews squinting at him from behind the duty desk.

Elizabeth Morley was reaching into her bag again. "If you are interested, I am to attend a meeting this evening. At the Empire Rooms at Covent Garden." From her purse, she handed Bowman a card, the details of the venue printed upon it in a flowery font. "I should be delighted to see you there at eight o'clock."

The inspector turned the card over in his hands, his habitual deep frown returning. "A Spiritualist meeting?" Bowman clearly wasn't sure.

"I believe it will do you good." For one moment, Bowman thought she was going to reach up to kiss him on the cheek. As it was, Elizabeth simply smiled. "Good day, Inspector Bowman."

With that, Elizabeth Morley stepped from the ordered chaos of Scotland Yard into the hubbub of the world beyond, leaving Bowman alone with his thoughts.

XV

Look Down

Just an hour later, Bowman was standing at the window in his office, gazing absently out across the canopy of trees towards the Thames. He usually enjoyed his view of the river and considered it, with its ebb and tide, one of the few predictable things in London. It held its course whatever the weather, rising and falling with every tide as if it were the city's heartbeat. Indeed, it often seemed to Bowman the very lifeblood of London, its banks the artery that conveyed the oxygen to the disparate parts of the metropolis. Trade thrived upon it, transport relied upon it. It was bountiful and generous. But not today.

Today, it was a secretive thing. Today it taunted those who would see below its surface. Only yesterday morning it had given up a secret, the severed head found just below the bridge outside Bowman's very window. Now, it was inscrutable again. Swollen with the dirty melt water from upstream, the Thames swirled and seethed its way past Scotland Yard, dangerous and unknowable.

A knock at the door drew Bowman's focus back to his room. "Enter," he barked.

Sergeant Anthony Graves was his chipper self once more. His morning by the river had brought colour to his already rosy cheeks. Glad to be of practical use once again, his earlier black mood had lifted.

"What news from the Embankment?" Bowman asked, walking to the bureau for a glass of brandy.

Graves pulled a notebook from his coat pocket and placed his hat upon Bowman's desk. "A headless body discovered this morning," he said, declining the offer of a brandy from his superior. "That of a young woman, in her early twenties."

Bowman walked back to his desk as Graves read on, the excitement in his voice seeming almost inappropriate.

"Loosely wrapped in torn sack and buried in the silt of the river bank - the same colour as the earth in our young lady's mouth." Snapping the notebook shut, Graves looked up with an expression of triumph. "Conjecture as to her stature and physical build has led Doctor Crane to conclude that both head and body belong to one and the same woman," he said pointedly.

Bowman nodded. This was progress at last.

His message delivered, Sergeant Graves was relaxing in the large leather chair Inspector Bowman reserved for guests. "How did Doctor Henderson takc the news of his daughter's murder?" he asked.

Bowman sat in his own seat across the desk from Graves, swilling the brandy in his glass as he recalled the morning's events. "It was a little... uncomfortable," he said, the very model of understatement.

"I'm sure it was," said Graves sympathetically.

"Doctor Henderson doesn't have a daughter."

Graves swung his feet from Bowman's desk and sat forward in his seat. "But Mrs Bessom - "

"Henderson claims she's a drunk." Bowman placed his glass on the table, guiltily.

"Do you believe him?" Graves asked.

Bowman puffed out his cheeks in exasperation. "I have no choice. Mrs Bessom left no address."

Graves made steeples of his fingers as he rested his elbows on Bowman's desk, lost in thought. "Then we have yet to ascertain the woman's identity."

Inspector Bowman could not but agree. "On that particular point, we're no better off now than when we first pulled her head from the ice."

The two men sat, helpless in the silence. Reaching for his glass again, Bowman narrowed his eyes. "Why do we deal in this ghastly business?" he asked, draining his brandy.

Graves shrugged. "Someone has to catch the rats, sir."

Bowman was staring into his now empty glass, as if inspiration might be found there.

"Nothing else has come from your piece in The Standard?" Graves asked, determined to rouse the inspector from his torpor.

"Nothing." Bowman rose from his chair and made for the window. Clasping his hands behind his back he continued. "I should like you to send to Doctor Crane requesting a full, written post-mortem of the body to the smallest detail." Casting his eyes to the ground outside his office window, he watched as an elderly woman fed the pigeons. "I'd also like you to liaise with Inspector Treacher from 'H' division to see exactly what he has on Hardacre and his gang."

Graves was surprised at this. "You're taking Isambard Fogg at his word? You think Hardacre or one of his gang might be responsible for her death?"

"There's no harm in listening to a dying man, Graves. After all, he has nothing to gain and nothing to lose."

London's sewers were in their infancy. The grand scheme to build embankments along vast stretches of the Thames had been completed, reclaiming many acres of swamp from its watery grasp. Beneath these embankments ran the wonder of the age, great subterranean tunnels that carried the city's effluent east and to the Thames Estuary. Hundreds of miles of tunnels had been constructed by the middle of the century. There was no feat of civil engineering anywhere else in the world to touch it. Many tons of Cornish granite had been quarried and conveyed on barges up the English Channel. Great cranes had been built to place them in situ. The pioneers and engineers who created this sprawling network of sewers would, upon its completion, be honoured for their pains, their names known throughout the land. They could never have known that, one day, the results of their endeavours would also provide the perfect hiding place for one of London's most nefarious villains.

Jabez Kane lay propped up against a buttress in one of the deepest sewers in the network, his face set into a grimace of pain. Beads of filthy sweat stood out from his face and ran in rivulets down the deep scar that traversed his forehead, over his eye and down his cheek. His eyes were wild and red-rimmed. His breath came in irregular gasps. His sodden clothes were caked in filth. His left arm was bandaged above the elbow with the kerchief he had previously tied around his neck, a desperate attempt to stop the blood flowing from a ferocious wound. The whole of his left side was caked in blood, both his own and that of the young Constable Evan, whose life he had taken not twenty-four hours earlier in Hardacre's den. Raising his eyes to the vaulted roof, Kane was sure he could hear a sound. In a moment or two more, it was clear there came a splashing behind him. Turning quickly, he strained to see in the half-light. The tunnel before him was swallowed in darkness. What light there was came from a single grill placed above Kane's head, but within a matter of a few feet it dissipated. Alarmed by the ever-increasing noise, Kane inched his way painfully around the buttress. Holding his wounded arm against him, he tried to slow his rattling breath so as not to give himself away. Kane weighed up his predicament. That one of the most dangerous criminals in London should be reduced to living like a rat in the sewers would scarcely have been credited just a day before. Jabez Kane, perpetrator of the most heinous crimes of the last ten years; the Shoreditch murders, the Brixton blaze, the death of several peelers, was reduced to nothing more than a fugitive, holed up in the least hospitable place in the whole great, stinking city. As Kane mulled over his situation in his delirium, the intruder came ever nearer. And then there was silence. The waters stilled, the splashing stopped. Kane held his breath.

"My, my. Haven't we gone up in the world?" Albert Hobbs' great, wide face peered at him through the gloom, his dirty, felt hat hanging over his eyes. "Thought I'd find you here."

Kane let his breath go and rubbed the sweat from his face with his good arm. "And that you have, Hobbs. What you got for me?"

Albert Hobbs pulled a hessian sack from his shoulder and took out a loaf of bread, which Kane declined, and a flask of gin from which he drank at once. "The South Bank is crawling with filth," Hobbs continued, watching Kane as he drank. "What did you do?"

Kane wiped his lips with a tattered sleeve. "Killed a young'un," he said. For a moment, his body shuddered with the thrill of the memory. The involuntary movement caused a spasm of pain to shoot up Kane's injured arm and he winced with agony. Seeing Hobbs had noticed the wound, Kane licked his dried lips before offering him an explanation. "A peeler," he began. "Took a shot at me in the alley."

"It looks bad, Kane," said Hobbs redundantly as he gently angled Kane's arm into what small light there was, the better to see the wound. "Very bad."

"I know," Kane winced again.

Hobbs let go his arm. "How many were they?"

"Four, five. Treacher was among 'em."

Hobbs' hat rose almost comically on his head as he raised his eyebrows in surprise.

"He's filth, Hobbs," Kane spat.

Hobbs nodded in understanding. A few things he had thought about Treacher now seemed to add up. "And what of Hardacre?" he asked.

Kane shrugged, then grimaced again. The pain was spreading from his upper arm into his shoulder now. "Dunno," he said, his voice now barely more than a dry whisper, "I helped him stash everything away, and then he made a run for it." Kane looked around, wildly. "Could be anywhere."

Hobbs thought, then turned to his companion in crime with a renewed urgency. It was clear Kane was not in a good way. "You can't stay here, Kane. You need to get that seen to."

Kane let a dry laugh escape his lips. "By who? The minute I step out from here, I'm as good as hanged."

Hobbs pushed his hat from his eyes. "Don't you worry about that," he said darkly, "I know someone who'll help."

A short time later, a young lad with curly red hair and dressed in rags approached a residence in St John's Wood. Weaving between the traps and horses, Thomas Crowley crossed the busy road with care and rang the bell outside number Fifty Five, Acacia Road. In time, it was opened by a stern-looking footman. Pollard stooped all the more to hear the boy's message and then, with a look of alarm, let him have admittance. Looking nervously up and down the street as he closed the door, it was clear that Pollard would be happier if this little encounter had not been witnessed. It took only the time taken for a cab to rattle past before the boy reappeared, this time accompanied by Doctor Henderson, resplendent in top hat and frock coat, a doctor's bag in his hand. As he closed the door behind him, he gave furtive glances up and down the street, then followed the boy across the road.

XVI

An Unexpected Confirmation

Sergeant Anthony Graves was never one to hide his light under a bushel. Tonight at The Silver Cross Inn, thought Inspector Bowman, he was plainly in his element. Bowman had thought it a good idea to join Graves for a quick dinner at the local public house. He had eaten there regularly for lunch, but an evening visit, he was finding, was a different proposition entirely. And he wasn't sure he liked it. He sat alone at a small table with a jug of porter and the remains of his dinner on a plate in front of him. Across the smoky, low-ceilinged room, he could just about make out Graves' head through the throng. He was seated at an aged piano, hammering the keys for all he was worth in a vain attempt to be heard above the crowd. They were currently two-thirds the way through singing 'The Ratcatcher's Daughter', a song that Bowman had never heard before, nor wished to hear again. He coughed in the fug of pipe smoke that hung in the air, and stroked his moustache thoughtfully. It had been a difficult day and Graves was obviously eager to put it behind him. Bowman couldn't help but agree but, to him, a Scotland Yarder was never off duty. Every now and then, he caught a glance thrown his way from one of the regulars, but Bowman was careful not to return the gesture. The last thing he wanted was company. As the song drew to an end, Sergeant Graves reached up with one hand to retrieve a foaming tankard of ale from the top of the piano. The assembled crowd whooped with admiration to see him play the final phrases with a single hand, downing his pint in one long draft as he held a low rumbling note at the end of the song. To great applause, he replaced the now empty jug on the piano and finished the tune with a flourish. Rising from his stool, Graves bowed theatrically several times and then, ignoring the cries for more, made his way through the pressing throng to join Bowman at his table.

"Very good, Graves," said Bowman above the din, "You obviously have a talent in - " he searched for the word. "Performing."

"Why thank you, sir," the young sergeant beamed, oblivious to any hint of cynicism in Bowman's tone. "I try my best!"

As he sat, the two men were joined by Harris the landlord. Graves was delighted to see he carried another pair of tankards, each full to the brim with the inn's distinctive brew. Harris had been the landlord at The Silver Cross for over thirty years, and his very skin seemed stained with the place. His leathery face might have been made from dried tobacco leaves, his hair hung lank to his shoulders.

"These are on the house, sergeant," he said, placing the tankards on the table before them. "Business is never better than when there is entertainment."

Graves' smile grew ever wider and he turned to the crowd behind him. "I'll drink to that!" he cried, to cheers from his grateful audience.

Bowman eyed his second jar with caution. He was never one to drink more than was seemly, and felt another pint might be one too far. As he was about to make his excuses and leave, the two men were joined by another visitor to their table. She was rather more comely than the last, and placed a hand on Sergeant Graves' shoulder.

"Hello, deary. What a performance you gave us tonight. Very professional, I'd say." Her eyes flicked across the table to Bowman. "And I see you've brought a friend." The woman glided across to Bowman's shoulder. "Pleasure to meet you too," she purred. "What d'you think of our star pianist?"

As she leaned flirtatiously to Bowman's ear she afforded the inspector a glimpse of her ample cleavage. Bowman was not convinced it was entirely accidental. The inspector took the opportunity to look at her in more detail.

As she moved into the pool of light cast from the lamp on the wall, flashing him a knowing smile, it was clear she was not as young as she had first appeared. In the hazy half-gloom of the saloon, she had presented herself as a young lady, smooth-skinned and elegant. In a closer light, however, it was apparent that she was closer to fifty than thirty, that her mouth had once enjoyed more teeth and that her skin had been the victim of one too many encounters with the pox. A heavy, sickly perfume hung about her in an almost visible haze, but this did nothing to mask the faintly musty aroma of her clothes.

"I think he has excelled himself," Bowman finally agreed, making a mental note to never visit this establishment in the evening again.

To Graves' evident amusement, their guest had pushed her way onto Bowman's bench beside him and the inspector now found himself the subject of many a wink and a nudge from those at the bar. As Bowman considered his next move, Harris appeared again at the tableside.

"Annie," he began, "I think you'd better move along." He took the woman gently by the elbow, attempting to steer her away to a more appropriate area of the room. "This is Inspector Bowman."

The introduction certainly had an effect on Annie, but perhaps not the one Harris had intended. She turned, eyes wide, to regard the inspector again. "Bowman? So, you're looking into this woman in the Thames, ain't ya?"

Annie's question pulled Bowman up short, and even Sergeant Graves stopped mid-sip to hold his tankard suspended in the air. The two men shared a look.

"I read about it in the paper. Or rather, I had it read to me." She gave a cackle.

"Come on, Annie," Harris tried one more time. "Let's leave the gentlemen in peace."

"It's all right Harris," said Bowman amiably. There was something about Annie's manner that seemed suddenly serious. Bowman was keen to know what she had to say, however it might look to the men at the bar. "What of it?" he asked of her.

"She was one of us, deary." Annie shook herself free of Harris' grasp. After taking a moment to assess the situation, the old landlord decided he had other, more pressing duties to perform and moved away, leaving Inspector Bowman with an apologetic look.

"One of us?" Bowman ventured, though her meaning was clear enough.

"You still wet behind the ears? She plied her trade with the rest of us. Catch my meanin'?" Annie stood with her arms crossed in front of her.

"Did you know her?" asked Graves, tentatively.

Annie slid onto the bench next to the sergeant, this time giving Inspector Bowman cause to raise a wry smile at Graves' predicament. "Well, that depends on what you've got in that there pocket for me."

To Graves' evident alarm, Annie reached over to pat his trouser pockets. Graves squirmed uncomfortably in his seat. "I beg your pardon?" he spluttered.

"Don't worry deary, I'm not on duty any more than you are. I only meant that a little payment might refresh my memory."

Bowman could barely contain his amusement as the young sergeant rolled his eyes to the ceiling. In spite of himself, the inspector was suddenly beginning to enjoy his evening. Graves pulled a coin from his pocket and held it up before him.

"So, how can you be sure you knew her?" he asked Annie. Whilst he was well aware of the import of the conversation, Graves was also relishing the playing of the game.

Annie snatched the coin from Graves' fingers and put it quickly in a purse secreted in her stocking tops. It took all Graves' self control not to stare. "Saw her picture in the paper, didn't I?"

Bowman leaned forward on his elbows. "And you're saying that she was a - " he fumbled awkwardly.

"Go on, say it love. I'm not ashamed."

Sergeant Graves came to his companion's rescue with a cheery smile. "You're saying she was a prostitute?" he asked, a touch too loud for Bowman's sensibilities.

"That's exactly what I'm saying. One of Hardacre's girls, like me." Bowman and Graves shared a look at the mention of the name.

"Hardacre?" Bowman repeated for clarification, "Jeb Hardacre?"

"Our lord and master," sneered Annie, her voice loaded with sarcasm, "He who must be obeyed. She was one of his, and had been for a good three years." As the two men took the news in, Annie reached for Graves' tankard and took a long draft. "Such a shame, she was a lovely girl."

"And her name?" asked Graves, "Do you know her name?" He felt the thrill of an imminent discovery course through him. Casting a nervous glance across the table, he could tell from his expression that Bowman felt the same.

"O'course I know her name," Annie replied as if it were the most ridiculous question she had ever been asked, although Bowman guessed she had been asked far stranger in the course of her work. "Only me memory's fadin'," she added mischievously. "What was it now?"

Shaking his head but secretly harbouring an admiration for her tactics, Graves presented her with another coin from his pocket.

"Yes, we're almost there," said Annie as she weighed the coin in her hand. "It's becoming a little clearer."

With a sigh, Sergeant Graves stood to empty the contents of his pockets onto the table and motioned that Bowman should do the same. Soon, there was a small pile of currency on the table, from which Annie took her pick.

"Do you never give anything for nothing?" asked Graves.

Annie flashed him a knowing smile. "Sorry, love. It's just not in my nature."

Her reward collected from the table, Annie closed her eyes as if deep in thought. Bowman was now enjoying her performance much more than he had previously enjoyed Sergeant Graves' at the piano, although he would never have admitted as much to his companion. Annie snapped her eyes open dramatically and held a finger in the air.

"Yes," she exclaimed, "That's it. I've got it now."

Holding her head in an expression of triumph, she looked Inspector Bowman straight in the eye. "Henderson," she said simply, "Mary Henderson."

With that, she deposited the remaining coins into her purse and moved away into the room, determined to pick up her night's trade where she had left off. Casting a look behind her, she couldn't help but laugh at the two Scotland Yarders staring at one another across their table, sharing a look of utter confusion. She smiled to herself as she moved into the throng by the bar. She had rather liked Inspector Bowman. There was a vulnerability about him that she had immediately found attractive. As she found her place by the counter the better to scan the room for trade, her eye fell across a face she knew. Even with his old, felt hat pulled over his eyes, there was no mistaking Albert Hobbs. Annie's heart leapt to her mouth. He had plainly overheard every word.

It took some time for the two men to gather their thoughts.

"It's too late to do anything more, Graves," said Bowman, having found his voice at last.

"Agreed," said Graves, downing the last of his beer. "But that's just about put a kibosh on the evening for me, sir. I've lost the taste for it."

The two men rose from their seats and shrugged on their coats.

"Any further plans tonight, sir?" asked Graves as he wound his scarf around his neck.

"Only getting home as fast as is practicable, Graves. No doubt I will see you in the morning."

Graves offered him a cheery "G'night" as they stepped from the inn and went their separate ways. The air was sharp now and Graves was in no doubt that there would be a frost in the morning. The paths would be treacherous. Above him, the sky was a clear, velvet black studded with bright stars. As he rounded the corner onto The Strand, a newspaper seller, keeping warm by a brazier, caught his eye. With almost impeccable timing, the boy took up his cry. "Standard! Late Extra! Read all about it!"

Graves lengthened his step, the quicker to be out of the cold.

"Scotland Yard in bungled ambush!" the boy cried, in full voice now.

Graves stopped mid-step and turned on his heels, in hopes he had misheard.

"Constable dead!" the boy brayed. "Read all about it!"

Digging in his pocket for what small change he had left, Graves reached out for a paper. “I’ll take one, boy,” he said.

The boy unfolded a copy from the pile on his arm and put Graves’ coins in a leather pouch tied round his waist. “There you go, sir.” He gave Graves a friendly, well-practiced wink as he handed him the paper. “Mind ’ow you go, sir. There’s some bad’uns about.”

Graves nodded, sagely. “Thank you,” he said. “I’ll bear it in mind.” As the sergeant leaned against a nearby lamp to scan the paper’s front page, the boy took up his cry again.

“Evenin’ Standard! Late edition!”

A mob of passers by poured from the nearest underground railway station. Many of them stopped to buy their evening news, jostling Sergeant Graves as he read the headline in despair; “INSPECTOR ADMITS TO BOTCH - CAN WE TRUST THE YARD?”

Folding the paper beneath his arm, Graves turned swiftly away and walked down The Strand towards home, hissing just two words under his breath.

“Jack Watkins...”

XVII

Behind The Veil

Inspector Bowman was feeling the cold. As he walked through Trafalgar Square to St Martin's Lane, he thrust his hands deeper into his pockets and buried his head further into the collar of his coat. This case was proving difficult. Bowman was used to dealing with a lack of solid information. Much of a Yarder's professional life was spent scrabbling in the dark, but contradictory evidence was never welcome. What was he to make of Annie's statement? Was she lying? Was Doctor Henderson lying and if so, why? If it were not for the detail of the eyes, he would be tempted to think there might just be another Mary Henderson, but Doctor Crane's observations made that unlikely. Everything pointed to the deceased being Mary Henderson.

Shaking his head to clear it, Bowman felt the sharp edges of a card in his coat pocket. Drawing it out as he walked, he saw it was the card that Elizabeth Morley had given him in the property store at Scotland Yard. He read it aloud to himself as he turned into Long Acre.

'THE EMPIRE ROOMS present
by arrangement with MADAM ROSE
a spectacle from beyond the grave.'

Bowman's natural instinct was to disregard the information, but he couldn't help but admit his curiosity had been piqued. Or was it that he wanted to see Miss Morley again? The address was printed in gold lettering along the bottom of the card and, with a start, Bowman realised he was just a five minute walk from the venue. Almost without thinking, he turned his step towards the Empire Rooms at Covent Garden.

In the lamplight, the central piazza of Covent Garden looked a romantic place. The stallholders were packing away the last of their wares as Bowman approached, but still the air was suffused with the earthy scent of heather and holly, the winter foliage sold by the garden traders in their covered market. As the empty crates were loaded onto waiting drays, their impatient horses – old nags and great Shires alike – pawed the ground. Apprentices sluiced the cobbles with steaming water and scrubbed them clean. Wandering tradesmen sold the last of the day's bread to passers by and chestnuts were roasted by scruffy young boys, eager to make an extra shilling before being moved on by the local bobbies. Even in the cold, Bowman saw couples out to take the air; the youngest of them stopping to catch a kiss beneath the lamplight, the oldest of them stopping to catch their breath.

Cobbles glistening beneath his feet, Inspector Bowman walked to the southern side of the covered piazza where he knew he would find the Empire Rooms, the venue for the evening's Spiritualist meeting. Having always considered himself something of a rationalist, he could scarcely credit the fact that he was going to such a meeting willingly. Several times the thought had entered his head that he should turn back and go home. Each time the thought was dismissed and he had walked on all the quicker.

Cabs rattled past as Bowman reached the Empire Rooms, a modest building tucked away from the main thoroughfare. The discreet entrance was marked only by a board propped up against the wall. It bore the same text that Bowman had read on his card, promising a 'Spectacle From Beyond The Grave', and written in the same antique font. Bowman hung back, watching from the shadows as the occasional pedestrian turned their feet to the door. Urchins ran between them, no doubt looking for easy pickings in the gloom. Bowman stamped his feet and blew on his hands to relieve the cold, when his attention was drawn to a smart brougham drawing up directly opposite. As the door swung open, Elizabeth Morley stepped from the footplate, bending to smooth her skirts before turning to thank the driver. Bowman slunk further back from the light, his mind a quandary. Should he make himself known now? Should he make himself known at all? Looking about herself, Elizabeth crossed the road with care and made her way through the entrance. As the brougham rattled away, Bowman stood in silence. Not for the first time, a question resolved itself in his mind, a question to which there would never be an answer. He whispered it aloud to the very air around him, as if that would elicit a response. "What would Anna think?" He felt like a child, lost in the night. Finally, and with a deep breath and a look of despair at his own actions, he followed in her footsteps, pushing open the door to the Empire Rooms.

The counter in the lobby was a hive of activity. Situated on the first floor, it afforded fine views of the market by day. As Elizabeth made her way up the stairs, she was greeted by the smell of burning incense and the hubbub of an expectant crowd. Behind the counter stood Elias Goldoni, proud proprietor of the Empire Rooms. Goldoni was of circus stock, his family being a clan of itinerants who roamed the country in more clement weather to entertain the masses. As a boy he had been trained in the many disciplines of the Big Top. He had in his time walked the wire, swung from the trapeze and entered the lion's cage. He could juggle and breathe fire if the occasion demanded but now, in his middle age, he had eschewed a life on the road for something a little more permanent. His skills as a showman had proved invaluable in putting the Empire Rooms on the map, and he was very much the public face of the establishment. And what a face it was. A broad lantern jaw was perpetually adorned with a whiskery shadow no matter how close he shaved, and a luxurious moustache hung down over a generous mouth. A monocle clung to his left eye, though whether this was due to necessity or affectation it was never known. His dark hair was neatly parted in the middle and smoothed on either side, and a fine pair of mutton chop sideburns adorned his face. In his tails and white tie, Goldoni was the very model of efficiency as he checked tickets, took coats and attended to all enquiries.

Goldoni assumed a sombre look as Elizabeth approached from the stairs. He fussed his way from behind the counter to take her coat. "Miss Morley, how grieved I was to hear of your father." Goldoni affected a hint of an Italian accent as he spoke, yet it was common wisdom that his lineage could be traced no further than the seaside resort of Margate. "You must accept my condolences."

Elizabeth accepted the platitude with grace and let Goldoni take her coat to the closet behind the counter. "Mr Goldoni," she continued as he returned to take her ticket, "We both know that death is only a door to another room."

Goldoni clasped his hands together in a gesture of heart-felt sincerity. "And perhaps tonight will bring you some comfort." Punching her ticket with a ticket inspector's hole-punch, Goldoni returned the piece of paper with a bow. "Have you seen Madam Rose before?" he asked.

Elizabeth shook her head. "I have not. Although I've heard all about her." She leaned in closer to Goldoni to whisper, conspiratorially. "And her Native friend." An almost visible thrill seemed to pass through her.

Goldoni removed his monocle to clean it on a pristine white handkerchief. "Mr Khy? He is a peculiar beast. From the Amazon basin, I believe. The sole survivor of a lost tribe."

"How exciting," breathed Elizabeth as Goldoni replaced his eyepiece. Now it was his turn to lean in.

"Are you hoping to speak with your father, Miss Morley?" he asked, delicately.

Elizabeth gave a smile, reaching up to brush some fluff from Goldoni's shoulder. "If death is merely the door to another room, Mr Goldoni, then perhaps Madam Rose will push it open a little."

A sudden commotion caused Elizabeth to turn. Behind her, Inspector Bowman had fallen up the top step and was now doing his best to recover his decorum.

"Inspector Bowman! How delightful!" Elizabeth exclaimed with a squeal of genuine delight.

Bowman returned the greeting with a nervous nod, his moustache twitching at his mouth as he punched a dent from his hat.

"Are you quite all right?" Elizabeth had advanced upon him in such a way that Bowman was sure she would offer him a kiss.

"Oh," he stammered, "I'm quite well, thank you. I just missed a step, that is all." He looked around at the small crowd that had gathered round him. They were a motley collection of all ages, but all dressed in their finest for the night's entertainment. "No harm done," he promised, brushing the dust from his knees. Elizabeth took his arm and led him carefully to the counter. Was Bowman imagining things, or was her grip especially tight?

"How wonderful of you to come," Elizabeth beamed. "I shall pay for your entry."

"I shall not hear of it," Bowman blustered, reaching into a pocket for his wallet. Before he could retrieve it, however, Elizabeth had called Goldoni over to take payment.

"You will soon learn, inspector," said Elizabeth with a playful look, "That I do not take kindly to being told what I can and cannot do."

With immaculate efficiency, Goldoni tore a ticket from a book at his counter and punched it with his machine. Standing almost to attention, he made great play of handing the ticket to the inspector and Bowman took it with a weak smile, already regretting his decision to come.

"Are you here to make a communication with the dead?" Goldoni asked from behind his luxuriant moustaches. The question took Bowman aback such that Goldoni felt obliged to ask it again. "Is there someone with whom you wish to communicate?"

Bowman felt his knees weaken. Is that why he had come? Was there a part of him that wished to speak to Anna? The rationalist in him knew it was impossible, and yet… "I am here only to communicate with the living."

The inspector shook his head, unsure of the veracity of his own statement. He fancied he could feel the burn of Elizabeth's gaze. Bowman was relieved to have the silence between them broken as Goldoni clapped his hands together. Puffing out his chest in readiness, he moved to a red velvet curtain that hung over a door in the corner.

"Ladies and gentlemen," he announced, "If I could have your attention." The hubbub died away as he cleared his throat dramatically. "Tonight I can promise you a glimpse into another realm. The realm of the spirits. Tonight, the dead shall walk among us and be as we are, corporeal."

Elizabeth gripped Bowman's arm more tightly and glanced up at him as he shifted uncomfortably on his feet. Her eyes, he noticed, were almost shining with a fervent, inner light.

"If you wish to take your seats," concluded Goldoni, stepping aside from the curtain to allow entry, "The demonstration is about to begin."

Beyond the curtain, the lobby opened out into an austere, wood-panelled room. Opulent sash curtains billowed like sails at the windows. Brightly coloured frescoes adorned the walls. The pride of the Empire Rooms was a large candelabra studded with electric lights which hung from the ceiling. It was decorated with plaster cherubs and, incongruously, ornate representations of bunches of fruit. The room, guessed Bowman, could be used for any number of functions both public and private, but tonight it had been pressed into service as something of a theatre. A makeshift stage had been erected at the far end and dressed with a wing-backed chair, small table and decorated modesty screen. A large tapestry of a hunting scene hung from the wall behind the stage, providing both a dramatic backdrop and, Bowman guessed, a screen between the improvised auditorium and a dressing area beyond.

Bowman led Elizabeth down rows of neatly positioned chairs and gestured for her to sit. All around them people jostled for position, and Bowman was amused to see a scuffle ensue over who should have the nearest seats. It was left to Goldoni to smooth things over in his inimitable manner, and the two parties were content to compromise.

"I knew you would come, inspector," said Elizabeth as she sat.

"Then you knew more than I," replied Bowman, folding his coat over the back of his chair.

Looking around him, Bowman could see the room was almost full. He was perplexed at so many choosing to spend a cold winter's night in such a place, and alarmed that, as he assumed, so many people would be willing to lend credence to such an idea as Spiritualism.

"Do you know any of these people?" he asked Elizabeth as he sat.

Elizabeth cast her eyes around the room. "Not all," she said. "The gentleman in the top hat is Sir Nathaniel Cokes."

Bowman strained to see across the room. There, sitting alone at the far end of a row, was an elderly man with a long white beard and whiskers. He sat bolt upright and looked straight ahead, seemingly unaware of the commotion around him as people settled into their seats in anticipation.

"Yes, I have heard of him," replied Bowman, his dark brows knotted together in thought. "But I thought him a man of science."

Elizabeth nodded. "A chemist and a physicist, I believe."

"What would he be doing here?" Bowman was confused. Did people leave their wits at the door to attend such a night as this? Could even the great and the good be duped with the promise of a tête-à-tête with the deceased? Bowman shrugged his shoulders in resignation and sunk back into his chair.

"Perhaps he's investigating."

"Investigating?" Bowman sat forward in an attempt to reappraise the man where he sat, but he was impassive.

"There are many who believe that spirits walk among us, inspector, but there are many more who don't. Unfortunately, they often conduct themselves with an all too fervent zeal and set about exposing the practitioners of the art."

"Is that not a good thing?"

"'There are more things in Heaven and Earth than are dreamt of in your philosophy.' Do you not know your Shakespeare, Inspector Bowman?"

"Plainly not as well as I should."

Looking round the room again in the ensuing silence, Bowman was sure he felt a cooling towards him from his lady companion. Had he been too harsh? He didn't think so, but resolved to be less outspoken if he could. As he glanced around, his attention was caught by a veiled lady in the front row opposite. Dressed entirely in black, she sat awkwardly, as if in fear of being approached. Even though her face was veiled, Bowman was sure she gave a start as she saw him.

"Who is the lady in the veil?" he asked Elizabeth. It was both a genuine enquiry, and an attempt to dispel the atmosphere that had suddenly grown between them.

Elizabeth looked across the room. "I have no idea. She looks recently bereaved. It is quite common to see such people here."

Bowman turned to face her. "How often do you attend these meetings, Miss Morley?"

Elizabeth looked square at him without apology. "Whenever I am in need of comfort, inspector." It was obvious to Bowman that he had no right to trample on the poor lady's beliefs if they brought her comfort, but he had to admit to a growing sense of unease at her evident commitment. As Bowman wondered how best to continue the conversation, he felt her hand on his arm again.

"Would it pain you greatly to call me Elizabeth, Inspector Bowman?"

Bowman looked around him, suddenly sheepish. "Would that be appropriate?" he asked.

Elizabeth Morley couldn't help but laugh at this. "How did such a sensitive man find himself a detective at Scotland Yard?

Caught by Elizabeth's direct manner, Bowman felt his neck burn beneath his collar. "Miss Morley," he began, "I - "

"The world weighs heavy on your shoulders, does it not, inspector?" Alarmingly, she was squeezing his hand now, as one might comfort a frightened child.

"I am simply tired," he said, gently lifting her hand from his.

Elizabeth looked down to her lap, suddenly disconsolate. "Not of me, I hope?" she asked quietly.

"No, Miss Morley. Not of you." Bowman sat back in his seat again, "Of London."

Elizabeth nodded sadly as if a sudden understanding had come upon her. "He that is tired of London - " she began.

"Ah yes," Bowman interjected, smoothing his moustache with his fingers. "The oft-quoted Doctor Johnson. But I do not tire of life," Bowman looked again at his companion. "I tire of death."

Elizabeth sighed as the electric light above them dimmed. "Oh dear," she said. "Then it seems I have brought you to quite the wrong place."

The auditorium was plunged in darkness. The only light came from candles placed around the stage. The temporary footlights cast their light upon the empty wing-backed chair, seeming to distil the atmosphere of anticipation pervading the room. A sudden turn of heads told Bowman that something was happening behind him. He let his gaze wander to the back of the room. There, he saw an elderly, grey-haired woman shuffling down the aisle. She was dressed in many layers and seemed to have an inordinate amount of colourful silk scarves thrown about her shoulders. Her bulky clothes gave her the appearance of one much larger as she tottered down the middle of the room. She held a pair of finger cymbals in each bony, brown hand which she sounded as she walked, giving the spectacle the appearance of a religious procession. Bowman guessed this was Madam Rose, an impression reinforced by the otherworldly glow that seemed to emanate from her bright, piercing eyes. Aside from the gentle, hypnotic tinkling of her cymbals, the room fell into a respectful hush. All eyes in the room were fixed upon this strange looking woman. As she walked into the pool of light illuminating the stage, Bowman could see she was accompanied. A frisson of excitement rippled around the room as Madam Rose's companion stepped into the light beside her. He was a man of a height much greater than six foot, guessed Bowman, and a stranger sight he had never seen. The man was dressed in what appeared to be animal skins. He wore crude sandals, trousers of soft leather and a waistcoat of a similar material. This covered his otherwise bare torso, which rippled with taut sinew and muscle. There were bracelets of bone at each wrist and brooches of feathers pinned to his chest. A belt of leather hung from his waist, to which was attached a long blade, shaped like a scimitar. Bowman had seen similar blades before in hauls of stolen property, but shuddered at the thought of ever seeing such a thing in action. The man's long, black hair lay over his brawny shoulders, braided with colourful twine and knotted with yet more feathers. Most alarming of all was the man's face. His tanned skin had the appearance of a rich, dark wood. Deep lines seemed etched upon its surface from which a pair of deep-set eyes sparkled like sapphires. This strange apparition stared absently over the audience as if his mind roamed over distant plains, as Bowman contemplated the most remarkable aspect of the man's features. It seemed a metal plate was lodged into his lower lip, causing it to protrude from his face almost comically, like a small saucer or receptacle. Bowman felt a shiver pass down his spine at the strangeness of the man's appearance. Glancing round the room, he saw the rest of the audience appeared quite unmoved.

"That must be Mr Khy," Elizabeth elucidated. "Madam Rose's psychic bridge to the spirit world." She looked at Bowman's wide eyes. "He is quite a sight, isn't he?"

Bowman, discovering his mouth was hanging open in surprise, snapped his jaw shut and swallowed hard to regain his composure. "Extraordinary," he said, quite aware that the very word was an understatement.

Upon the stage, Madam Rose had taken her seat. Her companion stood beside her, as if on guard. In the silence she surveyed the audience, commanding their attention. Just as Bowman was sure she would not speak, she opened her mouth to do so. She spoke with a cracked yet powerful voice, which hinted at the scale of the performance to come. And it was to be a performance, of that Bowman had no doubt.

"I am Madam Rose," she intoned theatrically. "I walk with the spirits."

Bowman felt a release of tension in the room, as if the audience's expectations had been met, and there was an outbreak of applause. He was alarmed to see that his companion was applauding the most energetically of all. As the sound subsided, he was interested to see Khy move wordlessly among the audience with a silver tray. Was there to be a collection?

Elizabeth caught his look of confusion and leaned across to explain. "It is common for a personal effect to trigger a communication from the dead," she said reaching for the chain at her neck. "It can act like a key to a door." Undoing the tiny clasp, Elizabeth placed her necklace onto the tray. Leaning forward in his seat, Bowman could see the attached locket. It was the same as he had returned to Elizabeth earlier in the Scotland Yard property store.

"Are you hoping for a communication, Miss Morley?" He noticed that Elizabeth did not meet his gaze as she replied.

"We shall see," she said simply and directed her attention very obviously to the stage.

Bowman was suddenly aware that Khy was standing before him, his hand outstretched for a personal possession. A musky animal scent hung in the air about him, and he fixed the inspector with an expectant look. With an almost apologetic shake of his head, Bowman waved him away. As the giant shrugged his enormous shoulders and moved down the line to recover rings, pocket watches and other effects from the assembled crowd, Bowman cleared his throat and settled back in his seat. He suddenly felt more uncomfortable than ever.

As Khy returned to the stage, he placed the tray of possessions on the small table next to Madam Rose's chair. With a bow, he stepped to one side so that all the audience could see her.

"Ladies and gentlemen," Madam Rose sat, impassive, as she spoke. "My assistant, Mr Khy, will shortly retire behind the screen to my left. This is to hide the grotesque distortions his physical form must undergo in order to become the living embodiment of the deceased."

There was a murmur of excitement among the audience and Bowman noticed several of the ladies fanning themselves. As he looked around, he felt a pair of eyes upon him and, when he turned to face the woman in the veil sitting on the front row opposite, he could tell by the attitude of her body that she had been staring at him. As he tried to look beyond the veil, however, she turned her attention back to the stage.

Madam Rose had lowered her voice almost to whisper, but still it was clear. The effect was to make the audience lean forward in their seats, enrapt.

"You may notice an emanation of vapours or ectoplasm," she intoned. "The material from which the physical presence of a spirit is formed. The spirit will then present itself to us." She raised a pointed finger directly before her, as if this were the very spot that such an apparition would appear. “At no point should you be alarmed.”

The ladies in the audience were fanning furiously now and even the men, Bowman noticed, had visibly blanched. Every eye was on Madam Rose as she leaned over in her chair and selected a silver fob watch from the tray of possessions at her side. The air was almost thick with silence as she held the watch before her. Bowman was sure that those around him could hear his heart pounding in his chest.

“To whom did this belong in life?” Madam Rose asked, her voice taking on a more dramatic tone.

A voice rang out from the back of a room, that of a man, sounding all the louder in the otherwise deathly hush of the auditorium. “To my dearest uncle!”

Bowman turned with the audience to see a handsome, middle-aged man standing in the very back row dressed in a long coat and pin-striped trousers. The flash of a coloured waistcoat marked him out as something of a dandy, and there was just a little too much pomade upon his hair for Inspector Bowman’s taste.

Madam Rose nodded, sagely. “Thank you, sir. He died a tragic death?”

The man nodded. “At sea.” There was a murmur of condolence around the room. “The watch is all I have of him.”

Fingering the watch thoughtfully, Madam Rose closed her eyes and turned to her assistant. “Mr Khy? We may begin.”

Bowman turned to look at Elizabeth, and saw her face was set in a mask of absolute concentration, as if she were willing the spirits to appear herself. Bowman felt a surge of disappointment course through him. If he were not hemmed in on both sides, he would have made his excuses there and then but as it was, he was forced to stay and observe the macabre spectacle being presented before him.

Madam Rose was rocking back and forth where she sat, her fingers stroking the fob watch in a rhythmical fashion. Her voice took on a sing-song quality as she attempted to make contact with the world beyond. “Spirits,” she pleaded, “spirits, come to us, your servants. Use us as your voice. Use us as your body."

There was a flurry of activity halfway down the room, and Bowman turned to see a woman had fainted. Goldoni was conducting something of a rescue operation, directing two flustered ushers to extricate her from the audience and carry her quickly from the room. Most unnervingly, the inspector saw that barely anyone else had noticed, transfixed as they were on Madam Rose's performance.

"Return to the Earthly realm and give us your secrets," she was imploring, her voice rising in both pitch and volume. "Come to us. Come to us!"

Everyone in the room was now on the very edge of their seats, holding their breaths in collective suspense. Slowly, almost imperceptibly at first, it was possible to discern that something was happening. Drifting from behind the screen, the first wisps of a milky white, gaseous substance could be seen. The effect upon the room was electric. As each member of the audience in turn saw the vaporous cloud appear, they gasped and nudged their neighbours. A number of them crossed themselves, some sobbed but none of them moved. They sat as if fixed to their seats, held spellbound by the appearance of a spirit before them.

"Behold, the dead are come among us!" cried Madam Rose in triumph. "They walk among us, in Earthly form!"

Bowman looked around at the audience about him, his sense of apprehension growing. Hands had been lifted involuntarily to mouths, eyes were opened wide. Madam Rose ceased her hypnotic rocking and held up a hand as if to bring the room to order.

"A spirit is among us," she announced portentously. "Show yourself! Show yourself!"

It took three hospital orderlies to lift Hardacre onto the trolley at Charing Cross. His corpse had been brought from Bow Street by Black Maria, a black wagon usually reserved for the transportation of living prisoners. He was to be transferred to the hospital's dissecting rooms on the orders of Inspector Edmund Treacher, so Doctor Crane could conduct a thorough post-mortem in the morning. The old, rusty trolley was wheeled through corridors and passageways, down to the dissecting rooms in the basement of the building. This was the coolest part of the hospital, and so the most apt for the storing of cadavers. It was lit by gas jets mounted on the walls that seemed to lend a deathly pallor to the very air. The walls and ceiling were tiled in the same pattern as the floor; small rectangular tiles, most cracked, some conspicuous by their absence, stretched over the vaulted ceiling. Four raised slabs, also tiled, were placed at regular intervals along the furthest wall with a basin between them. Looking like altars at some temple, these macabre plinths were of waist height and just long enough and wide enough to hold an adult body. Each of them had a raised rim to prevent the spilling of fluids over their sides. A small plug hole was set into the furthest end to funnel any seeping liquids away from the corpse and into a drain beneath.

At a signal, the three porters manhandled Hardacre's stout body onto the slab nearest the door. As he was still fully clothed, they bent to begin the task of undressing him, throwing his clothes into a basket by the door for disposal or distribution to the poor. Had Hardacre been alive to see it, he would no doubt have seen no humour in the irony. Once stripped, the body was washed with hot water from the basin and scrubbed with carbolic to minimise the smell from a night's stay in the dissecting rooms. It was debated whether the corpse should be shaved, but as the orderlies were keen to have an early night, the idea was abandoned as being beyond the call of duty. If Doctor Crane wanted the body shaved for his investigations in the morning, they agreed, he could surely do it himself. And so Hardacre was left upon the slab, his great mountain of a belly protruding monumentally to the ceiling. As the last of the orderlies left the room, he turned down the gas to the lights in the room and the body was left alone in semi-darkness. Several minutes passed after the soft click of the closing door had died away. A tap dripped into a basin. And then there was a distinct movement on Hardacre's body. Had anyone been present to see it, they might have noticed the tiniest flicker of a muscle in Hardacre's left cheek. An involuntary spasm, surely, they would have reasoned. Many were the stories of limbs jerking into life on the dissecting slab as the muscles contracted or relaxed. There were even tales of cadavers sitting up and exhaling whatever gases had been fermenting in their stomachs, then falling back to the slab again as if in sleep. But the movement in Hardacre's cheek was far from being the involuntary spasm of a long dead muscle. It was an indication of something more. Hardacre was alive. His great belly heaved as he took a breath. Soon, it had settled into a rhythm and was joined by a flexing of the fingers in each hand. Finally, his eyes snapped open. Looking around him, Hardacre assessed his situation. He was alone, at least. The timing had been perfect. Rubbing his face to encourage the blood to return to his cheeks, he swung himself round on the table with an effort and sat with his legs dangling down before him. The pins and needles in his feet subsided as he looked around. He was in the dissecting rooms, he guessed, though he could not think where. Steadying himself against the slab, he slowly got to his feet and stood for a while to get his balance. A triumphant smile spread across his face. Stroking the great beard on his chin, Hardacre made his way to the basket by the door and retrieved his clothes.

A scream pierced the air in the Empire Rooms. Madam Rose had completed her invocations and now, with hands raised, she beckoned towards the screen as if enticing a child to join her. To gasps, a figure stepped from behind the screen. It was shrouded by an almost impenetrable mist that hung about the stage, but Bowman could plainly see it was the mysterious Mr Khy. He hunched his shoulders a little and held his arms across his body in what seemed to Bowman a ridiculous attempt to disguise his great bulk. To the audience, however, it was entirely convincing.

"That's him!" called the man from the back of the room, on his feet and pointing towards the apparition on the stage. "That's my uncle!" His legs seeming to give way in his hysteria, he fell back in his chair, crossing himself feverishly. "May God forgive us."

Soon the air rang with cries of "May the Lord protect us!" and "Christ have mercy!" Even in this room of a hundred people, Bowman felt entirely alone. Feeling a hand on his arm and a tugging at his shirtsleeve, he turned to face Elizabeth. Her eyes were the widest he had ever seen them, and her other hand was at her throat in a gesture that Bowman had once found beguiling. He suddenly became aware of a weight pressing against his chest. He was finding it hard to breathe. Elizabeth gazed at Khy in an expression of genuine awe.

"Can it be?" she whispered. "I can see him, inspector. I see the spirit before us!" In her fervour, she stood to join in the chorus, swept along by the hysteria in the room.

Bowman opened his mouth to offer her some words of caution but couldn't find the breath. He felt a cold sweat prickle on his forehead. His hands felt clammy. As he shook his head and prepared to gather his coat from his chair in order to leave, his attention was again drawn to the veiled woman on the front row. Unlike those around her, she sat impassive, clearly unmoved by the events unfolding before her.

To take his mind off his sudden discomfort, Bowman forced himself to analyse the scene before him. Madam Rose's audience had abandoned all notions of individuality and seemed to behave as one mind; trusting, yearning and above all believing. It was going to be a productive evening. Soon the hysteria would die down and Madam Rose would question the 'spirit'. The questions would be vague enough and Khy would answer with nothing more than grunts and nods. Madam Rose had already gleaned enough information to impress the audience with her veracity. The man's uncle, they had heard, had died a tragic death at sea. The odds were that he was, if not a sailor, then a young man at least. Also, her fingering of the watch had yielded her another clue. As she had turned it between forefinger and thumb, she had felt the distinct edges of an engraving. Looking down briefly during her incantation, she could plainly see the words 'G.R. from E.W.' engraved on the back of the case. The initials would be useful. The man in the audience would unwittingly fill in the gaps in the narrative as her questions continued, convincing himself and those around him that this was indeed the spirit of his uncle. And so she would continue with the evening, taking a new possession from the tray and spinning a story that would prove vague enough to apply to someone in the audience. The high emotion in the room, Khy's appearance and the smoke hanging about the stage would do the rest. Before Madam Rose could fully embark upon her well-rehearsed routine, however, the proceedings were interrupted. The man that Elizabeth had recognised as the scientist Nathaniel Cokes leapt to the stage and began wafting the air about him with his hands. Bowman felt his mouth drying. As he watched the unfolding scene, he had the unerring sense that the walls were closing in. His heart beat against his chest.

"This is monstrous!" screamed Nathaniel Cokes above the din. "A sham and nothing more!" His snow-white beard jutted from his chin. The room was still and, for a moment, Bowman was unsure as to how the crowd would react. He clutched the arm of his chair, both in expectation and in an effort to control his breathing. Then everyone was on their feet, shouting with indignation at the usurper on the stage. There were cries of "Leave the stage!" and much booing and hissing. Bowman heard the man from the back of the room scream, "Be silent, sir! Return to your seat!"

"I will not be silenced!" screamed Cokes above the noise. He planted his feet firmly on the ground, setting his face into an expression of determination. Bowman could see that Goldoni, alerted no doubt by the braying of the audience, had entered the room again, jostling his ushers before him. The inspector could barely breathe now. He was sure something must be wrong. Turning to his companion, he tried to ask for help but saw that she was absorbed in the proceedings. Bowman's blood ran cold. He was certain he was dying. On the stage, Madam Rose had risen from her seat and approached the intruder.

"How dare you interrupt a communication from the spirits?" she growled ominously, pointing a finger of accusation. Nathaniel Cokes took a step away from her but was plainly not ready to give ground.

"Communication be damned," he replied, clearly unmoved by her portentous tone. "I repeat, this is a sham!"

Bowman felt Elizabeth lean forward beside him. "But the spirit before you," she implored Cokes. "Do you not see him?"

Bowman clutched at his chest. His clothes were stuck to his skin with sweat and the room seemed to have shrunk to half its size. The ceiling pressed down upon him.

Cokes fixed Elizabeth with a determined stare. "No Madam, I do not. Because I see through the eyes of a rationalist." Madam Rose seized her chance, accusing the intruder of the one thing guaranteed to disarm him in front of such a crowd.

"He is a non-believer!" she crowed in triumph. Despite this interruption to her well-polished routine, she was rather enjoying herself. "The spirit will not show himself to a sceptic!" There were more shouts for Cokes to leave the stage, and many men raised their fists in his direction. Two ushers jumped onto the stage and held Cokes by the arms, attempting to remove him from the room. Bowman knew he had to leave. He gasped for air in vain, the room now spinning before his eyes.

Cokes, though slight in stature, was evidently strong in his intent. "There is no spirit!" he yelled, looking towards the screen behind which Khy now cowered, uncertain of how to proceed. "You have all seen exactly what this fraud wanted you to see."

Madam Rose took a gasp of exasperation. "Fraud?" she bellowed with some force. "How dare you?"

A young man in a fine cravat and brocade waistcoat leaned forward towards the stage. "The ectoplasm," he called to the agreement of those around him. "How do you explain that, sir?"

"It is a substance called dry ice or fixed air." Cokes tried in vain to be heard above the abuse being spat upon him from all sides. "You may see it commonly enough at the theatre!" he concluded bravely.

Madam Rose turned to the ushers holding Cokes by the arms. "Gentlemen," she said with a generous smile, "will you kindly remove this man from the room and see to it that he leaves the building?" There was an outbreak of spontaneous applause as Cokes was bundled from the auditorium. Madam Rose seemed unmoved by his protestations, aware as she was that, although she may not have won the argument, she had certainly won the battle for audience support.

As the room returned to order, Inspector Bowman turned to his companion. “I am sorry, Miss Morley” he gulped, retrieving his coat, “but I have to - ” He couldn’t find the breath to finish. He needed air.

Elizabeth looked at him sadly. “But, inspector,” she began, plainly disappointed. “The spirits. Are you not curious to see more?”

Bowman rose from his seat and, throwing his coat over his arm, made his way carefully down the row of spectators. They each gave him room to pass, but Bowman could see the looks of suspicion on their faces. It was obvious to all who saw him that Inspector Bowman was not of their mind. Casting a final look back to Elizabeth, Bowman could see that she was once more absorbed with the proceedings on the stage. His vision now a blur, he pulled on his coat and headed for the door, leaving Elizabeth Morley and those around her to continue their commune with the spirit world.

In the lobby outside, Inspector Bowman leaned against the wall trying to calm his erratic breathing. He saw the two ushers attempting to manhandle Cokes down the stairs. Goldoni was standing over them, pulling himself up to his full height to direct proceedings.

Cokes was calling for his coat as Bowman approached. “I will not leave without it,” he spluttered.

“Let the gentleman go,” Inspector Bowman gasped, finding his breath at last. “I’m sure he has no wish to disrupt the evening further.” At a nod from Goldoni, the ushers released their grip, leaving Cokes to smooth his clothes.

“Please,” began Goldoni, pointing a finger towards the closet behind the counter. “Fetch the gentleman’s coat. Then I am sure he will see himself out.” Goldoni spat this out, leaving Cokes in no doubt as to what was expected of him once his coat was returned. Cokes offered his hand to Bowman in gratitude.

“Thank you sir,” he said.

Bowman cast a look to the ushers as he shook the scientist’s hand. “I trust you have come to no harm?”

Cokes was struggling into his coat now. Bowman noticed it was of a heavy material and came almost down to Cokes' feet. "I can assure you I have suffered no more injury than a glancing blow to my pride. And you, sir? You seem distracted."

Bowman swallowed hard. His anxiety was subsiding but he was concerned. He remembered such episodes from his time in Colney Hatch and he remembered the treatment, too. He shuddered at the thought. "I am quite well," he lied. "Thank you." Cokes fastened the buttons on his coat, produced a scarf from a voluminous pocket and threw it dramatically over his shoulder.

Just as Bowman was about to accompany Cokes from the room, he felt a blow to his elbow and was pushed momentarily against the wall. A figure pressed against him, pushing something urgently into his hand. Bowman blinked in surprise, about to voice his indignation, when the figure disappeared almost as quickly as it had arrived. As the inspector recovered his wits, he had just enough time to see the back of the mysterious, veiled woman disappear down the steps to the front door. He was about to set off in pursuit, if nothing else to see what she had intended by such strange behaviour, when his fingers closed around the object she had thrust into his hand. It was a crumpled piece of paper. Holding it close to a lamp that burned on the counter, Bowman slowly unfolded the paper to reveal a handwritten note, obviously scrawled in haste amidst the melee of the meeting. 'Highgate Cemetery,' it said simply, 'Noon tomorrow.' Bowman looked up with hopes of calling out to the unknown woman. As his eyes moved to the steps through the door, he saw that she had, quite simply, vanished.

XVIII

Dead Or Alive

The following morning saw a further change in the weather. It was barely possible to discern exactly when the night had finished and the day begun. Thick, thunderous clouds loomed over the city depriving the streets of light. The watery, ineffectual sun could do nothing more than lend a lighter shade of grey to one corner of the sky. The morning air was heavy with the expectation of a downpour. An ominous peal of thunder rolled over the city streets.

In the windowless dissecting rooms below Charing Cross Hospital, Sergeant Graves and Inspector Treacher stood downcast next to an empty slab, a haughtier than usual Doctor Crane at their side.

"This is it, gentlemen." Doctor Crane peered over his glasses at them as he spoke. "This is where the orderlies left him. I fancied you might want to take a look."

Sergeant Graves looked around the room. The only way of effecting exit or entry was through the very door through which they had come. Ever conscientious, he took a notebook from his pocket. "What time was he brought down here, Doctor Crane?" he asked.

"At approximately half past eight last night," the doctor responded archly, his clipped Scottish vowels betraying his annoyance at being summoned at so early an hour in the morning.

"And you know for sure that he was dead?"

"Of course he was dead." Treacher was standing dumbfounded at the slab, his eyes cast down as if some clue to Hardacre's whereabouts might lie on its stained surface. "He dropped like a stone in the cell, foaming at the mouth and fitting something terrible." He looked up to Graves who was scribbling furiously with the stub of a pencil. "It was all over in an instant," he continued. "No sign of any pulse, not a breath from his body."

Graves finished the sentence with an energetic stab at the paper then looked up to meet the doctor's gaze. "Your immediate thoughts, doctor?"

With a sigh, Doctor Crane removed his glasses to pinch at the bridge of his nose with a bony hand. Graves was clearly testing his patience. "Unfortunately, Sergeant Graves," he began, "it seems the only piece of evidence we had simply got up and walked away."

"You mean the body was removed?" asked Treacher not unreasonably.

Doctor Crane replaced his spectacles and smoothed an errant hair over his balding head. "That would be entirely conceivable, Inspector Treacher," he said magnanimously enough, "if it were not for the fact that an orderly saw him walk out the front door of his own accord."

The two men couldn't help but stare at the doctor, their mouths wide open.

"And he made no attempt to stop the man?" Treacher was aghast at the news.

Doctor Crane looked down his nose. "Would you?" he asked, pointedly.

Graves was writing furiously again. "So, the orderly could offer a positive identification of the man?"

"You must talk to him yourself, sergeant, but he told me the man's appearance exactly matched that of the cadaver he took delivery of last night. He recognised the clothing and the tattoo."

Graves stopped writing, his pencil poised. "Tattoo?"

Doctor Crane sighed again. "It seems your friend has a very distinctive tattoo on his right forearm. The orderly saw it as the man put on his coat. A picture of a mermaid on a rock, beneath a single word. 'Nimrod'."

Graves continued with his notes, scratching the word "Nimrod" in bold letters upon the paper.

"It cannot be possible," Treacher complained, his hands on his hips. "A dead man cannot simply get up and walk away." He puffed out his cheeks in exasperation. With Kane disappeared, Fogg dead and now Hardacre himself on the loose, the time he'd spent in their den gathering evidence that may have hanged each of them was slowly coming to nought.

Crane pushed his spectacles further up his nose as he spoke. "I would not discount it so readily, Inspector Treacher."

Treacher looked up, his eyebrows raised in expectation.

"There are compounds and substances," the doctor continued, "which, if ingested in particular amounts, may produce the appearance of death for a while, but preserve the subject in perfect health."

Sergeant Graves chewed on his pencil. "So he could, to all intents and purposes, be mistaken for dead?"

Doctor Crane sniffed. "By the layman, yes."

"Where could one find such a drug?" asked Graves, pencil poised once more.

"That is a question for you, sergeant," Doctor Crane concluded, heading for the door. It was plain that he at least thought the meeting over. "Though it would be easy enough, given the right friends in the right places."

As Doctor Crane left the room, Graves turned to Inspector Treacher. An expression of resignation had clouded his broad face. Despite everything the doctor had told them, it was obvious that they were both none the wiser.

St John's Wood seemed a different place in the storm. Gone were the calm, orderly streets that Inspector Bowman had seen the day before. Now, the roads were awash with rainwater. The drains, ineffective against the deluge, had quickly clogged with leaves and detritus. Twigs and even whole branches had been wrenched from the elm trees that had seemed so sedate only a few hours previously. Now they swayed perilously in the wind, providing precious little shelter to passers by beneath. The lack of sunlight gave a sickly pallor to the air, the pressing clouds seeming to deprive the smart townhouses of their roofs. It was difficult, thought Albert Hobbs as he looked up, to see where the houses ended and the clouds began.

Hobbs crossed the road to the Henderson residence, oblivious to the puddles around him. His feet were already soaked to the skin and his clothes so wet they clung to him. He felt their weight bear down on his shoulders as he raised an arm to ring the bell. The rain stung his face as he waited. Fat drops slapped against the doorstep. Blowing water from the end of his nose, Hobbs removed the hat from his head to wring it out. As he wiped the hair from his forehead the door opened and there stood Pollard, imperious as ever.

"Yes?" he asked, not bothering to hide a look of disgust.

Hobbs leaned into the old footman, his broad face graced with a threatening snarl. "I want to see Henderson."

Pollard raised an eyebrow. "Doctor Henderson is a busy man," he responded with a look down his long nose. "And so am I."

Hobbs prevented Pollard from shutting the door in his face with a well-placed foot. He had half a mind to throttle the old bird there and then. Looking up and down the street, he saw there would certainly be no witnesses. "Tell him my name is Hobbs," he rasped. "That should get his attention."

"Oh?" Despite himself, Pollard felt himself in thrall to the repulsive man on the doorstep.

"Tell him that Kane is dead," Hobbs continued. "Died in the night in the greatest pain."

The drawing room at number Fifty Five, Acacia Road gave out onto the street. Through the net-curtained windows, Doctor Joshua Henderson heard every word of the altercation on his doorstep. Sitting in his chair by the window where he had spent a good hour leafing through the paper on his lap, Henderson leaned a little further forward and to the right in order that he might have a cleaner view. He could see Hobbs gripping the door now as he delivered his message. Pollard, thought the doctor with a sly smile, was earning his keep today.

"Well, I am very sorry for you, of course," continued Pollard from the hall.

"And tell him one of the girls has been squawking, but she squawks no more. I've seen to it."

Pollard was aware of the threatening tone in the vagrant's voice. "Very well," he conceded with a sigh. "I will pass on your message. Now, if you will kindly remove your foot from the door, I shall wish you a good day."

At this, Doctor Henderson noticed Hobbs shift his weight on his feet and lean away from the door to the window at which he sat. For a moment, he was sure that Hobbs could see him perfectly well through the heavy net curtains.

"Tell him," Hobbs continued pointedly, "that Hardacre is free and likely wants to settle a score. Seen him with me own eyes, I have."

As Pollard finally closed the door on this most unwelcome of callers, Henderson picked up a cup of tea from a small table at his side and took a sip. So Kane was dead. That was all to the good. Henderson knew he wouldn't last long. The wound had turned septic and there was little he could have done. As it was, he'd simply given the man sugar pills and a bandage, certain he would be dead by the morning. He cared nothing for the girl that Hobbs had mentioned. She was not important. But Hardacre was different. Replacing his cup back on its saucer with a controlled precision, Doctor Henderson rose from his chair and headed for the door.

XIX

Revelations

Inspector Bowman stood at the window in his office, straining to see through the rain to the streets below. A fierce wind was whipping across the Thames, blowing spray on to the few passers by who were fool enough to brave the morning. Sergeant Graves had come straight to Scotland Yard after his meeting with Doctor Crane, eager to deliver his latest news. He sat, knocking the rain from his hat, in the large, wing-backed leather chair before Bowman's desk.

"Disappeared?" growled Bowman in exasperation as Graves finished his report. "He can't just have disappeared. Do they not have any security at Charing Cross?"

Graves shook his head. "They've evidently not considered it a priority, sir."

"So we have no idea where Hardacre may be. Nor in what condition."

"Doctor Crane was of the opinion that he may well have affected a complete recovery."

"Really?" Bowman raised a quizzical eyebrow. "So, death is now considered a temporary condition?"

"Hardacre might have had access to certain drugs which may give the appearance of death."

Bowman gnawed his bottom lip in frustration as he thought. "There are fewer people abroad in this weather, so he'll be conspicuous unless he goes to ground. I will have 'H' Division comb the streets around the hospital and beyond. He's Treacher's quarry. I would not do him the injustice of denying him his prey."

"If we could stop every man and ask to see his forearm, then our job would be all the easier," offered Graves, breezily. Usually one to enjoy being gainfully employed in the pursuit of a criminal, he was happy enough on a day such as this to remain at the office and let others do the fieldwork.

Bowman turned to look at Graves, perplexed. "Why would you do such a thing?"

Graves leafed through his notepad, licking his fingers to turn the pages until he found the relevant information. "Hardacre had a very distinctive tattoo upon his right forearm. A picture of a mermaid on a rock beneath the word 'Nimrod'."

Bowman took a step closer to his companion, his fingers twitching as if straining for something just out of reach. "Nimrod? You're certain it said Nimrod?"

"According to the orderly who saw him walking out." Graves noticed Bowman's brow crease with thought. "Is there anything of import about it?"

"Only that that is the second time in as many days I have heard mention of it." Acknowledging Graves' blank look, Bowman continued. "The Nimrod is a schooner. Doctor Henderson told me he had spent some time on board as ship's surgeon, though what he has to do with Hardacre is anyone's guess." Weighing up his options, Bowman decided on a course of action. "Sergeant Graves," he began, "I want you to go to the shipping office at Somerset House. Find out all you can about the Nimrod, particularly with regard to crew and passenger manifests. This has to be more than mere coincidence."

Graves sighed. So he would have to brave the rain again, after all. As he rose to leave, a thought seemed to occur to him. He took the previous day's Evening Standard from the folds of his coat. "You might want a look at this, sir. Jack Watkins has been a busy man." Graves unfolded the front page. As Bowman read the headline, his features bunched into an expression of consternation.

"Ignatius Hicks will be the death of us all," he grumbled. "I take it he was the source of this information?"

"I'm guessing so," nodded Graves, throwing the paper to Bowman's desk. "I gather he spent some time with Watkins after we met at Chelsea Embankment. Said he was 'keen to develop a relationship with our finest evening paper'."

Bowman was pacing now. "And I should imagine he was handsomely rewarded for it, too. Watkins is not above procuring a story via his chequebook. If that turns out to be the case, Hicks will be disciplined. I've been working hard to build up the public's trust in the Force." Bowman's voice grew thick with rage. "Hicks has undone all that with one fell swoop." In a fury, Bowman pounced to his desk, sweeping the paper into the air with a fluid movement of his arm and throwing it against the window. Suddenly aware of his actions, he stood for a while, feeling Graves' gaze upon his back. He felt a muscle twitch involuntarily at his eye. "I'm sorry, Sergeant Graves," he said, not daring to turn. "The past two days have been rather trying."

"For us all, sir," Graves concurred, slowly. "In fact sir, if Watkins himself had been in this room, it would have been more than his blessed newspaper I would have thrown to the window."

Bowman turned to see Graves' eyes sparkling. His blond curls and flushed face gave him something of a cherubic appearance, quite at odds with the sentiments he expressed.

"Indeed." Grateful for Graves' expert defusing of the situation, Bowman made his way to his chair and sat, thoughtfully. "Then perhaps it might be best if I went to see him this afternoon."

Before Graves had a chance to respond, there was a hurried knock at the door. At Bowman's command, it swung open to admit Harris, the landlord of The Silver Cross, his head and shoulders sopping wet from the short walk to Scotland Yard. He reminded Graves of a wet dog as he shook the rain from his hair, but his grim expression soon brought the young sergeant up short.

"Inspector Bowman," Harris began, steeling himself for the news he had to deliver.

"What is it, Harris?" Bowman responded, rising from his chair.

"Begging your pardon sir, but it's Annie."

Graves tensed as he turned to Bowman. "The girl we spoke to in The Silver Cross last night," he said by way of explanation.

Bowman nodded. "What of her, Harris?"

Harris tried hard to steady his breath. "She's dead, sir. Found strangled not quarter of a mile from The Silver Cross. A bobby found her in the alley between Whitehall and the Embankment."

As Harris stood, dripping water to the floor, Bowman turned again to face the window and the rain outside. This was turning into a very grim business, indeed.

By noon, the rain was torrential. It hammered against the windows of Bowman's brougham cab, an excusable expense he had reasoned, given the conditions outside. Still, the rain gained access where the windows were not sealed as robustly as perhaps they might have been. The inspector wiped away the odd drop as it splashed against his face, such was the force of the torrent outside. Great cedars lined the road, standing like sentinels at the entrance to Highgate Cemetery. As Bowman glanced out the window he could see them, massive as they were, bending in the wind. The rain lashed against their branches, weighing them down with its force such that the trees themselves seemed to reach at the ground in an effort to remain anchored there.

As his cab pulled up against the sturdy iron gates that stood at the cemetery's entrance, Bowman saw a rather handsome private carriage standing in a far corner of the drive. Although it was parked beneath a canopy of branches, the rain still thundered against its roof. Curiously, noted Bowman, the driver was still sat in his seat, seemingly impervious to the deluge. Pulling his collar closer around his neck and tugging the brim of his hat over his eyes, Bowman jumped from his cab and walked briskly through the rain to the waiting carriage. Looking in through the window, he saw nothing but his own reflection staring back, wet and bedraggled already despite having only been in the rain for a matter of seconds.

"Hello, there!" Bowman called against the hissing of the rain. The door remained firmly shut. Feeling drops of water trickle down his neck, Bowman rapped on the door with his knuckles and awaited an answer with growing impatience.

Nothing.

Bowman turned to the driver perched high on his seat, the horse's reins resting in his lap. He wore a large, black overcoat with shiny buttons done up to his chin. A great scarf was wound around his face and neck and tucked into his collar and a top hat was jammed on his head. With no hint of any flesh visible save a beak-like nose protruding from his scarf, the man looked like nothing more than a bundle of clothes piled on the driver's seat.

"Hello, there!" Bowman repeated, but still the driver didn't move. "I say!" he began again, shaking the rain from his upturned face as he called. The only answer came from one of the horses tethered to the carriage beside him. Plainly unhappy at being asked to work in such conditions, the mare cast a mournful look at the inspector and gave a whinny of disapproval. Turning away, Bowman's attention was caught by a figure standing beyond the gates. It was a woman, dressed in black like the lady he'd seen at the Empire Rooms. She stood, sheltering beneath a great umbrella, inscrutable in an ankle-length coat and wide-brimmed hat. Just as Bowman was about to call out, the woman turned and made her way further into the cemetery, picking her way carefully between the long grass and weeds that encroached upon the path. Reasoning that he should follow, Bowman wrapped his coat tighter about him and stepped gingerly across the drive to the great iron gates by which one may enter the Kingdom of the Dead.

Highgate Cemetery had been open for just half a century, but already it had the appearance of an ancient site. Although certain areas were tended to, great tracts had been left wild such that Nature had, in all its manifestations, begun to slowly take back what had been tamed. Gravestones and tombs not twenty years old were entwined with ivy, great mausoleums were adorned with lichen coats and the paths grew narrower with every step. Had Bowman been here at another time of year, he would no doubt have marvelled at the view from the top of Highgate Hill across London. He may well have stood in silence to hear the birdsong, or muse at the profusion of wild flowers that grew among the graves. As it was, the wonder of the place was quite lost on him. He walked stealthily, his head down against the rain, looking up now and again to try and catch a sight of his mysterious quarry. Reaching a fork in the path, Bowman looked about him. Immediately before him, a great stone angel knelt in perpetual prayer. At its feet, an open book of carved granite proclaimed the names of those who were buried beneath. A fresh bouquet of flowers denoted a recent visit. Around him, ornate crucifixes studded the ground and rose like saplings from the ankle-high grass. His coat all the heavier from the rain, Bowman stood a while to catch his breath. He raised his eyes further up the hill towards a section of the cemetery dug into the surrounding hillside. A promenade of granite had been pressed into the escarpment, a series of imposing entrances giving access to the vaults beyond. It was here he saw her. Sitting in a pagoda for shelter, the woman in black was bolt upright, facing him, gazing impassively at the view at his back. Her umbrella folded neatly at her side, she rested a gloved hand on its handle as if she were awaiting an audience. Bowman approached cautiously, noticing the gentle rise and fall of the woman's shoulders as she recovered her breath from the chase. The hem of her dress was visible beneath her coat as she sat, and both were wet to her knees. Her boots, dainty and no doubt expensive, thought Bowman, were caked with mud. As his eyes rose past her prim waist and shoulders, he found himself confronted by a handsome but care-worn face. Standing outside the pagoda looking in, Inspector Bowman felt rather like an observer to some private play.

"For pity's sake, Inspector Bowman, come out of the rain." The woman's voice was clear and direct and served to bring Bowman's attention back to the matter in hand. Stepping into the pagoda, he shook the rain from his hat and smoothed his moustache with a gloved hand.

"You have me at a disadvantage," he said.

The mysterious woman held him in her gaze, a look of faint amusement passing over her features. "Yes, I am sure I do," she said, simply.

Bowman studied her carefully. Her dark brown hair, streaked with an iron grey, was scraped back over her head beneath her hat. She was perhaps fifty years old, but her eyes looked older. Where once they had obviously been a startling blue, they were now fading to a watery grey. The skin on her face was stretched tightly over her prominent cheekbones, but still there were lines about the eyes and mouth. Her head was held high on an elegant neck.

"However, inspector," she continued, "I have seen you twice before."

Bowman's eyebrows knitted together, the dark crease between them becoming all the more prominent in thought. "Twice?" he asked.

The woman nodded before she spoke, giving her the air of one humouring a rather slow child. "Once, of course, during that dreadful business at the Empire Rooms last evening," Bowman winced at the memory, "but firstly in the morning through the bow window to my bedroom."

The inspector was taken aback at this. A bow window? The only place he had been within the last two days that might make boast of such a thing was Doctor Henderson's residence in St John's Wood.

"Mrs Henderson?" he stuttered in surprise.

"Oh bravo, inspector. You're quite the detective, aren't you?"

Feeling suddenly rather foolish, Bowman realised he had quite forgotten to ask the doctor if he had been married. He recovered himself in a moment to address Mrs Henderson. "Why did you wish to meet me here today?"

He could see Mrs Henderson's hand alternately grasping and releasing the handle to her umbrella in agitation. Bowman had long ago learnt that a physical gesture may very often give an insight to the workings of the mind.

"To tell you the truth, inspector."

"The truth?" Bowman enunciated the words carefully.

Mrs Henderson lifted her head in an apparent moment of decision, her hand finally coming to rest at her side. "The truth about my husband. And the truth about my daughter."

It took Inspector Bowman a moment to collect his thoughts. "Mary?"

At that single word, Mrs Henderson's demeanour crumbled. She slumped forward on her seat and reached to her coat pocket for a handkerchief. Where only moments before she had been impassive and inscrutable, now she sobbed into her hands, the tears coursing freely from her eyes. Thinking to offer some comfort, Bowman sat beside her.

"I saw her picture in The Standard," she whispered. "Unmistakable, of course. It was Mary." Bowman nodded slowly. "My husband thought as much too," Mrs Henderson continued, folding her handkerchief in her hand as she spoke. "But he told me to put it from my mind."

"Why would he say such a thing, Mrs Henderson?" Bowman was leaning forward now. Mrs Henderson took a breath and turned to him.

"I believe he advised you that he had no daughter. How can a man deny his own flesh and blood?" There was a sudden silence as she contemplated her own question. For a moment, Bowman was convinced she might give an answer. Then, just as suddenly, her grief returned. "And she was so lovely a girl." Burying her face in her handkerchief again, Mrs Henderson turned away from the inspector, her shoulders heaving as great sobs escaped her. Bowman thought it best to do nothing but sit and wait. Looking around him, he took stock of what his companion had told him. So Mary was Doctor Henderson's daughter. What possible reason could he have had for lying? Thinking back to his earlier interview with the doctor, Bowman remembered the odd look on Henderson's face as he had heard the news of his daughter's discovery. What was that look? Bowman felt a movement at his side and turned to see Mrs Henderson settling herself again.

"My husband is a distinguished surgeon," she continued. "He is well known for his good works and his devotion to the poor."

Bowman remembered Pollard's comments from the day before. "So I hear."

Mrs Henderson couldn't help but hear the tone in Bowman's voice. "You must understand, inspector," she said sternly, "that he has worked very hard to attain his position. He is, therefore, always very careful to avoid scandal and insinuation, and presents himself at all times a decent, honest man."

Inspector Bowman couldn't disagree with that. Henderson had indeed presented himself as a very respectable man. "And Mary?" he asked.

Mrs Henderson looked out through the pagoda towards the city beyond the environs of the cemetery and from there to the horizon. As the rain fell in sheets around them, she held her handkerchief tightly in both hands as if it were some memento of the daughter she had lost.

"She was the sweetest blessing the Lord has ever seen fit to bestow upon either of us. The apple of her father's eye and she knew it. He was never a strict father, Inspector Bowman. Of course, he knew that a child has its place and should know it, but never a gentler, sweeter father have I seen."

"Mrs Henderson, what happened?" Bowman was afraid he might feel some resistance at the question, as if he might be pushing too hard against something not yet willing to give. To his surprise, however, Mrs Henderson answered him directly.

"Mary fell pregnant," she said, simply. "She was not yet eighteen and she had fallen with a child."

"I see." Bowman knew such a development would be hard to bear for a man of respectable reputation.

"My husband could not allow it." Mrs Henderson sat stock still, her eyes seemingly focused on events long past. Bowman felt obliged to press her again.

"And what became of the baby? Your grandchild?"

"It was never to be, inspector. My husband, as I said, is a surgeon of note. His knowledge of anatomy is unsurpassed." Again she turned to him, her eyes red with grief. "I must leave the rest to your imagination."

Bowman swallowed hard under her gaze and resisted the strange urge to clear his throat. "I understand. And what of Mary?"

Mrs Henderson gave a sigh and pursed her lips in the face of a painful memory. "She was removed from the house by force, and led to believe that it would no longer be her home. I had no further knowledge of her until I read of her discovery in the Thames."

Bowman nodded. "And your husband has denied having had a daughter ever since?"

"All trace of her, all memory, was removed. Her name has not been mentioned in my house again." Mrs Henderson cast her eyes to the ground around her. Even under the cover of the pagoda, the rain ran in rivulets to the stone bench where they sat.

"Does your husband know that you are here?" Bowman asked, delicately.

"He does not, and I would not wish him to."

"Of course."

Mrs Henderson drew another deep breath, as if trying to gain strength from the cold air. When she turned to face the inspector again, he saw a steely look of determination in her eyes. "And now, inspector," she said, gripping tight to the handle of her umbrella. "What became of my daughter?"

Bowman felt his mouth dry as he thought how best to proceed. "We are still in the early stages of the investigation," he blustered, his moustache twitching as he spoke.

Mrs Henderson looked downcast again. "I see. You think it best that I am kept in the dark."

"No, not at all." Bowman shifted uneasily on his seat. "Mrs Henderson, some things are far from clear. Many things in fact." The admission made him feel more uncomfortable still. "I will tell you all I know for certain." Swallowing hard, Bowman collected his thoughts as Mrs Henderson gazed at him, expectantly. As he spoke, she studied his lips intently as if she did not want to miss a word. "Your daughter was buried in a shallow grave some days ago at Chelsea Embankment." Bowman paused as he considered how best to approach the details.

"That is all you can tell me?" asked Mrs Henderson, her eyes wide.

Bowman swallowed again and felt the heat rise beneath his collar. "The details are - "

"How did she die, inspector?" Mrs Henderson was leaning towards him now, her mouth set in an expression of grim determination. "I have to know or I shall never rest."

Bowman gazed out to the cemetery beyond the pagoda, reluctant to meet Mrs Henderson's eyes as he continued. The haphazard graves and monuments gave the impression of leaning closer to hear, as if the dead themselves were witness.

"Once the body was recovered, we discovered bruising to the neck," Bowman cleared his throat. "It was hard to see initially due to some discolouration of the skin, but it would indicate that your daughter died from strangulation just days before. And then it seems, her head was struck from her body." Bowman had lowered his voice to a whisper, unwilling to give voice to such awful words. He felt a jolt pass through the woman at his side. A wave of horror shook her body, her hands moving involuntarily to her mouth. Bowman could see the conflict in her eyes.

"Please," she whispered, barely audible above the rain. "Go on."

Bowman wished himself anywhere but on that stone bench. "She had also had her tongue removed."

Now Mrs Henderson gave vent to her grief. "What kind of a beast - " she exclaimed through her sobs. Her body rocked as she gulped through her tears. Mrs Henderson was clearly doing her best to retain some semblance of control. Bowman fought the urge to hold her, settling instead for resting a hand upon her elbow. "Why?" Mrs Henderson asked in a pained whisper as she recovered herself.

Bowman felt helpless. "We don't know. She was then carried to Chelsea by a vagrant and buried."

"Did he kill my daughter?"

"We suspect he knew her murderer. While in our custody he admitted to the burying of a body in a sack. He also gave us the name of one in his gang. A Jabez Kane. He may have killed your daughter."

Mrs Henderson raised an eyebrow. "May?"

"Until we trace the man and bring him in, it's all we know for now."

Calmer now, Mrs Henderson nodded. "Do you know anything of Mary's life since she left my house, inspector?"

Bowman was surprised by the question. Strangely, he hadn't considered that she wouldn't know. But, now she had asked, just how much did he know himself?

"Tell me, inspector," Mrs Henderson pleaded. "Tell me everything."

Inspector Bowman frowned as he struggled to put his thoughts in order, stroking his moustache absently as he spoke. "Once she was turned out of your home, she naturally had nowhere to turn. With no one to protect her, she found herself on the streets where she soon drew attention to herself. It seems she may have found herself at the mercy of a man named Jeb Hardacre. Kane was one of his gang." Bowman could sense a picture building as he spoke. How precise the picture was he could not tell, but he was almost ashamed to admit to himself that he was finding the conversation useful. "Hardacre was known to us previously. We had an inspector watching him and his gang when your daughter's body was found. He heard tell of his involvement in everything from extortion to prostituting young ladies for money. He was, I'm afraid, a thief, a murderer and a pimp."

Mrs Henderson nodded again. "I see."

"He was once in our custody, but I regret to say he escaped from the cells."

"You're suggesting my daughter resorted to selling her body." Mrs Henderson's face had turned a ghastly white.

Bowman tried his best to offer some small comfort. "That's not certain. She was three years in his -" he chose his words carefully, "*Employment*. In that time, it seems her health deteriorated dramatically."

Mrs Henderson searched the inspector's face, as if his meaning might be found in the very lines around his eyes. "Thank you for your candour, inspector."

Rising suddenly from her seat, Mrs Henderson straightened her coat about her and moved to the balustrade that marked the pagoda's edge. Comprising almost the entire circumference of the edifice, it was hewn from granite and marble. At intervals, iron columns rose from the balustrade to support the roof, a wooden canopy painted on its underside with Biblical scenes. Bowman watched her for some minutes as she stood, gazing out at the tombs before her.

"Why were you at the Empire Rooms last night?" he asked, suddenly.

Mrs Henderson remained with her back to him, but he could tell the question had surprised her. "I have never before had any regard for such matters," she began. "But yesterday I saw a white feather float in at my window and I thought it was a sign." She turned, a look of apology on her face. "Mary always wore white as a child," she explained with a smile, "and she was pretty and delicate as a feather." Mrs Henderson shrugged at her explanation, keenly aware that it made no sense at all. "I went to the Empire Rooms in search of answers," she continued. "I found nothing there but arrant trickery. And you, Detective Inspector Bowman? Were you there to consort with the dead?"

Bowman shook his head, suddenly uncomfortable. "I thought only to consort with the living." He looked out onto the ragged tombs about him. "But the dead got in my way."

"I saw you leave the room," Mrs Henderson ventured. "You seemed distressed."

"I was - " he searched for the word Nathaniel Cokes had used in the foyer of the Empire Rooms that night. "Distracted."

Bowman offered the word by way of explanation, though truth be told he was far more worried by the incident than he would have her know. He had had such episodes at Colney Hatch, where Doctor Taylor had prescribed bromide for 'nerve weakness'. He had hoped to have seen the last of them.

Evidently deciding that the interview was over, Mrs Henderson made to move toward the pagoda's entrance. "Good day, inspector," she said, curtly. "And thank you."

Bowman rose to his feet as she passed. "Mrs Henderson. Would it be possible to speak with your husband today?"

"He is a busy man, forever at his surgery or his lockup in Lambeth." Bowman noticed a muscle twitch involuntarily at her cheek. "Come this evening, if you must, but I beg you inspector, not a word of this meeting."

As Inspector Bowman nodded his assent, Mrs Henderson smiled in thanks, unfurled her umbrella and stepped out into the unrelenting rain.

XX

A Deal Broken

Inspector Bowman slammed the newspaper down on the desk before him, sending up a plume of dust to mingle with the smoke from Watkins' cigar. The editor of The Standard had been scribbling in a large notebook, his weasel features set in an expression of deepest concentration. At Bowman's interruption, he put his pencil down and looked at the newspaper, folded so as to display its front-page headline. The inspector had bought the offending issue on his way back to Scotland Yard from Highgate. 'DEAD MAN WALKS! - SCOTLAND YARD BUNGLES AGAIN!'

Watkins recognised it as that day's early edition. He had, of course, been expecting a visit from Scotland Yard since the paper hit the stands, and now he regarded the inspector with barely concealed amusement. Bowman reached across the desk to extinguish Watkins' cigar in its ashtray.

"Yes, Inspector Bowman," Watkins asked, affecting innocence, "How may I be of service?"

His teeth set in an expression of exasperation, Bowman glared down at him, struggling hard to contain his rage. After the morning he had just endured, he was in no mood for Watkins' games. "Steer clear of Inspector Hicks, I said. I presume he was the source for this material?" Bowman waved the newspaper in front of Watkins' face to give emphasis to his words, sending several sheets of paper fluttering to the floor in his fury.

"He was a veritable mine of information," replied Watkins calmly, his hands held wide in innocent supplication. "And all of it offered freely."

Bowman planted his fists on the desk and thrust his head closer to the editor's face. "What's your game, Watkins?" he demanded, his voice a growl.

Watkins held Bowman's gaze a while, then stood to retrieve a box of safety matches from a shelf behind him. "If I remember correctly," he said playfully, opening a drawer at his desk as he spoke, "I was told the Yard could bear some criticism." Watkins took another cigar from the drawer, holding it to his ear and rolling it between his thumb and index finger.

"You were also told I was to have the final say on what you print." Bowman unfolded the paper and held the front page aloft. "I don't recall giving you permission for this."

Judging it to be of adequate freshness, Watkins bit the end from his cigar and spat it to the floor. "It was the truth, inspector," he said simply as he lifted the cigar to his lips. "Truth needs no permission."

"You are completely undermining my investigation, and I will not allow it." Bowman moved to the window as Watkins lit his cigar, sending clouds of smoke billowing into the room about him.

"You have yet to find a credible witness to the young woman's murder; you have no positive identification, no motive and no suspect." Watkins sat on a corner of his desk, perfectly at ease in his own domain. "I serve our readership," he continued, "and I think they should know."

"The investigation of a murder is a delicate matter," Bowman hissed. "And we have discovered more than you know, Watkins."

"Really, Inspector Bowman? And do you not think that would be of interest to our readers?" Watkins looked down at his cigar, rolling it between his fingers again as if deep in thought. "As would the explanation as to why one of Scotland Yard's most eminent inspectors was consorting with phantoms at the Empire Rooms last night."

There was a silence in the room, broken only by the rattling of the rain against the window. Watkins looked up from his cigar. Bowman was plainly taken aback at his remark. "You had me followed?" he asked, incredulous.

"Tut, tut, inspector," Watkins tried his best to look hurt. "We would never stoop so low. Douglas McCrimmon is our theatre critic and was there in an entirely professional capacity." He leaned across to reach for his notebook, leafing through its pages with a half concealed smile. "These Spiritualist meetings are becoming quite the rage. It's only right that our readers see them represented in our pages. Although I cannot say it was worth the entry price, McCrimmon's copy makes for fascinating reading. It was obviously an extraordinary event." He looked up at the inspector pointedly. "I've no doubt our readers would be most interested to hear of it."

Bowman eyed the newspaperman warily. "I was performing a duty," he said, suddenly worried.

"As an inspector?" teased Watkins.

"As a friend." Bowman's jaw was tightening as he spoke.

Watkins threw his notebook down on the desk and stood to join Bowman at the window. Standing toe to toe with the inspector, he thrust out his chest, evidently enjoying the moment. "Can you not imagine for a moment," he began, a self-righteous tone in his voice, "how such a thing might look to the public?"

Bowman was determined not to be intimidated. "What is it to them how a man spends his time?" he retorted, standing his ground beneath Watkins' gaze.

"They pay your wages, Inspector Bowman!" Watkins barked, pacing back to his desk. He smoothed his red hair with the flat of a hand and turned to regard the inspector with something approaching contempt. "I think they will be concerned that Detective Inspector Bowman is at a loss. That he has given up all hope of finding the murderer by conventional means and so, in desperation, has turned to the unconventional. Is Scotland Yard now looking for answers in the spirit world, inspector?" He gave emphasis to his words with a jab of a yellowing finger.

"That's preposterous," Bowman scoffed. "Is that all you have?"

"By no means, inspector."

Bowman's eyes narrowed. What was Watkins playing at now? As he watched, the wiry newspaperman was walking to a set of drawers by the door. Reaching inside and leafing through some papers, Watkins drew out a facsimile of a front page from The Evening Standard. Wordlessly, he slid it across the desk. Bowman leaned in to read the headline; 'INSPECTOR ADMITTED TO LUNATIC ASYLUM AFTER DEATH OF WIFE.'

"It's from May of last year," Watkins purred. "The morning edition, just a few days after your incident in Whitechapel."

Bowman felt he was suddenly at sea. The room seemed to pitch and roll. He braced his legs against the swell and grabbed the sides of the table before him, forcing himself to breathe. One word stood out from the page; 'LUNATIC'.

"The commissioner has faith in me," hissed Bowman through clenched teeth.

"Really?" continued Watkins, rolling his cigar between his fingers. "Our readers have long memories, Inspector Bowman. I think they will be concerned that a madman has been left in charge of a murder investigation. And if that decision can be laid at the commissioner's door, it's all the worse for him."

The inspector took a breath as he considered the import of Watkins' words. "Is that what your leader will suggest tomorrow?" he asked, steadily.

Watkins could see the byline now; 'Who would send a madman to solve a murder?' He took a draw from his cigar, peering through the resultant fug at the disconsolate figure by the window. "Unless you can convince me otherwise by this evening," he said with a shrug, "it is."

The row of arches stretched as far as the eye could see. Above them, the suburban lines of the London and South Western Railway spread out like the tendrils of a web. From Waterloo, it raced away to Richmond, Staines, Datchet and Windsor, as if fleeing the very city that sustained it. Where it crossed marshy land, great tracts of line were set upon arches, and so the railway strode like a colossus across the landscape.

Jeb Hardacre loped into the yard that ran alongside the arches outside Lambeth. Fat beads of rain slapped about him as he walked with weary steps, pulling a hospital blanket about his head for shelter. Picking his way between the puddles, Hardacre cursed himself for not stopping to pull on his boots at the hospital. At the time, speed had seemed of the essence but now he regretted not taking the time to effect his escape with more care. His feet were bloodied, filthy and cold. Steadying himself with a shaking hand against the arches, Hardacre scanned the yard before him. There, in the furthest corner, a set of doors stood ajar. Making his way along the line, he brushed the spray from his eyes and shook the rain from his great, matted beard. Looking nervously about him, Hardacre knocked at the partially opened door. Pulling the blanket tighter around him as he waited for a response, Hardacre felt the chill reach to his very marrow. Growing impatient at being left to wait in such conditions, he was about to push against the doors and make his way inside, when a pair of hands reached out to him from within. Clutching him by the lapels of his ragged coat, the hands pulled him almost off his feet and into the lockup beneath the arch, the doors slamming shut behind him.

XXI

The Penny Drops

The log fire at The Silver Cross popped and spat from the grate. As Sergeant Graves warmed his feet on the hearth, he looked about him at the bustling scene. It was a testament to Harris the landlord that The Silver Cross was always busy. There were many public houses within a stone's throw of Scotland Yard, but Harris had established himself as one of the more trustworthy landlords in Whitehall. The beer was never less than foaming and there was seldom any trouble from the clientele. As a result it attracted, he liked to think, a better class of customer, with more than half a dozen of Scotland Yard's finest among them. Harris tipped a wink to Sergeant Graves from the bar where he stood, towel in hand, drying a tray of freshly cleaned glasses and tankards. Graves smiled in acknowledgment and sunk even deeper into the high-backed leather chair by the fire. The rain streaked down the window behind him, collecting in pools on the sill before dripping to the street. Reaching out to the table at his side and lifting his glass to his lips, Sergeant Graves could think of nowhere he would rather be. His thoughts were interrupted by a flurry of movement at the door. Inspector Bowman stood, stamping the rain from his feet, water dripping to the floor from the brim of his hat. As he cast around for a sight of his colleague, Graves caught his eye and motioned that he should join him at the fire. As Bowman approached, Graves gave a nod in the direction of Harris, a signal to bring another glass to the table.

"A flood of Biblical proportions, Sergeant Graves," Bowman said archly as he hung his coat on a hook by the chimney breast.

"It is that, sir," Graves replied, amused to see the inspector's hat beginning to steam in the warmth of the fire. "I'd be glad enough to spend the rest of the afternoon at this table."

Bowman agreed. "And after my encounter with a certain Mr Watkins this afternoon, I'd be inclined to join you."

"Any word on Hardacre?" Graves asked.

Bowman took a breath. He shook his head and wiped the rain from his moustache with a handkerchief. "He appears to be rather fleet of foot for a dead man. What news from the Shipping Office?" Bowman pulled his chair up to the table and rested his chin thoughtfully on his hands, eager to hear Graves' report.

Sergeant Graves pulled his notebook from a pocket. "Plenty," he replied. "Though how much is of use remains to be seen."

"I'll be the judge of that, sergeant," said Bowman leaning back in his seat as Harris delivered a full jar to the table. "Just tell me all you have."

Graves squinted hard to read his scrawl. Even in his inside pocket, the rain had soaked through to dampen the pages, causing them to pucker and stick together. Graves lifted and turned each dimpled page with care until he found his place. "The Nimrod was registered at Southampton in July 1854. She belongs to the Indies Trading Company and has, over the past thirty-five years, completed more than thirty voyages to the Indies and Bengal to trade for spices, coffee and jute. According to crew manifests which, I have to say, are far from complete, one Jeb Hardacre was recruited to the galley staff some twenty five years ago."

"Galley staff?" Bowman's brow knitted together in thought. "So, he was the ship's cook?"

"Nothing quite so grand, I'm afraid. He's listed as the kitchen porter. The lowest of the low, I would suggest." Seeing no response from Bowman save for a look of impatience, Graves cleared his throat and returned his attention to his notebook. "It appears that there was some incident on board. Hardacre was implicated and placed in confinement on board by the captain, a Mr George Biddel of Tilbury, since deceased."

"Very thorough, Sergeant Graves." Bowman sipped from his beer as he thought. Just what was the connection with Doctor Henderson?

"Once ashore, though," Graves continued, spurred on by his superior's words of encouragement, "he escaped. Nothing more was heard from him until we had word of his activities in Southwark. But, for twenty years, he just disappeared."

"Not for the last time, it would seem." Bowman stared into the fire, as if the answers he sought could be found in its dancing flames.

Graves thumbed through the pages of his notebook, a look of concentration on his face. "Then I spoke to Inspector Treacher from 'H' Division."

"Oh?"

Graves paused to down the last of his beer, wiping the froth from his upper lip with his jacket sleeve before he spoke. "From the information he gathered in his time in Hardacre's den, it was clear to him that Hardacre had placed himself at the very heart of the criminal community. Treacher knew of various petty thieves and pickpockets who answered to him, and there was talk of him providing murderers and blackmailers for public use."

"He offered criminals for hire?"

Graves nodded. "And charged a great deal for the pleasure. He grew as rich as he grew fat, but kept it all in his den as we saw."

Bowman remembered the collection of treasure in Hardacre's cellar. "To what end?"

"Treacher believes that he planned to sell up and move abroad."

Bowman pushed himself back from the table, stretching his legs out towards the fire to warm his still damp feet. "What's Treacher's next move?"

"Hardacre's whereabouts is his prime concern," Graves replied, snapping his notebook shut. "He is going to talk to anyone suspected of having any recent contact with him. Prostitutes, petty thieves, hospitals."

"Hospitals?"

Graves nodded, almost enthusiastically. "He acquired bodies for dissection. Criminals, usually." In what Bowman thought was an entirely inappropriate gesture, Graves flashed him a mischievous smile. "People tend to turn a blind eye." Not for the first time, Bowman noted Graves' propensity to enjoy the more macabre aspects of his job.

"Quite the jack-of-all-trades, isn't he? Any clues as to where he might be?"

"He's got several hideouts, apparently," Graves continued. "The den in Southwark of course, but we're guessing he won't be going back there any time soon. The location has been sealed and 'H' Division are keeping watch. He is also a deft hand at navigating the sewers."

As Sergeant Graves spoke, Bowman's attention was drawn out the window, across the rain-beaten street to the other side of the road. As carriages and cabs rattled past, his eye alighted on a butcher's shop. In the failing light of the day, lamps had been lit at the window, illuminating the scene within as the butcher struggled to his block with a side of pork.

"He also visits a lockup vault just outside Lambeth," continued Graves as Bowman watched the scene unfold in the butcher's shop. Light flashed on blade as the butcher reached for his knife. The great hatchet was held high in anticipation and, for a moment, Bowman felt himself holding his breath. A moment later and the hatchet fell. The head was dispatched with a clean, professional stroke and the carcass prepared for another blow. As he watched from his chair in The Silver Cross, Inspector Bowman became aware he was sitting stock-still, his glass of porter paused in its transit from the table to his lips.

"What did you say?" he asked.

"A lockup," Graves repeated. "At Lambeth."

The butcher's hatchet fell again and a leg was severed. Bowman seemed in a trance. As Sergeant Graves leaned forward in his chair, it was as if he could see a thousand thoughts collide in Bowman's eyes. "Sir?" he offered, concerned.

"Why?" Bowman turned to face his companion, his brow creased into his habitual frown.

"Why what, sir?"

"Why does Hardacre visit a lockup in Lambeth?"

"Treacher wasn't sure. He just heard talk of it amongst Hardacre's gang."

Bowman was suddenly galvanised into action. Turning to the chimney breast, he grabbed his coat from the hook. "Drink up, Sergeant Graves, and come with me."

Graves looked through the window to the rain beyond. "In that?"

Inspector Bowman was almost to the door already. "Yes, in that."

"Where are we going?" Graves rose reluctantly from his chair by the fire.

Bowman fixed him with a determined glare. "To catch a rat," he said meaningfully.

The lockup was one of eight that ran the length of the arches beneath the London and South Western Railway. At first glance, there was little to distinguish it from the others; all were in possession of a stout pair of doors, one of which contained a single window. All were of the same height and interior dimensions and all gave out to the rain-spattered railway yard containing surplus wood, bricks and metal. One particular lockup was, however, distinguishable from the others in one important respect. It contained the body of a dead man.

The carcass lay on a makeshift table in the centre of the room. Around it, wooden shelves groaned with boxes of medical equipment and nautical mementos. Syringes and flasks stood alongside sextants and maps. Bottles and vials crowded onto every available space next to burners and test tubes, each carefully labelled with a neat, cursive hand. Cobwebs were strung from post to beam and a thick layer of dust lay over every surface. With the window in the door obscured by a tattered strip of curtain, a single lamp lit the gloom. It hung from an improvised hook in the middle of the ceiling, illuminating the grisly scene beneath. Hardacre's body lay on the narrow table, its arms hanging loose at his side. His great mountain of a stomach protruded up to the ceiling, pulling his shirt tails from his waistband to expose an expanse of belly. His bare feet hung over the table's end, calloused and dirty from his walk in the rain but, most apparent of all, was the thick slick of blood that oozed from his neck to drip to the floor. It ran in viscous gobs from a wide wound running from one side to the other. This time there was no escaping it. Jeb Hardacre was dead.

Doctor Joshua Henderson stood in a corner just beyond the reach of the light, a long-handled, bloodied knife at his feet. It lay where he had dropped it, amongst the dust and filth that had accumulated over years. Henderson stood panting, his breath condensing in the cold air. The sweat on his forehead betrayed the exertions of the previous few minutes. Moving silently to a corner shelf, he took a syringe and bottle from an unmarked box. Uncoiling a length of Indian rubber tubing to use as a tourniquet, Henderson rolled up a coat sleeve to expose an arm and dropped to his knees, unscrewing the lid from the bottle and fumbling to remove the protective casing from the needle as he did so. Pulling the tubing tight above his elbow, Henderson drew the liquid from the bottle to the syringe and let it slip deep into the vein. A gentle pressure on the plunger, and he let the tubing go to feel the drug coursing through his body. A familiar warmth enveloped him. For a moment, Henderson gave himself completely to its effects, his eyes rolling back into their sockets as he succumbed to its sweet oblivion. Then, with a sudden vigour he rose, shook his head and looked around him with a sense of urgent clarity. The body was in need of disposal, but it would be a long process and his absence would surely soon be noticed at home. It would not do to arouse suspicion now. Confident that Hardacre would not be found that night, Henderson straightened his coat sleeve over his arm, wiped the dirt from his knees and resolved to return in the morning to complete his grisly task.

"Any idea which one?" Bowman pressed his back hard against the wall as he looked out at the railway yard before him. He and Graves had found the yard by a process of elimination, following the line by cab through Lambeth. A row of lockup vaults stretched away before him in the thumping rain, each the same as the one before save the numbers chalked upon their doors.

"No idea at all sir," rasped Graves from his position behind him. "But there aren't that many."

Bowman wiped the rain from his face with a look of exasperation. He had thought of calling upon Mrs Henderson for details of her husband's whereabouts, but felt any further delay might well prove costly. "You take the last four, Sergeant Graves, I'll take the nearest." Graves gave a cheery nod and stepped out into the full force of the rain. "And be careful," Bowman hissed after him, but he was already beyond hearing.

As Graves ran across the yard, keeping out of sight as best he could, Bowman made his way to the first vault in the line. Finding it locked, he set his shoulder to the door and pushed. The inspector was surprised to feel the doors give beneath his weight and open sufficiently so that he could squeeze through the gap between them and gain access to the lockup beyond.

The first thing he noticed was the smell. From long experience of gaining access to such places, Bowman immediately recognised the acrid tang of varnish. Waiting a moment for his eyes to grow accustomed to the gloom, Bowman looked around as best he could for any signs of life. The lockup was lined with shelves of tools; lathes and saws and others Bowman did not recognise. An object was placed in the middle of the floor. Measuring perhaps six feet long and four wide, it stood almost five feet tall. It was covered in a large, greasy sheet. Moving cautiously towards it, Bowman reached out to the object, carefully lifting a corner of the sheet to peer beneath. Even in the dark, he could see it was an ornate pump organ such as one might see in a small church or chapel. From its condition, Bowman could tell it was in the midst of renovation. The foot-pumped bellows at the base of the instrument were torn and misaligned, the wooden panelling in various states of repair. Bowman let the sheet drop and cast a final look around the room. Satisfied it was otherwise empty, he moved towards the exit, sliding his feet through the sawdust on the floor in the half-light so as not to lose his footing. Just as he put his hand to the door, however, he felt a pressure against it from the other side and a panting Sergeant Graves squeezed through the gap to join him. Placing a finger to his lips to indicate that Bowman should remain quiet, Graves pointed with the other hand to the small window in the door, pressing himself into the darkness of the wall as he did so. Bowman joined him, pulling to one side the rag that hung at the small window by way of a curtain. He peered through, anxious to see what Graves had found.

"Looks like fortune is with us," whispered Graves with his customary smile. He was plainly enjoying the subterfuge. Out in the yard, Bowman saw Doctor Henderson walk briskly past the lockup, a top hat on his head and an umbrella in his hand.

"Did you see where he came from?" asked Bowman as he watched the doctor leave the yard, his purposeful stride increasing with every step. But Graves had already put his shoulder to the door and eased himself through the gap, motioning with his head that Bowman should follow.

In the stinging rain, Graves pushed against the doors of the last vault in the row. The padlock held them fast. While Bowman kept a lookout for any sign of Henderson returning, Graves looked around amidst the mud for a brick large enough to smash the lock. A suitable candidate found, he hurled it against the padlock until the mechanism gave way and the door swung open on its hinges. The two men pushed their way in and looked around. Medical implements and nautical instruments lined the walls and even hung on hooks from the ceiling. Sergeant Graves whistled at the eclectic collection of surgical saws, lancets and rasps, dividers, astrolabes and almanacs. Soon, however, his eyes were drawn to the middle of the room and the body that lay on its rickety bier.

"His throat's been cut." Bowman was standing beside Hardacre's body, gesturing towards the slick of blood on the floor. "And recently, too."

"Well," Graves took a step closer, wiping the rain from his face with a sleeve. "He won't be walking out of here again."

"Graves, stay here with the body and be on your guard. I'm going after Henderson." Bowman was already at the door.

"Then he's our man, sir?" Graves turned to his companion with a look of wide-eyed enquiry.

"Oh yes, Sergeant Graves," Bowman smoothed his moustache with a gloved hand. "He's our man for sure."

XXII

On Lambeth Bridge

Lambeth Bridge had been in a forlorn state for many years. Crossing the Thames between the Palace of Westminster and Lambeth Palace, its steep approaches and doubts about its safety had been enough to deter all but pedestrian traffic. As a result, revenue from the tollbooths at either end had not been enough to pay for its repair. It stood on an historic site, its termination on the Lambeth side being just a few yards north of an old Horseferry landing stage. Originally an impressive sight, the bridge was divided into three spans along its length, each one resting on immense piers that rose from the waters beneath. It was a shadow of its former self. The road was pitted and cracked and the great twisted cables were coloured with rust. Great lumps of masonry had fallen from its side exposing the rusted iron girders that held the piers in place.

Doctor Henderson had known he was being followed for several minutes. As he approached the bridge from Lambeth Road, he had turned to see a familiar figure not a hundred yards behind him. Even with his hat pulled down and his collar up, Henderson had easily discerned the figure of Inspector Bowman, his face set into a determined expression as he strode through the rain in pursuit. Henderson had quickened his step in response, but found himself matched for speed as he turned into the bridge approach. Behind him, he had heard Bowman blow on his whistle to summon help and now, as Lambeth Bridge came into sight, Henderson knew he was running out of time. Weaving between the few passers by who were braving the rain, he threw his umbrella ahead of him and darted down an alley off the main road. The tenements rose up ominously at either side as he broke into a run. Beneath the relentless rain, only the hardiest of ice still clung to the roofs and windowsills above him. The melt water ran from the walls and broken gutters to the ground, making the passageway treacherous underfoot. Taking no heed of the water as it splashed around his ankles, Henderson thought to double back upon himself and emerge back onto Lambeth Road behind Inspector Bowman. Beyond that, he had to admit, he had no plan. As he rounded a corner, however, Henderson felt something clutch at his coat tails as they billowed up behind him. Bowman had made up the distance between them. Losing his footing on the wet ground, Doctor Henderson crashed to the floor, splaying his arms ahead of him in a vain attempt to break his fall. Inspector Bowman, now scrabbling on the floor with him, held him fast by his waist. As his hat rolled away before him, Henderson looked up to see a pair of legs running swiftly towards him.

"I've got him, Graves!" Henderson heard Bowman shout. Narrowing his eyes against the rain, he could see Graves coming ever nearer, his trouser legs sopping wet from the puddles around him. Lifting a knee to his chest, Henderson summoned his strength and slammed a foot into Bowman's shoulder. With a yelp of pain, the inspector released his hold and Henderson was able to scramble to his feet. Momentarily losing his balance, his momentum sent him crashing into Sergeant Graves who fell against the wall behind him then slid to the ground, winded by the impact. Seizing the advantage, Henderson broke into a run towards Lambeth Bridge, leaving his two pursuers sprawled on the ground behind him.

"Are you alright, sir?" Graves found his breath and crawled to where Inspector Bowman lay, clutching at his shoulder.

"Yes, Graves," Bowman winced. "Go after him." Graves hesitated, concerned at Bowman's condition. "I'm with you," entreated the inspector. "Go!" As he rose slowly to his feet, Bowman saw Graves take a deep breath to compose himself, then disappear round the corner back onto Lambeth Road in pursuit of his quarry.

As quickly as the rain had begun, so it stopped. The heavy, grey clouds, still pregnant with their load, loured ominously over the city as Graves approached Lambeth Bridge, but no rain fell. He could hear the water cascading from gutters, but he was grateful not to feel the sting of rain upon his face. As he swept his hair back from his forehead and wiped his face with a hand, Graves focused on the bridge ahead. There, clinging to the outside of one of the great piers that supported the structure, he could see a figure. Turning to his side, Graves saw his companion at his shoulder. Bowman was clutching at his upper arm and panting for breath. Since their struggle in the alley, both men had found themselves soaked to the skin and Inspector Bowman couldn't help but shiver against the cold. Through all this, Sergeant Graves was certain there was something wrong. Despite his exertions, Bowman's breath was just too erratic, his eyes too wide.

Graves regarded him cautiously. "Shall I handle this, sir?"

Bowman shook his head. "Together," he panted, clutching at his chest. "We'll do it together".

"Well, there he is." Graves raised an arm to point at Henderson. He was leaning out over the seething Thames, both hands clutching at the bridge behind him. "I think he's going to jump."

"We must prevent that at all costs," gasped Bowman, wincing against the pain in his chest. Inspector Bowman noticed the daylight beginning to fade around him. Soon the lamplighters would be about their business, even in this most inclement of weather. In the gathering gloom, he walked cautiously to the side of the bridge, peering over at the river beneath. Oblivious to the water dripping onto him from the trees above, the inspector could see that, after the deluge of the last few hours, only the shallowest water was still frozen. Even at the banks, the thin ice was cracking and breaking away to join the seething waters. The river churned and boiled, a tumult of such force that Bowman knew Henderson wouldn't stand a chance if he jumped. In spite of the urgency of the situation, his attention was drawn inexorably to the water beneath the bridge. The swirling motion turned his stomach and he gulped as the gorge rose in his throat. It took an effort of will to turn his eyes from the swell.

"We've got to get to him Graves, but if he sees either one of us approaching - "

"Leave it to me sir," Graves interrupted. "Keep him talking."

Bowman turned to his companion, a look of concern playing about his face. "What do you have in mind?"

"The unexpected." With a nod and a wink quite out of keeping with their circumstances, Sergeant Graves walked away, plainly mindful that Doctor Henderson should see him do so. Affecting a nonchalance that Bowman would have found almost amusing under other circumstances, Graves sauntered back down Lambeth Road, away from the bridge and back towards the alley where they had first accosted Henderson.

Standing alone at the river's edge, Bowman became aware that Doctor Henderson had seen him. Reasoning that it was too late to hide, Bowman decided to make the best of the situation and engage with the doctor. He walked slowly to the middle of the road and, holding his hands out by his side to show that he was not armed, proceeded towards the bridge. With each step, Bowman felt his legs grow weak. His vision was blurred. When he had come within twenty feet of Henderson, the doctor turned his head to meet his gaze.

"That's quite far enough, Inspector Bowman," Henderson cautioned, his teeth set into a grimace of determination. Bowman could see that, like him, the doctor was soaked to the skin. His long frock coat was beginning to steam in the slowly warming air and his hair was plastered flat against his head. Gone was the immaculately presented, professional gentleman Inspector Bowman had met in the drawing room of Acacia Road just twenty-four hours before.

"Doctor Henderson," Bowman began, coming to a stop as directed. "That is a foolish thing to consider."

Henderson stared down at the swirling maelstrom beneath him. "There is a comfort to be had in choosing the place and time of one's death, inspector," he said, his hair blowing about his ears in the wind.

"That's not a comfort you afforded to Jeb Hardacre." Bowman looked about him for a sight of Graves. Just what had his companion meant?

"Interestingly," began Henderson, "there are several distinct ways of drowning. In perhaps a tenth of all cases, the victim dies of asphyxiation due to the reflex closing of the vocal cords."

As the doctor spoke, seemingly oblivious to his situation, Bowman moved slowly to the opposite side of the bridge. Casting his eyes downwards, he glimpsed a hand grasping at a ledge beneath the main span. Below him, Graves was almost bent double in the space between the iron supports. Struggling to find purchase on the ledge above in order to keep his balance, the sergeant stepped gingerly out over the river. Bowman could see that, as he made slow progress towards the centre of the bridge, Graves was able to come to his full height, feeling his way carefully along the wet girders with his feet. Turning back to Doctor Henderson, Bowman could see he was being watched.

"Do not come a step closer, inspector," intoned the doctor, "or I shall slip from your grasp forever."

There was a calm, sing-song quality to his voice that Bowman found unnerving. It was as if the doctor was perfectly at ease with his predicament. Thankful that Henderson had mistaken his movements as an attempt to edge closer, Bowman made great play of coming back to the centre of the bridge. "I spoke to your wife today," he began, aware that if Sergeant Graves was to stand a chance of reaching the doctor before he fell he would need all the time he could get. "She would miss you."

Quite unexpectedly, Henderson threw his head back and laughed. When he finally spoke, Bowman noticed a manic gleam in his eye and an edge to his voice that belied his outward calm. "If you really spoke to my wife today, then you will know that she feels no love for me, nor I for her."

"She spent three years aching for news of her daughter."

"And now she has it," Henderson replied simply. "Mary is dead."

"Killed by your hand." Bowman held the doctor's gaze. A slow, uneven smile spread across Henderson's face as he contemplated Bowman's words.

"I see you fancy yourself as quite the master detective, inspector."

"No more than you the master surgeon." Bowman needed Henderson to stay exactly where he was. He took a guess that he was not a man to let such insinuations stand. As long as

Bowman appealed directly to the doctor's own sense of superiority, he knew he would not jump.

"I have a reputation, inspector. Something that you have yet to earn."

"Of course. Your reputation." Bowman looked down at the cracked and crumbling bridge surface with forced nonchalance. "The only thing in your mind when your daughter presented herself to you in her pregnant state. How the tongues would wag." Raising his eyes again, Bowman could see his words had hit their mark.

"What else do you know, inspector?"

Henderson's eyes burned with a ferocious intensity. Shuffling where he stood in spite of himself, Bowman resisted the urge to clear his throat and tried to affect an authoritative air as he spoke. "I know that during your time as ship's doctor aboard the Nimrod, you met a certain Jeb Hardacre. I know there was an incident on board and I know that from that moment, Hardacre has been in your debt. You will need to enlighten me further as to the nature of the contract between you."

Even from twenty paces, Inspector Bowman could see that Henderson was transported in his mind to events long ago and many miles away. Knowing that Graves needed every precious minute to scale the bridge beneath him, Bowman was content to indulge the doctor in his reverie.

XXIII

NIMROD

Joshua Henderson had much to celebrate. Having recently received his accreditation with the Royal College of Surgeons, he felt vindicated in his choice of a career in medicine. A hard and expensive training had left him almost penniless, his private savings spent and his family unwilling to lend him more. But with his accreditation came the most valuable commodity of all; opportunity. Throwing himself upon the world with all the energy of one half his age, Henderson considered himself at a turning point at last. In truth, at almost thirty years old he was already middle-aged, but opportunity could be found at any age if the wind was fair. The metaphor was apt, thought Henderson, as he lay in his cabin on board the merchant vessel Nimrod, en route to Bengal. The voyage out to Chittagong had been as uneventful as a journey of three thousand miles might be expected to be. In his post as ship's doctor, his concern had been for the welfare of the eleven-man crew that manned the Nimrod, and in particular their diet. Henderson had had no say in the stores and provisions that had been loaded aboard at Southampton, and the first few days at sea were marked by uninspiring food served unenthusiastically by the surly galley staff. No fresh fruit or vegetables had been allowed for in the inventory and the resultant grey, floury broths had been almost unpalatable to a man of higher tastes. Moreover, Doctor Henderson knew that such a diet would result in him being far busier than he intended. His motivation in accepting his post on board the Nimrod had been entirely selfish. To see the world and receive an income for it had seemed an ideal opportunity for a man with time to spare, and Henderson was determined that it would not be spoiled by having to administer to a shipload of sick and dying sailors. Speaking with the captain, a large, thickset man with fewer teeth than any living man Henderson had ever met, the doctor had been able to arrange the taking on of more nutritious stores at Lisbon. He had overseen the buying of fruit in person, even allowing himself to break into a rare sweat as he helped load the crates aboard. Spanish oranges and grapefruits were soon regular accompaniments to the otherwise uninspiring meals the crew had to suffer, and Henderson made a mental note to argue for the purchase of spices as soon as they reached their destination in the East. He was determined that the voyage home at least would be characterised by a more varied and palatable menu. In the light of a more nutritious diet, Henderson was spared being presented with the usual ailments of travel by sea. He saw none of the vitamin and mineral deficiencies about which he had read with horror before his voyage began. Instead, he found himself troubled only by the occasional crewman complaining of sunburn or of having received a bump to the head in the course of his duties. As a result, Henderson was free to peruse at length the many books he had brought aboard, sketch the shores of foreign lands as they rolled past and stand on deck of an evening to watch the sun set over strange waters.

It was never his intention to get to know the crew. Beyond the odd, formal dip of the head in the morning as he encountered each man going about his business, Henderson contrived to have as little to do with them as possible with the exception of Captain Biddel whose company, despite appearances, was pleasant enough. Henderson was content to tolerate his rather exuberant manner and tall tales in exchange for the opportunity to eat at the captain's table each night. As captain, Biddel had a part share in both the ship and its cargo, and was pleased enough to have all his crew in good health as they docked at Chittagong. He was astute enough to realise that this was in no small way due to Henderson's insistence they be fed a decent diet and he had agreed to give the good doctor a small portion of his personal profits the moment they made landfall back at Southampton. It was a gesture Henderson had appreciated but, as one also made under the influence of drink, not one by which he had set any great store.

Aside from Biddel, Henderson saw little to recommend in the crew. With the exception of the purser, a stuffy, officious man with the air of one dissatisfied with his station in life, all the crew were taken from the lower classes. They drank to excess when they could and spent much of their time, it seemed to Henderson, devising excuses by which they might be relieved of their duties. Chief among them was the kitchen porter, a rough barrel of a man with a thick beard that obscured a good half of his face. Spending his time below decks scrubbing pans and preparing the food with the cook, he was only seen at mealtimes when he would serve the food with a distinct lack of enthusiasm and, more often than not, an air of genuine menace. It was rumoured among the crew that he would spit on the food if he was crossed and Henderson believed him to be the cause of many a black eye in his time on board the Nimrod. He was plainly a man to be avoided. Henderson came to know him as Jeb Hardacre.

A week out of Lisbon, Doctor Henderson had the opportunity to study Hardacre's fabled temper at close quarters. At dinner one night a young able seaman, Perryman, was found to have cheated at cards. Rumbles of discontent had emanated from the ship's crew and from Hardacre in particular. An inveterate gambler, he had lost the contents of his small purse to Perryman with a week's ration of rum besides. It was discovered that Perryman had been hiding cards up his sleeve. Goaded by the men around him, Hardacre had launched a ferocious attack upon the poor man. His fist had landed again and again upon his face, splitting his nose and cracking a tooth. The purser, a lean man of principle, had intervened and the matter was brought before the captain. Biddel sat behind his desk, his large hands clenched into fists of frustration as Hardacre and Perryman stood before him. Doctor Henderson was granted a seat in the corner as witness to the proceedings. Hardacre's skin shone like burnished leather in the lamplight, his great beard cascading over his heaving chest. Perryman was altogether a different prospect. Standing at no more than five and a half feet tall, he had a head of thick, blond hair. His normally bright, rosy complexion was spoiled by a great swelling across his face and, despite having been attended to by the doctor, blood still seeped from his bloated nose. Standing with his hands at his side and his eyes to the floor, he had the air and appearance of a naughty schoolboy who had been called for admonishment to the headmaster's office. Biddel fingered the great Bible on the desk before him. It was richly decorated in gold leaf with the ship's name and the picture of a mermaid on a rock. Also on the desk between the men, Henderson could see the coins that Perryman had won from his opponent in a game of cribbage.

"He cheated, sir," Hardacre growled. "Pure and simple."

Biddel thumped his fist down hard on his Bible. "I will not have insubordination aboard the Nimrod, Mr Hardacre," he growled. Hardacre fell silent, though his eyes still burned with a dangerous disobedience. "In matters such as these," continued the captain, "I defer to a higher authority than maritime law." His great fingers leafed through the pages of his Bible until he found a marker he had placed there earlier. He had plainly rehearsed his arguments. Placing a pair of half moon spectacles upon his nose, Biddel read from the yellowing pages, tracing each word with his finger so he did not lose his place. It was an endearing affectation, thought Henderson from his corner. "Timothy; Chapter six, verse ten; For the love of money is the root of all kinds of evil." The droll captain leafed through the pages again, pulling at another marker to find his place. "Proverbs tells us, "Wealth gained hastily will dwindle."

"Chapter and verse will not get my coinage back. Nor my week's worth of rum, neither."

"Your coinage is forfeit. It will be divided among the purser, myself and Doctor Henderson." Hardacre let out a low, rumbling growl. Captain Biddel rose from his chair and leaned towards the two men. "I will not have gambling aboard the Nimrod!" At this, Hardacre launched himself with a mighty roar at Perryman. Grabbing the unsuspecting able seaman by his tousled hair, he proceeded to kick, punch and bite his quarry with almost animal-like ferocity. It took the captain and two ratings to hold him down. While Perryman slid unconscious to the floor, Biddel hollered his orders to his men. "Take this beast to the brig and there let him stay without food or water for three days and nights. If he is disagreeable or resists confinement, feed him to the sharks!"

As Jeb Hardacre was dragged from the room, globules of spittle and blood flying from his foaming mouth, Doctor Henderson was left to tend to Perryman's wounds as best he could.

Once at port in Bengal, the crew worked hard to load the sacks of jute to be transported home and sold. As Henderson sat on the dock, reclining in his deck chair reading, he would occasionally lift his gaze to survey the industry around him. The harbour workers bustled their way between makeshift, ramshackle offices, directing the crew to warehouses full of the golden, sinewy fibre that was to be the Nimrod's load for the voyage home. It amazed the doctor that such an innocuous cargo could be so valuable, but Captain Biddel assured him that, with the rise of the Merchant Navy, jute was in demand. If dried and twisted, it could make excellent rope. If pressed and woven it could be sewn together to make strong sacks. Henderson marvelled that fortunes could be made in the production and sale of such base material, but he was willing enough to believe the captain when he told him it was so. As he drew the brim of his hat further over his forehead to shade his eyes, Henderson let his imagination wander to the future and how he might expect to spend his fortune.

Three days passed quickly and without much by way of incident. Henderson swiftly found a routine by which to live that included morning trips into the Bengali interior. Before the sun was at its highest, he would find and sketch flora and fauna indigenous to this particular coast. Trees, shrubs and palms provided shade and shelter for snakes, spiders and a greater variety of insects than Henderson had ever seen. Within those three days, he drew and catalogued no fewer than fourteen species of beetle alone and carefully collected specimens of the more interesting poisonous plants for future study. Henderson had heard how natural poisons could be harnessed for medicinal purposes and he hoped to be a contributor to the field. Local myth had it that a particular compound of plants even had the capacity to give the appearance of death in subjects still living. On one such expedition inland, he halted in the shade of a magnificent Knema bengalensis tree to watch a herd of elephants pass on their way to a watering hole. It was on such occasions that he cursed himself for neglecting to pack his box camera. Henderson made the most of his time ashore knowing that, within a mere thirty six hours, he would be condemned again to share the company of another dozen or so men of varying worth and sobriety.

On the final night at port, Henderson was napping in his quarters. The exertions of the morning had taken their toll and, after a light lunch of curried vegetables, he had sought the refuge and cool of his cabin. Having written up the day's discoveries in his journal, Henderson kicked off his shoes and lay back in his hammock. Motes of dust danced lazily in the beams of the sun that entered through his porthole, a luxury afforded him on account of his standing with the captain. Just as he drifted into sweet oblivion, a cry served to raise him from his slumbers. At first he was disoriented, caught somewhere between sleeping and waking. Sweat had drenched his clothes in spite of the cool in the room and his throat was dry. Swallowing hard, Henderson leaned upon one arm. The cry came again, and this time, he could discern it was a cry for the captain. Swinging from his hammock with a single, practised movement, the doctor stepped into his shoes and jammed his wide-brimmed hat upon his head. As he stepped into the short corridor beyond his cabin and turned towards the main deck, Henderson was knocked aside by a hurrying Jeb Hardacre. The galley porter barrelled past him to the lower decks breathing hard, but not before Henderson had noticed he was trying his best to conceal a sharp blade in his apron. As Henderson stepped blinking into the early evening sun, he was greeted by such a commotion that at first it was difficult to ascertain exactly what had happened. Looking down through the large hatch in the main deck into the hold, Henderson saw several men struggling to lift a large crate of jute from the planks. A rope swung wildly from a crane above his head. Catching the end in his hand, Henderson could see the fraying hemp had been cleanly cut through with a knife.

"Doctor Henderson!" Captain Biddel was calling up at him from below decks. Casting his eyes downwards, Henderson could see the captain had his shoulder to the large crate in the hold. "This crate must weigh a ton and there's a man caught beneath it. He'll need your help!" As the doctor looked closer, he could plainly see the lower portions of a man protruding from beneath the container. A slick of dark red blood was seeping into the planks below.

Henderson sprang down the steps at speed. Those not engaged in moving the huge crate gave way and he was soon pressing his weight against it. With a final heave it moved to reveal the crushed remains of one of the ship's crew.

"Perryman." It was clear he was dead. Several of the men blanched at the sight of the body and one or two ran to the sides of the ship to heave the contents of their stomachs into the sea. It was plain to Henderson that Hardacre had wrought a deadly revenge for Perryman's misdemeanour.

Arrangements were made with the Governor of Chittagong that Perryman be buried in a grave near the makeshift local church. A simple service was held at which there were some three or four attendees including Henderson, Captain Biddel and a vagrant who, it appeared, had made his home in the hallowed ground of the churchyard. Using a finger to lead his eye across the page, Biddel read a favoured passage from his Bible and Henderson threw a handful of dry dust upon the simple coffin when he had finished. As distressing an interlude as it had been, the doctor was keenly aware that the crew of the Nimrod had been lucky enough to come this far with only one fatality among them. The fact that this death, as Henderson was sure, had been caused by another member of the crew only served to make the fact more bitter still.

One evening after dinner some three weeks into the voyage home, there came a visitor to Henderson's cabin. Just that day, the Nimrod had successfully rounded the Cape of Good Hope. Henderson was only too aware of the sea's reputation in these parts and had led the galley in a toast of thanks to the captain at dinner. Biddel had accepted the compliment with all due modesty. Now, the young doctor sat at the desk in his quarters to continue cataloguing the various specimens he had gathered in the forests of Chittagong. For much of the evening, he had been consumed with a line drawing of an indigenous plant, lulled by the pitching and creaking of the ship as it breasted the waves of the great Atlantic Ocean. As he paused to draw upon his pipe, he heard the faintest knock at his door. Henderson let go his pen and swivelled on his chair. "Come!" he barked. At this, the door swung slowly open on its salt-rusted hinges to reveal Jeb Hardacre, filling the frame with his bulk. Henderson stood gingerly, his fingers involuntarily twitching at his side.

"No need to call for help, doctor," rumbled Hardacre. "I'll do you no harm if you can help me."

Henderson looked closer at the kitchen porter before him. The nut-brown colour had gone from his face to be replaced by a sickly pallor. Beads of sweat stood out against his forehead. His beard was straggly and matted. The pupils of his yellowing eyes were wide and his breathing shallow. As he stood in the door in his regulation overalls, Henderson could see that Hardacre was but half the man he had been some days previously.

"Are you ill?" he enquired gently, taking the spectacles from off his nose and placing them carefully on the table beside him. His movements were slow and studied so as not to alarm the figure that stood before him. "Are you sickening for something?"

"That I am," replied Hardacre, a sudden shiver passing through his body. Henderson was beginning to recognise the symptoms of an all too common ailment.

"And how can I be of assistance?" Henderson kept his distance. He was relieved to see Hardacre remain at his door rather than attempt to enter the room.

Hardacre cleared his throat of phlegm. "Time was that the men would share their provisions with me," he rasped. "Before the accident with Perryman. And now my own supplies are spent."

Henderson's eyebrows rose. "Provisions?" he asked, knowingly.

"The Tincture."

So Henderson had been right. Hardacre was exhibiting signs of opiate withdrawal. It occurred to the doctor that he could take advantage of the situation. Bravely, he turned his back on the man at the door and gazed at the heaving horizon through the porthole above his desk. "What is the word on Perryman's death?" he asked. Behind him, Henderson heard a deck plank creak as Hardacre shifted his weight uncomfortably.

"They have their suspicions," he growled, "and have had nought to do with me for weeks."

"I would say their suspicions are well-founded, wouldn't you?" Henderson turned slowly to the door. "Did the captain order a search of your quarters, Hardacre?"

"He did not."

"Had he done so, would he have recovered a very particular knife?" Henderson was sweating now, too. He knew he was playing with fire.

"There's many a sailor aboard the Nimrod with a knife."

"But none with so murderous an intent as you. And while every man was running to Perryman's aid, you were running away. If it were brought to light, you'd surely hang." Henderson was making his way across the cabin as he spoke. Opening the door to an elaborate bureau that stood quite at odds to his otherwise sparse quarters, he drew a bottle containing a reddish brown liquid from a compartment together with a long silver box.

"And how might a man prevent such a thing?" rumbled Hardacre from the door.

Henderson gestured to his visitor that he might enter the room. Shutting the door behind him, Hardacre took a step into the middle of the floor, keeping his head low for fear of hitting it upon the low beams of the ceiling. The doctor opened the box to reveal a syringe in three parts. Moving to Hardacre, he carefully rolled up the sleeve on the man's left arm and used a rubber tube from another compartment to tie a ligature just above the elbow. Turning to assemble the syringe, Henderson then drew a quantity of the liquid from the bottle. Peering closer, Hardacre could plainly make out the word printed on a label on its side. Laudanum. The beginnings of a smile flickered at the corners of his mouth in anticipation.

"I think you could be of use to me once ashore," Henderson began as his needle made contact with the skin on Hardacre's forearm. "I wish to make a reputation for myself as a surgeon, but I lack experience." The needle slid easily into a vein. "Upon my return to England, I shall need access to cadavers. So that I may learn my craft." Hardacre's eyes began to flicker as Henderson squeezed his thumb on the syringe.

"I could find them for you."

Henderson released the ligature to allow the drug full flow. Hardacre shuddered as the laudanum was delivered. His eyes rolled back in their sockets and a deep sigh shook his body. The doctor withdrew the needle and placed it in a dish on the bureau. "You are to come to me every three days at this time. I shall be waiting."

"Then your silence is assured? With regard to Perryman?" Hardacre fixed an unwavering gaze on the doctor. Henderson nodded.

"If the bargain is maintained, you will live a free man."

"Then I am in your debt." As Hardacre turned to leave the cabin, he was interrupted by a gentle cough. In the fading evening light of his quarters, Doctor Henderson was holding up the bottle of laudanum, a sly smile on his face.

"Doubly so, it seems."

XXIV

Fall From Grace

Bowman's head was spinning. His vision was narrowing to a point as he gulped for breath, clutching at his chest. "Such a practice is wholly illegal," he gasped, his brows knotted all the tighter. He had barely heard the doctor's story above the seething tumult of the river below, but the salient points had been clear.

Henderson threw back his head and laughed, the rain falling from his head in fine droplets to his shoulders. "I envy you your view of the world, inspector. The law is an artifice, drawn up by those who do not have to live within its bounds." Henderson released his grip on the bridge to wipe the moisture from his face. "Hardacre escaped capture once ashore. Perhaps he thought me false in my intent and feared I would hand him over to the authorities. I would never have done such a thing, of course." He puffed out his chest, "I, inspector, am a man of honour and principle."

The doctor's hubris was astonishing, thought Bowman from the road. "And by chance," he called, "you found him."

"I have never put my trust in chance, Inspector Bowman. After three years at sea, I found myself in practice at St John's Wood and in need of specimens on which to perfect my craft. In my line of work, I often deal with the most unsavoury of individuals. It was easy enough to make discreet enquiries of my own. I was quite the investigator." Henderson chuckled to himself as if he were doing no more than sharing a private joke with a colleague. "The greatest criminal on the South Bank and I had him in a most unfortunate position. I found him and reminded him of our bargain."

"He agreed to provide you with certain services." Bowman glanced at the edges of the bridge for any sign of Sergeant Graves. Outwardly, he hoped, he was presenting a calm countenance. Inwardly, he was panicking, unsure whether he could stand the confusion any longer. He clutched at his head as if to stop the world turning about him. There was a chill in his blood. As the doctor continued, the detective inspector fancied he could hear horses' hooves.

"Let's not bandy words, inspector. He provided me with bodies for dissection. Criminals, I expect. I cared not where they came from. In return, he would visit me periodically for his medication."

Bowman narrowed his eyes. "I was not thinking of those kind of services."

As the rain had eased, so the city around them had come to life. Bowman could see people hurrying along the Embankment towards Westminster. He fought the impulse to call for help. He must not show weakness. Soon, those on the south bank would wish to cross the river. The inspector knew he had only minutes to ensure Henderson's safe recovery. He couldn't risk untimely interruptions from curious members of the public. The doctor was leaning out dangerously over the river, his face into the wind and his coat tails flapping behind him.

Henderson turned his troubled eyes to the inspector in a silent challenge. Even from this distance, Bowman could tell he was under the influence of some powerful narcotic. "When I turned Mary away from our home, my wife turned cold towards me. There was no place for me in her heart, nor in her bed neither."

"You procured women from him, didn't you? In return, you sated his opiate addiction." Bowman dared to stagger nearer his quarry. Again, he heard the sound of approaching hooves but this time, there was something else. The rattle of a carriage. As his mind was pulled back to that fateful night in Whitechapel, Bowman fought to remain in the present.

"And I had my favourites. But a week or so ago, he sent another, and that proved my undoing." Releasing his grip again, Henderson let go a scream and swung dangerously out over the river. Even over the churn of the waters below, the sound carried to the banks. Those who heard it stopped and turned their attention to the bridge. Enthralled by the spectacle of a man clinging to its side, some quickened their step towards the scene of the commotion. There was no hope now of this being resolved beyond the public gaze, thought Bowman. He took the opportunity to step closer to the doctor, fighting every impulse to turn and run. His legs felt weak and he thought that he might vomit. There were mere yards between them. In the meantime, Henderson's scream resolved itself into a word at last, a word that seemed to be torn from the very depths of the doctor's tormented soul.

"Mary!"

Bowman could barely see through the ghosts. Anna stood before him, about to step from the curb to the Women's Refuge across the road. If he stretched his arms to their full extent, he fancied he could touch her clothing, her face. And still the hooves approached.

Henderson screwed his eyes up against the memory of his daughter. "We met in my usual place. The lockup, away from prying eyes. And at first, in the dark, I did not recognize her. But she knew me. Her own father." Henderson reached out as though he could see her before him. "I lifted the veil she wore over her head and there I saw the face, the eyes, of my daughter."

Bowman was moving between two worlds now, the past and present. He flicked his eyes to the edge of the bridge, but there was still no sign of Sergeant Graves. He could feel the cobbles of Hanbury Street beneath his feet. Anna was stepping into the road now. The sounds of Whitechapel broke through the tumult of the river below. Bowman knew this was his chance. He had to act or risk losing her forever.

Henderson bent at the waist and let out a sob of pity, though whether for himself or his daughter it was difficult to tell. "She broke into a frenzy, lashing out like an animal. She threatened to run, to betray me." The sobs stopped suddenly and Henderson looked out across the city with a cold, hard glare. "I knew she could not leave alive." Shifting his feet on the ledge, Henderson gazed down into the depths of the swirling morass beneath him.

Bowman had moved slowly to the edge of the bridge. Stealing a furtive glance at the girders beneath, he spied Sergeant Graves making his way stealthily to where Henderson stood. Just a minute more and he would be there. Bowman panicked. He didn't have a minute more. The carriage was almost upon them, its driver slumped forward, dead at the reins. With an effort of will, the inspector forced himself into the present.

"Your only thought was your reputation," he spat.

"She screamed and screamed such that I feared discovery." Henderson lifted his hands before his face. "I put my hands to her neck," he was quiet now, almost whispering, "and I squeezed the life from her." He looked to Bowman, "But still she accused me."

"You murdered your own daughter."

Henderson was manic now, his voice and body quivering as if wracked with pain. "Even as she lay dead on the floor, I could hear her. She reproached me as a man and a father. I cut out her tongue." As if in disgust at himself and his actions, he looked away. "A terrible thing, but it wasn't enough. Still she accused me."

Bowman finally understood. "So you struck her head from her body."

"And finally, she was quiet."

"A clean cut, struck like a butcher." Bowman's confused mind was drawn back to his revelation in The Silver Cross and the butcher's window across the road.

"No, inspector." Henderson drew himself up to his full height. "Like a surgeon."

Below them both, Sergeant Graves was now in position. Listening to their conversation with ever-greater disbelief, the young sergeant considered his next move. Clinging to the girders beneath the main span of the bridge, he thought a sudden strike his best option. The only question was, when? Too soon and Henderson might be spooked, too late and the river might have him. Graves craned his neck for a better view of proceedings, but found his line of sight blocked by masonry and ironwork. Listening intently, he knew he would have to judge for himself when the time was right.

Above him, Bowman continued in his attempts to keep the doctor talking. "And then you ran to Hardacre." He swallowed hard. Time was running out, he was sure, but to move any closer would be to risk Henderson jumping. "But he was not to know she was your daughter. To him she was just another girl."

"He sent a boy to the lockup to dispose of the body."

Bowman nodded. "Isambard Fogg."

Henderson gave a dry, mirthless laugh. "He buried her body too shallow. And then the floods came." His teeth were gritted in anguish. "I had to make things right. It was fortunate that Fogg was already dead, killed like a dog by his master. Hardacre evaded me for a while, but eventually he came to me like a wasp to honey. Kane was easy enough. As luck would have it, inspector, I think you fired the fatal shot yourself."

Bowman thought back to the altercation in the alley just two nights before. So he had mortally wounded Kane. He couldn't find it within himself to feel sorry.

"And so I thought myself free from implication. Clearly I was wrong. The whole story is one of misfortune, don't you agree, inspector?" Henderson gave a wry smile. "I had everything within my grasp at first. A model wife, a promising career." For a moment, his face seemed to soften. "Ah well," he said simply, "The best laid plans…"

As his eyes glanced down once more to the river, Henderson caught a movement. Below him, Sergeant Graves swung into view in an attempt to climb onto the bridge, his hands grasping for purchase on the stonework. As the young sergeant found a foothold on the masonry and struggled to haul himself up, Henderson gave a cry of alarm and kicked furiously at his hands, attempting to loosen his grip on the bridge. Graves' voice rang like a bell through the air.

"I have him, sir! Don't move!"

But Bowman was hurling himself towards the doctor, his eyes blazing with a manic light. In his mind's eye, he was back in Whitechapel. Before him stood his wife, her hands reaching out, her eyes alive and dancing in greeting. The hooves were louder now, bearing down upon him as he clutched at her clothing.

"Keep back, sir, I have him!" Sergeant Graves had Henderson by the ankle now and was attempting to prevent the doctor from falling. A few passers by had reached the south side of the bridge and were standing like spectators at some great contest. With a look and a wave of his arm, Graves cautioned them to come no nearer. Time slowed.

Bowman's boots skidded across the flagstones as he barrelled into his wife. Her expression changed from one of confusion to fear as she looked beyond her husband to see the approaching carriage. "No, George, no!" she was shouting. Bowman knew he was putting himself in harm's way. It was as it should be. Just one push and she'd be safe.

Henderson looked around to see Bowman hurtling towards him. From below, Graves thought he caught something in the doctor's eyes. What was it? Surprise? Fear? Bowman piled into him, the full force of the blow tipping him off balance.

"No sir, no!" Graves felt Henderson's ankle slip from his hand. Looking behind him from his foothold, the sergeant watched helpless as Henderson pitched towards him. The doctor let go a scream, his hands flailing at the air.

Bowman shook his head. The scene around him cleared. He felt the ground beneath his feet. Turning, he saw Henderson's coat tails billowing around his shoulders as he fell. Someone screamed. Instinctively he reached out, clutching at the doctor's coat as he tipped from the balustrade. With some force Bowman pulled him back, every sinew straining to prevent the doctor's fall. Henderson became a dead weight, hanging limp and heavy from the bridge. Bowman could feel him slipping from his grasp. With a cry of anguish he tightened his grip. Suddenly, he felt the weight easing. Henderson was being dragged back over the balustrade by a force from behind. Bowman turned to see Sergeant Graves had joined him on the bridge. With a grimace of effort, he was pulling Henderson's limp form over the balustrade and to the ground. The sergeant collapsed upon him, his breathing laboured.

"He's alive," Graves was saying. "Just out for the count."

Bowman could feel himself slipping away. His vision was clouding. Dropping heavily to his knees, he felt his senses failing. The sky was pressing down upon his back and the ground was rushing up to meet him. He heard a crack. Somewhere, he had the thought that it might have been his head making contact with the ground.

Bowman felt the pressure of his cheek against the dirt. He stretched his face and forced his eyes to open. The ringing in his ears subsided. Had he saved her? He must have saved her. He dared to look behind at the oncoming brougham, but saw nothing. The streets of Whitechapel had dissolved. Lambeth Bridge stood cold and bare before him. Sudden realisation dawning, Bowman staggered to the opposite side of the bridge and leaned against the balustrade. He remembered colliding with Henderson, but there was no sign of him below. Had the river claimed him already?

Sergeant Graves had joined him at the bridge's edge, panting for breath after his exertions. "We got him sir, we got him."

Bowman could say nothing. Looking to his right, he saw two constables dragging Henderson from the bridge, his feet bumping across the flagstones behind him. His head rolled from side to side.

For a while, the two men stood in silence, the blood rushing furiously in their ears. Beneath them the swollen, foaming Thames continued on its course to the city, unknowing, uncaring. Bowman gazed to the distance. "He was right, Graves," he said in a small voice.

Graves took a deep breath. "How's that, sir?"

"The best laid plans. They all come to nothing." The inspector looked wildly about him. "I'm sorry, Graves. I'm sorry."

Tugging his hat down over his eyes and pulling up the collar on his coat, Bowman took a breath and turned to walk away. His gait was unsteady. There was a tremor in his hands. Sergeant Graves watched him leave, his eyes wide with confusion, then turned to disperse the crowd.

XXV

Coda

Sergeant Graves sat in Bowman's chair, his feet resting on the inspector's desk. Gazing around the office, his eyes fell upon the map of London on the opposite wall. Chewing on his lip, he mused how the events of the last few days had all occurred within a stone's throw of each other. From the discovery of the head beneath Westminster Bridge to Hardacre's Southwark den to Henderson's final stand at Lambeth, the whole affair had taken place within the radius of a mile. How many other crimes might even now be being committed within that small area on Bowman's map, he wondered. Might they never be brought to light? Graves shook his head to clear the thoughts from his mind. Most unlike me, he thought. Perhaps the job is getting to me.

Startled by a sudden noise from the corridor beyond the office, Sergeant Graves swung his feet from the desk and moved to stand by the window. A second later and he would have risked a disapproving look for his slovenliness. Within moments, the door had flung open to admit Inspector Bowman, his brows knotted in their customary furrow.

"Inspector Hicks has been reprimanded for jeopardising the success of our case." Bowman walked to his chair. Seemingly reluctant to meet Graves' gaze, he made great play of removing some dirt from his desk, left there by the sergeant's shoes. Graves cleared his throat, guiltily.

"I take it Watkins was good enough to speak against him?"

Before Bowman could reply, Inspector Hicks himself joined them in the room. His eyes blazed with a ferocious defiance as he wrenched the smoking pipe from between his teeth.

"The man is nothing but a weasel and I've thought so all along," he thundered. Shutting the door behind him, he turned to spread his great hands wide in an appeal for support. "There's just no trusting some people."

Bowman shared a look with Sergeant Graves and was about to reply when he was cut short by a knock at the door. Rolling his eyes at the interruption, Inspector Hicks took it upon himself to grant admittance to Bowman's office. "Come!" he barked. Not for the first time, Inspector Bowman marvelled at Hicks' complete disregard for the social graces. The door swung open to admit a tall, young woman with a slim waist, sharp eyes and a subtle cleft at her chin. She held herself with a poise that was unmistakable.

"Miss Morley!" Bowman swallowed hard and felt suddenly awkward. He moved towards her, his hand outstretched in a clumsy attempt at a greeting. Elizabeth returned the gesture with amusement.

"Inspector."

Bowman was at a loss. Desperately, he looked to the other men in the room for support or inspiration. Sergeant Graves stood with his arms crossed. Inspector Hicks left Bowman to his discomfort for an inordinate length of time before finally breaking the silence with a salacious grin.

"I shall leave you to your business, inspector," he leered. With a look to Elizabeth and a ghastly wink at Bowman, Hicks sauntered from the room with an affected swagger. Bowman swung around his guest to shut the door before Hicks could change his mind, then motioned to Elizabeth that she should sit in the leather wing-backed chair before his desk. Sergeant Graves took a step closer to the window and feigned a sudden interest in the view below. Bowman sat at his own chair, facing Elizabeth across the desk. He marvelled at how the sun from the window was playing about her hair.

"How may I be of service?" Bowman smoothed his moustache between his finger and thumb in a vain attempt to calm his nerves.

"How formal!" laughed Elizabeth. Bowman threw a look to Graves' broad back at the window. Elizabeth took his meaning and acquiesced but the faintest smile still danced about her neat lips. "I have come to thank you, inspector."

Bowman cleared his throat. "For what?"

"For accompanying me to the meeting last night."

Bowman flinched at the memory. "Did you stay long after me?" He thought he saw Sergeant Graves shift uncomfortably at the window. Perhaps he was regretting not leaving the room with Inspector Hicks when he'd had the chance.

"Yes," replied Elizabeth. "All night. After the initial disturbance, the evening proceeded as planned." Bowman was surprised. That the event had continued at all after such a disruption seemed hardly credible. Elizabeth leaned forward across the desk. Inspector Bowman could smell her perfume. "And I spoke with my father."

"I see," replied the inspector, quietly. He felt nothing but pity for the elegant creature before him. To bear the loss of one's father in so gruesome a manner would be hard enough, but to then fall victim to such shameless bunkum as he had witnessed the night before seemed a double cruelty.

"Yes, and he is well." Elizabeth's eyes shone. "His death was quick and he says he did not feel a thing. It was of great comfort."

"I'm pleased for you." Elizabeth noticed Bowman's moustache twitch. After studying his face for what Bowman thought to be an age, she rose.

"And what of you, inspector? Where will you find your comfort?"

Feeling suddenly very uncomfortable indeed, Bowman contrived an interest in the gold inlay of his desk, picking at it with his fingers in a studied attempt at nonchalance. "Not here," he murmured, not daring to meet her gaze. "Not in London." He could almost feel Graves' eyebrows rising in surprise behind him. Elizabeth could not conceal her disappointment.

"Then, where?"

"Who knows?" Bowman cleared his throat and summoned the courage to look up. "I have just resigned my place here at Scotland Yard." He knew that Graves had turned to face him at his place by the window.

"Oh." Elizabeth was crestfallen.

Bowman nodded, warming to his theme. "I am to move to a provincial force, although it has yet to be decided where. I am hoping for the West Country. It is very pretty there."

"London too can be pretty, inspector. In the right company."

Now Inspector Bowman stood at his desk, his face softening. "I am sure it can, Miss Morley. But I do not care for the rats." Rather stiffly, Bowman extended his hand.

Elizabeth nodded slowly, sensing their meeting was over. "I see. Well, I shall wish you good day. And thank you again." Removing a glove, Elizabeth reached for Bowman's hand. The inspector noticed how soft her skin was, and how small her hand.

"Thank you," he said simply, swallowing hard. They stood for a while as if they were the only two people in the room. Then, slowly, Elizabeth Morley turned and walked from the room.

"Sergeant Graves, would you be so good as to see Miss Morley safely home?"

"Of course." Graves moved to the door but then faltered, puzzled. "You're not really leaving us, are you sir?"

"No, Graves. I am not."

"But - "

Bowman sighed and ran his fingers through his hair. Graves noted that Bowman looked the saddest he had ever seen him. "Life is complicated enough," he said.

Acknowledging the point with a rueful smile, Sergeant Graves moved to leave the room.

"Sergeant Graves," Bowman called after him. "Anthony."

Graves stopped sharp at the use of his Christian name. It was the first time he could remember Bowman having ever used it.

"We've never spoken about Whitechapel," the inspector continued. Graves shuffled nervously on his feet. "About Anna."

"I wouldn't think there was much to say, sir," Graves said, cautiously.

Bowman nodded slowly. "I've never thanked you. It has been remiss of me." His eyes were cast down at the floor. Graves turned to face him square on.

"No thanks are needed, sir. I did what I thought I should."

"It was for the best," muttered Bowman none too convincingly. "You saved my life. You have my gratitude." An uneasy silence hung in the air. Bowman took a breath. "And yesterday, on Lambeth Bridge."

"Yes, sir?"

Treading carefully, Bowman struggled to find the appropriate words. "I was somewhat… overcome."

Graves nodded, "Yes, sir. I should think you were."

"Will my behaviour be recorded in your report to the commissioner?"

Graves regarded his companion sadly. "I think Henderson got everything he deserved, sir." Inspector Bowman seemed to have shrunk by a good few inches before his very eyes. "I shan't mention it to the commissioner," Graves continued, quietly. "If you can promise me that you are quite recovered."

"I can, Sergeant Graves," Bowman whispered. "I am quite recovered."

Nodding in silent understanding, Graves reached into a pocket to retrieve a folded up newspaper. Bowman could tell it was The Evening Standard. Unfurling it in his hands, Graves placed it gingerly on the desk before him then turned on his heels too quick to notice the tremor in Bowman's hand. He closed the door behind him with a soft click, leaving Bowman to consider the headline; 'SCOTLAND YARD REDEEMED'.

Alone in his office, Detective Inspector George Bowman stared at the door then let his eyes pass along the map on the wall to the window. He fancied that, somewhere beyond the horizon, he could sense a life that might have been. His thoughts were interrupted by a dove landing on the sill beyond the window. The inspector was struck by how clean it looked, its beady eye scanning the streets below for food. And then it took flight over the city. Over the river towards the south bank it flew, along the course of the Thames for several seconds before soaring back to the city and on towards the horizon. The morning sun flashing on its feathers, the bird wheeled away into the bright blue January sky.

End Note.

In researching the care of those with a mental illness in the latter half of the nineteenth century, I was very interested to learn that treatment was not so barbaric as one might expect. The Lunacy Act of 1846 established the Commissioners in Lunacy to inspect plans for asylums and required them to be registered with the Commission. Asylums were to have written regulations and to have a resident physician. The Commission monitored the conditions in the asylums and the treatment of the patients and made a point of reaching out to patients in workhouses and prisons and getting them to the proper institutions where they could be treated. 'Life In The Victorian Asylum' by Mark Stevens offers ample evidence of the Victorians' surprisingly progressive attitude to mental health.

Bowman's visit with Elizabeth Morley to a Spiritualist meeting at Covent Garden was a pleasure to write. Whilst The Empire Rooms are entirely fictional, the Victorians' near obsession with the Spirit Realm is not. Famously, none other than Arthur Conan Doyle himself had a fascination for all things paranormal, attending a lecture on the subject as early as 1881. In 1887, he published an article in The Light, a spiritualistic magazine, detailing a séance that he'd attended. In the early decades of the twentieth century, he would likewise develop an interest in subjects ranging from the infamous Cottingley Fairies to the contacting of Harry Houdini's long dead mother by means of automatic writing.

Finally, I am often asked whether Jack the Ripper has any bearing on Bowman's world. In fact, I have to admit he doesn't. Anyone looking for Jack the Ripper in the Bowman Of The Yard series will be disappointed. I decided to set my series of books four years after the Ripper murders, giving the stories, I felt, sufficient distance so that they wouldn't be mentioned. That meant I could introduce each new investigation without the reader (or indeed, the characters) thinking, 'It must be Jack the Ripper!' Secondly, I wanted to be very clear that Bowman's world is a work of fiction. Besides the odd historical character

(Queen Victoria being mentioned, for example, or Sir Edward Bradford, the Scotland Yard commissioner from 1890-1903) every character and just about every event in the series is fictional. That's not to say Jack the Ripper never existed in Bowman's world, just that perhaps it's enough that he existed in ours.

Richard James, March, 2020.

SUBSCRIBE TO MY NEWSLETTER

If you enjoyed The Head In The Ice, why not subscribe to my newsletter? You'll be the first to hear all the latest news about Bowman Of The Yard - and I'll send you some free short stories from Bowman's Casebook!

Just visit my website **bowmanoftheyard.co.uk** for more information. You can also search for and 'like' Bowman Of The Yard on **Facebook** and join the conversation. I would love to hear your thoughts.

Finally, I would appreciate it if you could leave me a review on Amazon. Reviews mean a lot to writers, and they're a great way to reach new readers.

Thanks for reading The Head In The Ice!

Richard

Printed in Great Britain
by Amazon

68752435R00135